WICKED
CHARM

AMBER HART

WICKED
CHARM

Entangled Publishing, LLC
2614 South Timberline Road
Suite 105, PMB 159
Fort Collins, CO 80525

Entangled Teen is an imprint of Entangled Publishing, LLC.

Visit our website at www.entangledpublishing.com.

Edited by Karen Grove
Cover design by Cover Couture
Interior design by Toni Kerr

ISBN 978-1-63375-896-4
Ebook ISBN 978-1-63375-897-1

Manufactured in the United States of America

First Edition January 2018

10 9 8 7 6 5 4 3 2 1

an imprint of Entangled Publishing LLC

For Rodolfo

1

WILLOW

THE SWAMP BEATS AND THROBS and hums with life. Sickly hot air meets a limitless blue sky, and below, a forest of teeth and limbs reaches toward a jagged scar of land that separates two properties.

One belongs to my family.

Gran lives on the edge of the Okefenokee wetlands in a damned city named Waycross, Georgia, in a damned county called Ware, as she would say. A place where nothing exciting ever happens, life trudges on, resisting change, and the people like it that way. It's a world built on legends and secrets that run like a vein through the heart of history.

Most claim only the craziest live this far out. And they're partially right.

"The brightest light casts the darkest shadow," Gran says.

I eye our property through the kitchen window. I happen to like the shadows, the seclusion of the trees, the whispers of the forest. Especially at night, when everything takes a less defined form, when the swamp comes to life.

"I'm telling you, this world would be better off if they remembered that. 'Specially that neighbor of mine, never mindin' his own business. Telling me I need to stop feeding the gators. I can feed the gators any damn time I want. It's my land. I wish he'd just move on already, bless his heart."

I'm a replica of Gran. Except Gran is much older, wrinkled like a rippled reflection in water. My hair is hers, dark and thick, though hers has now faded to gray. And our eyes are identical, a solid brown—so brown that my pupils bleed into them. I am younger and more beautiful, she would say. But Gran says all kinds of things.

"By 'move on'"—I pause to turn off the stove and shuffle eggs onto Gran's plate—"do you mean 'die'?"

"Hell right I do," she says, grabbing a biscuit, a scoop of sausage gravy, and four pieces of bacon. "Maybe then I'll have some peace around this godforsaken swamp."

"Gran, it's not nice to wish people dead."

Gran despises the next-door neighbor, Mr. Cadwell, making sure to ignore his greetings and glances. He's nice enough, I suppose. But I don't know him like she does. Word has it they even dated once, long before she decided that he was evil.

"You're new here, Willow," she says. "Just you wait and see. Twisted, that's what that family is, the whole lot of them."

It's true that I'm new. I've been here five days, though I've visited plenty of times over the years. Never long enough to know the old man next door for anything more than a passing hello lost on the wind. I glance outside again. Marsh is everywhere, pushing the smell of earth and fungus through the open window. Patches of water are blanketed in green algae, alligator eyes popping up like floating marbles. Cypress trees protrude from the murky water, reminding me of notches of bone, little leaves growing from them. Lifeless branches float along for the ride. The swamp is the kind of place a girl can get lost in and never find her way out.

Though Gran's land is mostly wet, there's solidness, too. My eyes trace the long path that cuts the property between Gran and Mr. Cadwell in half. I'm expecting to see nature—the kinds of birds Dad and Mom study, snakes, grass, and forever sky—the same things I've seen every morning since moving here with Dad and Mom to help Gran, who's ailing but doesn't like to admit it.

I get halfway down the path with my stare before my eyes snag on something. A serving spoon falls from my hand with a clatter into the sink.

"Who," I whisper, "is that?"

Across the way stands a boy. He's staring at me, wearing a twisted grin like he knows me. The wind ruffles his depths-of-the-ocean black hair. He's wearing a dark shirt and dark jeans, and I cannot tear my eyes from his.

Gran hobbles over and looks out the window. "What is *he* doing so close to our side?"

"You know him?" I ask.

I can't stop staring out the old, weathered screen.

"Hell right, I do. Grandson of the evil next door. Trouble in living form. Someone oughta hand that boy a Bible. Change his life forever and ever, amen."

Gran curses a lot. "Hell" is her favorite word.

"Hell, you'd better look away first," Gran says. "B'fore he snares you for good."

I wonder if she's right. I want to look away first. Okay, that's a lie. I don't want to look away at all.

"Mother!" Dad's voice enters the room a moment

before he does. "Did I just hear you cursing around Willow again?"

I rip my eyes away—though it's hard—to see Dad clad in shorts and a T-shirt, ready for another day of observation. He and Mom are ornithologists, scientists who study birds. Mom follows Dad into the kitchen and takes a seat at the table; her strawberry-blond hair is braided and slipped through the adjustable hole in her hat. Dad's hair is like Gran's and mine, his eyes, too. Mom's eyes are blue, and I'm secretly glad mine are not. I enjoy being like Gran.

"It's not good to curse around her; she's only seventeen," Dad continues.

In Florida, Dad and Mom studied birds so much that I hardly ever saw them. Here's no different, but at least now I have Gran to keep me company.

"Doesn't matter, and you know it," Gran says. "A heart is a heart is a heart. A few words here and there won't change that."

My stare goes to the window again. The boy is gone.

"Quit looking for that boy, you hear?" Gran says, knowing.

"I'm not looking for him," I reply. But I'm a lying liar.

"What boy?" Dad asks.

I join him and Mom at the table.

"No one," my lying self answers.

Maybe I should take him a Bible and say it's from Gran, and then I'd have a reason to meet him.

"Stop thinking about him," Gran says.

"I'm not!" I say, frustrated. But only because she knows me so well that I can't hide myself from her.

"Are too, girl. I'm no damn idiot."

Dad shakes his head and sighs. "Mom, the cursing.

And what boy?"

"There's a new neighbor," I say. "Or maybe he's an old neighbor. Who knows? I've never seen him before today. But he was there on the path and now he's not. That's all."

Mom smiles. "Well, how old is he? Maybe you can make a friend."

We all look to Gran for the answer.

"Don't need to know nothin' about him. He's rotten like the mushrooms 'round here. Soul black as the night," she grumbles.

Clearly Gran isn't a fan. We drop it and eat our breakfast, Dad and Mom jabbering about some new species of bird they think they've discovered. Gran watching me like a hawk. And me wondering about the gorgeous black-souled, trouble-in-living-form grandson of the evil next door.

2

BEAU

I KNOW THE MINUTE SHE ENTERS the classroom because all eyes swivel to her, though she's only a devil's minute late.

"Hi," she says, smiling at the dull-as-death teacher who's droning on about the history of blah blah blah.

"Hello," Mr. Dull says. "Are you Willow?"

"I am."

It's odd of her to show up for her first day on a Friday.

There's only one high school in our county. Each new student is sent here. That's not why she's interesting, though. It's because she's the girl I saw next door, the one who looks like the old lady, if the old lady had tripped over time and fallen backward.

"Great," he says. "I've been looking forward to meeting you ever since they notified me of your arrival. Please find a seat. We've only just started. And here, take this."

He hands her a textbook like he's giving her a baby, something precious. No one but him cares about the required reading, but she's polite enough about it.

"Thank you," she says, and turns to find a seat.

That's when her eyes loop with mine. I see that she remembers me, too.

"Hi," I say boldly.

There are whispers. My friend Grant, sitting in front of me with a head of curls, turns around with a smile that says, *This should be interesting.*

Mr. Dull says something about everyone being quiet in order for him to continue to bore us to absolute death. Or maybe that's how I heard it. Willow moves to take a seat a few down from mine in the back.

"Mind moving over a couple of seats for the new student?" I whisper to the girl next to me. Rachel or Raquel or something similar.

Rachel-Raquel begins to laugh, thinking I'm joking, but stops when she sees the serious look in my eyes. Quickly, she swipes up her book and moves to the other chair, forcing Willow to sit in the only available seat—next to me.

"Hello," I say again, flashing a grin.

Mr. Dull is talking too loudly to hear me.

With a small laugh, Grant whispers, "Here we go."

"Hi," she says, opening her book.

"Willow." I say her name, testing it in my mouth.

Her dark hair brushes her desk and hides part of her face. But I already know she's beautiful.

"What's your last name, Willow? Is it Bell? Are you related to Old Lady Bell?"

She is, and I know it. And she knows it. I just want to show her that I realize who she is, I suppose.

"That's none of your damn business," she says with a small smile.

They're definitely related.

"Didn't your mom teach you it's impolite to curse?" I tease.

"Didn't your mom teach you to read a Bible?" she fires back. "From what I hear, you need that and more with your black soul."

I can't help it. I laugh.

"Is that what Old Lady Bell is saying these days?" The woman never has liked my family much. Hasn't had any reason to.

"What's your name?" Willow asks.

People are staring, but I don't care.

"Beau Cadwell. Grandson of Parker Cadwell next door. The evilest family in all the swamp."

Or so people say.

Willow bites down on her pencil eraser, and I find my eyes drawn to her lips.

"Well, Beau," she says in a sweet tone. "I don't think we're supposed to be friends."

"I suppose not."

Her eyes are darker than anything I've ever seen. They're the type of dark that takes over the swamp after the sun falls from the sky.

"You might be trouble for me," I say, joking. "And I am not nice," I add, not joking.

"Everyone is part good, part bad," she replies.

I don't think she realizes just how offset those parts of me are.

"Even so, you should probably not associate with me," she says. "My gran would hate it."

"Would you hate it?" I ask.

Willow twists the metal-clothed eraser between her teeth for a moment before speaking. She holds my stare like she holds her breath. "I'm still trying to decide, Beau Cadwell."

I like my name on her lips. I like her tongue on her

lips. I'd probably like my tongue on her lips, too.

"You are trouble, after all, I hear." But she doesn't say it like she's scared of trouble.

"Then we definitely shouldn't be friends." I don't mean a word of it.

"Okay." Her eyes leave mine. She looks around the dingy classroom, like she's just now taking it in, walls buried behind history posters and a chalkboard covered in something that is supposed to pass as legible handwriting.

Half the class is staring at her. Some of the guys look like they want to order her up for dinner. Some of the girls look like they want to burn her alive for talking to me. Just because things ended badly between most of the girls and me doesn't mean they need to hold a grudge. What does it take to get girls to move on around here?

"Do you want to be friends anyway?" I ask.

She lets her eyes find their way back to me. "Okay."

And just like that I have an in with the new girl, Willow Bell.

Grant fist-bumps me when Willow isn't looking.

From across the room, near the front of the class, my twin sister is watching. She sends a razor-sharp smile my way, knowing that I'll probably do to Willow what I do to all the girls here, which is break her perfect little heart into so many pieces that nothing can fix it.

3

WILLOW

"HI, I'M JORIE," says the girl who plops down next to me on the concrete bench.

Around us, people talk, most rehashing the details of the day as they wait for the bus home. I catch bits and pieces of conversations—a football pep rally, a bake sale, an opening on the school debate team.

"I'm Willow," I say. "How do you get your hair to do that?"

Jorie's hair is like a zebra, black with white stripes, or maybe it's the other way around. I never could tell that about zebras—black and white or white and black? And her hair is the same.

"It's a weave. My momma's a stylist." She pops her gum loud-like. "She does all kinds of hair but specializes in African American techniques, learned from her momma. They're as black as the night sky all the way back as far as time goes until me. I got a bit of my daddy in me. His skin is light like yours."

I like her skin. It's not quite light or dark. I like her accent, too, though I can't place it.

"Where are you from, Jorie?" I ask.

"The bayous of Louisiana originally, but I don't remember it. Was just a baby when we moved here. You?"

"I'm from Georgia originally, a county two hours north of here. Moved to Florida for a bit before coming back. My parents study birds, and that's a good place to do it." It's a lame thing to say, but it's the truth.

"Wanna sit with me on the bus?" Jorie offers. "Then you won't have to worry about people bugging you about Beau."

"Why would they do that?" I have no idea how she knows that I've met him.

"Because he's Beau," she says.

Like that explains it.

Jorie's all elbows and knees and sharp angles. I wonder how she stays in shape. I'm curvy and always carrying around what Gran calls biscuit weight. Not that I'm overweight—I'm not—I'm just soft. I once asked Gran over the phone what I could do to lose ten pounds after I saw this quiz in a magazine that said I could look my best with a little weight shed. She said I'd have to quit eating biscuits. But that's crazy talk. Who has ever heard of giving up biscuits? No, thanks.

The bus pulls up, and we pile on. It's not completely full, so I don't think I need to sit with Jorie to avoid sitting by someone else, after all. But I'm happy to, all the same.

"What did you mean about Beau?" I ask, once we're settled in, bags down between our legs to make room. The bus jerks away from the curb.

Jorie pops her gum three times before she answers. Her kohl-rimmed eyes remind me of almonds dipped in chocolate.

"You really don't know, do you?" she asks.

"'Course not," I reply. "Just moved here a week ago, and today's the first time I met him. He seems nice."

Jorie laughs. It's a boisterous sound that turns heads. She smacks a hand on her thigh and says, "Girl, stop playing. Beau is *not* nice. Never is that boy nice unless he needs something. Hot? Yes. Taken? Yes. Smooth as a pearl shined? Yes. But nice? Never. Not once."

I hear all of Jorie's words. Each one after the other, but the only one that sticks is this: *taken.*

"He has a girlfriend?" I ask.

"I knew it." Her eyes slide my way. "You like him. Every girl who likes boys does. It's not just you. But you have to learn to fight it, or he'll devour you."

I'm not so sure I consider that a bad thing.

"And yes, he's taken. Every day of the week. The girls don't last more than a couple of weeks, but they are always there. One after the other," she says.

The thought irks me. Don't ask me why, because I don't know.

"Well, he and I aren't anything to each other, so I'm sure there's nothing for me to worry about," I say. "I don't even think he's hot."

Yes I do.

"Atta girl," Jorie says. "Keep lying to yourself and eventually you might actually believe it. It's a start."

"I'm not lying," I say.

"You're lying now," she says.

"Maybe," I admit.

"Like I said," Jorie continues. "Almost all girls fall for him. But be careful. He's an inch shy of as wicked as they get."

Maybe I like wicked. Maybe I top my pies with

wicked, and maybe I order wicked every day; she doesn't know. *I can handle it*, I tell myself. But that might be the lying liar in me.

"Him and that sister of his, both," Jorie says. "You'll mostly find him with those two goons, Grant and Pax. I'm sure you've seen them. One looks like a bird and the other like a gorilla. You might get a chance to see him alone more than most people, though, because he's your neighbor, right?"

"Hard to tell," I say. "I've never seen him before, and I used to visit often."

A memory hits me. A stringy young boy—same age as me at the time, eight—running around the yard, chasing squirrels as though he means to catch one.

"If you're looking to eat it, you have to set a trap, you know," I say. *"And try being quiet when you approach them—it helps. Plus, who are you and why are you on my gran's property?"*

"I'm not. I'm on my grandpa's side. See?" he replies. "That's the dividing line back behind you."

He was right. He *was* technically on his side.

"Unless he was the boy I once met years ago," I say to Jorie. "I'd always thought he was visiting before. I never saw him afterward."

"Well, you're Old Lady Bell's family, right?"

"Yes," I confirm. I'm proud of Gran. Don't care what anybody says. And I've heard it around town, how my gran's the crazy lady who lives in the deep swamp, who's taken to feeding the gators and yellin' at anyone who tries to trespass her land. Doesn't mean she's bad. Just means she likes privacy and animals. She can't help it if most of the animals in the swamp are of the reptilian kind.

"Then he's been your grandma's neighbor since he was ten," she says. "I knew your grandpa, by the way. He was a good man. My grandpa used to frog hunt with him. He'd stay for dinner from time to time."

"Sounds like Grandpa," I confirm. "May he rest in peace, amen."

I was taught to give respect to the dead and attach amens to the ends of sentences like periods.

"When was the last time you visited here, before actually moving, I mean?"

"More than a year ago," I say. I wonder why Gran never mentioned having neighbors my age next door, but then I remember how she warned me away from Beau. She must not have wanted me to befriend him or his sister.

My hands shoot out to stop my body from hitting the seat in front of us as the driver slams on the brakes at a stoplight. Jorie grabs a sheet of paper and begins writing her number.

"Here, call me if you want to hang out sometime. I live down the way from you, about ten miles."

I take the paper and fold it until it fits tight-like into my jeans pocket. My red-and-white-striped shirt sticks to the back of the seat as I scoot forward. The bus seems to have no air-conditioning, even though it should because senior year is only three weeks in and summers in Georgia are brutal.

"Anyway," Jorie says, "Beau's family—him, his sister, momma, and poppa—moved in with his grandpa when his parents fell ill. Rumor has it that they eventually died."

What a wicked-sad thing to have happen. If it's true, maybe that's why Beau supposedly isn't nice? Grief can make a person act all sorts of ways.

"No one reliable has seen his parents there or around town. 'Course you always get those few looking to tell a juicy tale, aching for attention, who want to say they've seen them. No proof, though. No pictures. Supposedly seeing them when there are no witnesses to back up their claims. You'll learn that some folks 'round here are as good at lying as they are at breathing, and they're not afraid to show it. Carry it around like a prized medal for winning best pie or something."

I can tell the exact moment we leave the city part of town and enter the swamp because the driver stops roughly and lets most of the kids off. Only eight of us remain. Like a demon straight out of hell, the driver takes off again, leaving stoplights and houses behind for trees and water encroaching on both sides.

"I guess the mystery works for him, though. He has half the girls at our school in love with him."

"Must be more than his mysteriousness." I watch the muddy water bubble and pop. "If girls are falling that hard."

Vines slither and wind their way around trees, choking the trunks. Very little light enters the cover of leaves, making daytime appear more like dusk. The road is the only thing lit by the sun, save a few breaks in the vegetation.

"Do you know what it's like to be in love, Willow?" Jorie asks.

It's a personal question, but I answer anyway. "No."

"Neither does Beau," she replies. "For all the girls he's broken, he doesn't know a thing about love. You'd be wise to remember that."

I have no idea what she means, but I realize that people in the Georgia swamp are simply different than the people I knew back in Florida. They speak their minds here. Leaving Georgia when I was only nine affords me few memories of small-town life. What always did stick was my accent. Tried scrubbing it away with many years in Florida. Tried not standing out, but it never worked. Always felt forced.

"Jorie," I say. "If all girls fall for him at one point or another—if they like boys, that is—how have you not fallen?"

"Oh, I have," she says. "You think I don't look? It's too hard not to. I'm not immune, but I've learned how to avoid him. How to not draw his eye. Maybe when he's made it through all the girls here, he'll come for me. But for now, I'm safe."

"What's that supposed to mean?" I ask.

"It means that he's not finished breaking hearts. That's what."

She looks me over, eyes resting on mine.

"Or maybe I'm not safe at all anymore now that we're friends," she says. "We are friends, right?"

"Sure." She's the closest I have to a friend here.

Jorie twists the bangle bracelets on her wrist in a nervous kind of way. "Then maybe I'm not safe. I will be in his line of sight now. He might be too preoccupied with you, though. He's taken to you already. That's not a good thing, by the way."

"Maybe it could be a good thing."

"You think that now," she says. "But your tears will tell you differently later."

Maybe she's right. But maybe she's wrong. I think

about Beau's disarming smile and how I could hardly look away from him. Yes, she's probably right. She is most likely absolutely right.

And somehow, I don't care. I'm going to talk to him again anyway.

4

BEAU

"YOU'RE WAITING ON THE NEW girl to get home from school, aren't you?" Charlotte joins me at the old window, peering out of the smudges made by age to see the house in the distance. Thankfully we drive to school and don't have to wait on a bus to make several long stops. "We only have one neighbor within two thousand acres, and a new girl our age happens to move there when most of the people around here are as old as time. What do you think the odds are?"

"Slim."

I lean farther back in the purple chair that faces the window. Charlotte sits in a matching one.

"She was talking to you in class," she says. "What a fool."

My sister is kind to no one. Well, that's not the full truth. She is sometimes kind to family—what she has left of it, Grandpa and me—but to no one else. She is perhaps meaner than me, which is saying something.

Her long pink nails *tap, tap, tap* on the wooden armrest of her chair. Her eyes roam our home, a small wooden cabin. The place where my dad was raised.

My mind flashes to my parents.

The swamp hisses at us from all angles, wind rushing through trees. Charlotte and Mom paddle a canoe ten feet away, Mom at one end and my sister at the other. Neither of them is wary of the bog, as though they've lived here their whole lives instead of where we actually live, Atlanta proper. Grandpa is the one who lives here, paddling a canoe of his own, leading the way.

Dad sits across from me, a slight smile on his face. He's more relaxed here, in his element. We've visited enough times to not frighten when alligators curiously venture near or when fish jump out of the water, belly flopping back in. I wonder if they're being chased beneath the surface. I can't see through to tell. The water is a patchwork quilt of algae-green and muck-brown.

Dad looks at me with a face just like my own, only older, with wrinkles and hair as black as moccasins. His rough blue eyes focus on nothing in particular.

"Nice out here, isn't it?" he says.

I nod. It really is. What eight-year-old wouldn't like this?

Mom reaches out a hand and brushes a string of branches that spread toward her canoe. I can hear her laugh ping off bark, and it might be my favorite sound. Charlotte smiles widely and stretches for the leaves, too. Their canoe nearly tips, and they collapse into a fit of giggles, the two of them.

I wonder if there will ever be a day when we don't have to leave, when we can pack our bags and make this our daily life. I certainly wouldn't mind.

I never intended to live here without my parents.

"Will you break her heart today?" Charlotte asks.

Charlotte often talks to me like she's the older one, though I was born minutes first.

"So soon? Where's the fun in that?"

She laughs. "Go on then, here she comes."

Willow emerges from the path and steps onto the porch attached to her small home, sunshine pouring over her. She looks back toward my house.

"If only a guy had moved next door," Charlotte says. "That would have been much more fun. For me, of course."

She leaves me with my thoughts, her bare feet smacking against the wooden floor beneath her.

Willow stands there for a moment before I step outside.

I don't walk all the way to her property. That wouldn't be wise. Mostly because I'm not a fan of Old Lady Bell, and the feeling is mutual. She's always been quick to yell at me to get off her land. I wait for Willow halfway, at the line where the properties are severed.

She comes to me.

"Hello, Willow Bell." I smile.

"Hello, Beau," she says, amusement skating across her lips. I wonder if I'm imagining the way her pupils dilate the slightest bit with my closeness. "I heard a funny thing today."

She turns, leaving me to follow after her. I don't know quite what to do, so I just stand there.

"Are you coming or not?" Willow flips her dark hair over her shoulder and flashes me a sweet smile.

"I haven't decided," I say honestly.

"Okay." She shrugs. "Then I suggest you go back home because Gran will wake from her nap in about five minutes, and she won't be happy about you crossing her property line. She's not a fan of trespassers."

"What are you talking about, Willow?"

She glances at my feet.

I look down. Well, what do you know? I guess I had taken a few steps toward Willow after all. I'm now on Old Lady Bell's side.

Hell with it.

I run after Willow. She smiles because she knew I'd come. I decide, when I catch up, that I like her smile, her plump lips. I think I even like the tiny gap between her two front teeth. I hadn't noticed that before. I guess I hadn't been close enough.

"There's a place just past here, 'round a bend of water lilies, where we can sit. Would you like to do that, Beau?"

"I would," I say.

Willow approaches a tiny, dingy, metal boat with rust eating at the sides, stained where the water has touched the bottom. She pushes it toward the marsh, her feet squelching in mud. She's wearing the right kind of shoes—snake-proof, water-resistant boots—I'll give her credit for that. Her shorts are short and her hair is long and her look is deep, just the way I like it.

"Fair warning." She pulls back her shirt just slightly to reveal a sheaved knife tucked into her shorts. "I'm not afraid to use this if I need to."

I like her already. "Why would you say something like that?"

"Like I said, I hear things," she replies. "And I don't know you well. But I suppose I oughta give you a chance and judge for myself, right? If I listened to all the gossip 'round this town, I'd never have any friends."

She has a point.

Willow hops in when the boat begins to float, and I join her. Our boots leaky-faucet drip onto the inside metal as we grab oars to row. The water is as murky as triple-steeped tea, teeming with gators, vipers, and fish. Frogs bask on cypress roots that grow out of the water like fingers, protecting the creatures that live underneath. Dragonflies whir past us, and mosquitoes swarm.

"You just moved here," I say, offering up a conversation.

"And you moved here almost eight years ago, I hear," she replies.

"You seem to hear a lot of things."

She surprises me with a smile. "You don't know the half of it."

"Tell me some of it?"

I row steadily through the marsh. Eyes open and ready. Never can be too careful. Once had a coral snake drop out of a tree and into my canoe.

"Okay, for starters, do you really think you should be in this boat with me?"

"Why shouldn't I be?"

Willow doesn't lose her grin or her sharp wit. She says exactly what she wants, and I happen to like that in a place where people will bless your heart at the same time that they're muttering curses under their breath.

"Would your girlfriend like it if you were here?" she asks.

I didn't realize she knew yet. Guess word does spread fast. The funny thing is: she waited to ask until I was already in the boat, so what does that say?

"Are you hitting on me? Because otherwise, why would it matter if I have a girlfriend? I thought we were just beginning to become *friends*."

She blushes swamp-berry red.

"I thought maybe we were going for a boat ride as friends, and you could tell me all about why you're here in this swamp." I make sure to catch her eye.

"Okay, then," Willow says, turning back to the water.

The bend of lilies takes only a minute to get to, and soon we're docking the boat and climbing out into gurgling mud, grabbing onto tree branches to not sink into the quicksand that lines the shore.

I watch the way Willow knows just what to do. How to relax and to not fight the mud. How to slowly get herself out. How to climb the cypress tree roots and take a seat atop so that she's safe from the water. She begins scooping mud off her boots and flinging it back into the depths. Her hands are dirty, and she smears muck across her cheek by accident.

"You look as though you've done this a hundred times."

"I might have."

"Tell me how that's possible?"

I haven't seen her in the swamp before. She must have been here, though, I reason as I climb the tree roots. They're not wide, so I cozy up next to her. Thankfully, she doesn't send me toppling into the water.

"You tell me something first," she says.

I find myself wanting to tell her anything.

5
WILLOW

I THINK BACK to the conversation I had with Gran yesterday.

"It's just an apple pie, Gran," I say. "Don't you think it's nice that I baked him one? You always tell me to be kind. I thought I could take it to him and introduce myself. Maybe make a friend."

"He doesn't deserve kindness," Gran replies. "Don't you have anything else to do instead of spending an hour in the kitchen making that good-for-nothin' boy a treat? He'll steal your soul, that's what he'll do."

I laugh. "Gran, that's a little far-fetched. I thought you said the devil's the only one powerful enough to do that."

"Who says he's any different?"

"It's just a pie."

Gran walks up to me slowly, relying heavily on her cane.

I don't see the fork in her hand until it's too late. She scoops a bite and chews. I don't know how she expects

*me to give it to him now that she's taken a chunk out of it.
"Delicious, that's what this is. Sweet, so sweet."*

*She sets the fork in the sink. Then she picks up the pie
quicker than I would have expected her to and throws it
in the trash. It melts and crumbles against the plastic bag.*

*"Let me tell you something about boys like him, Willow
Mae." I stare at her, slack-jawed. "They're attracted to
sweet more than anything. The sweeter, the better. That
boy will make you feel crazy-wonderful, all right. Yep,
sure will. And then he'll break you."*

Gran hobbles to her room and slams the door.

"What is it you want to know?" Beau asks.

I probably shouldn't trust the way he makes my
insides quiver. I place a hand against my stomach to try
to steady myself.

"Maybe the things I heard today are true." I think
back to what Jorie told me, hoping he doesn't plan to
chew me up and spit me out like the others.

"And what kinds of things are those?"

His look twists me up, and so I glance into the trees,
instead of his eyes, distracting myself with the moss that
hangs like tinsel.

"Things like how you break girls for fun."

Beau laughs, dragging my stare back to him.

"Maybe I want to break you like they say," he replies
with a disarming smile.

"You won't break me." He won't. I mean it.

He runs a finger along the dip behind my ear. Though
it's hard, I take his hand from my skin and place it back
at his side. I need to know if the rumors are actually true.

"Do you really have a girlfriend?" I blurt.

His eyes twinkle, wicked-like. "Maybe."

"What's her name?" I'm curious.

"Samantha," Beau replies. "But maybe I don't really like her."

"Is that so?" I can't rightfully judge his words yet, but I think he might be messing with me, telling me what I want to hear while doing the complete opposite.

"It could be so," he says.

"Or you could be a liar."

Beau pushes hair away from my face and rubs a thumb against my cheek. It comes away grimy. This swamp is always getting pieces stuck all over me. Mud in places mud should never be. His touch doesn't linger.

"I *am* a liar," he says. "You're a liar, too. We all are."

I like the way he presents the truth. Beau has a funny way of looking at me that makes me want to lean into him like I lean into a pillow at night.

"Where'd you get this scar?" I reach up to point at a spot on his forehead.

"There might have been a day when I was climbing the roof to replace a rotten piece of wood and I fell and split my forehead," he says. Then, "Or there might have been a day when my sister, Charlotte, threw a cup at me in annoyance."

Well, which one is it? I wonder.

"Or," he continues. "There might have been a time when I wasn't nice to a girl and her daddy found out and punched me good in the head to remind me to stay away."

I look into his riverbed-brown eyes, wondering about the strange boy who lives next door.

"Is one of those possibilities true?" I ask.

He shrugs. "Could be."

Above us, a bird trills. The swamp, thick like split-pea

soup, brushes the shins of the trees, occasionally gurgling and plopping.

"You're not nice to girls very often, are you?"

"Not too often," he says.

I think he's being honest, but it's hard to tell. "Are you being truthful now?"

He grins wickedly. "I could be."

"Do you often talk in so many damn riddles?" I ask.

"Do you often curse with such a sweet tongue?" he asks.

"Sometimes."

I pull my hair up into a high bun to get the sticky sweat off my neck. There's not much of a breeze today, and the swamp feels especially hot, but I can't think of another place I'd rather be. Beau respects the distance between us, even though I can see in his eyes that he's curious about me. Well, he's not the only curious one. My fascination with him is palpable, as thick as the muggy air around us.

"You're beautiful, Willow. Where do you come from?"

I choose to save some things for myself. "Does it really matter?"

"I want to know about you."

Since I'm no good at keeping my mind straight, I tell him. "I'm from Georgia, moved to Florida, then back to Georgia."

"Why are you here now?"

My skin tingles with excitement, happy that he wants to know more. Or maybe it's the mosquitoes.

"Nosy, aren't you?"

"How will I ever break you if I don't know more about you?" he says.

I'm not actually sure if he's joking.

"Like I said, there's not a chance of you breaking me, Beau Cadwell. I have too much Bell blood running through me for that sort of thing."

"Old Lady Bell is a strong one, I'll give her that. And you are her all over again, that's for sure. But I think you might be nicer."

I spot an otter swimming slow-like through the water, marveling at how it seems to float with no effort at all, until it disappears back beneath the surface.

"I think you might be right," I agree.

We watch the swamp, quiet to catch the noises. Mostly, the frogs croak and silence follows. But only for a few seconds before an osprey calls to the sky and mosquitoes buzz and water laps. It's a peaceful place to be. So we do just that: be.

Beau and me. The swamp and nothing else.

Beau seems content with the swamp, too, like this is where he belongs, and so it's only natural for him to close his eyes and lean on roots like he does. His smile tells me next to nothing about him but makes me want to know everything.

I study his face. Short lashes and thick lips. Soft freckles on his cheeks and a slightly wide nose if you look at it just right. His olive skin and features make me wonder where his family relocated from before settling here. His jaw is strong, and his eyes are sure when they pop open to find me staring.

"I heard you moved here when you were ten," I say. "Where'd you come from?"

"I was born in Atlanta. My dad, too. But my mom is from the Philippines."

I see it in his features. "Have you been to the islands? I've never traveled outside of the US."

"A couple of times when I was younger." Beau smiles like the memory is something special to him. "Mostly, the island is with me in stories told by my mother."

I want to ask about his parents. I haven't seen them once since moving across the way. But Beau edging closer interrupts my inquisition. I look away quickly.

"Willow," he says, less than an inch from my ear.

Something tells me that if I turn back to him, he'll kiss me. Or maybe I'll kiss him. But I'm not ready to kiss Beau, thank you very much. *Yet*, that is. I need to know a boy first. And I still can't tell if he's messing with me about having a girlfriend. I think I now understand Jorie's statement: *he has half the girls at our school in love with him.* Mysteriousness does work well for him. Makes a person want to know more.

"Better get back," I say, ignoring the fact that he just said my name. For now, I like the idea of us being friends. "Gran will be up."

It's true. She'll know that I'm gone, and the boat, too.

I stand up and work my way back through the mud to the boat. Beau follows. Until I can resist him, I avoid looking at his face. Being instantly attracted to someone I hardly know makes me uneasy and isn't something I have experience with—the rope tethered to my navel, dragging me toward his look, his touch, his crooked grin.

I pick up the oars and begin rowing home. Only boys I ever kissed had been friends of mine first. And while that was nice, the whirlwind in my gut tells me that this might be something nicer. More enticing. More exciting. I always did have to be drawn to mystery, didn't I? And Beau is that, a complete and total mystery.

"Willow." His voice is deep, and I finally turn his way. "You want to ride with me to school on Monday?"

I think of Jorie. I'd like to see her again. I'd also like to ride with Beau.

"I can't," I say. "I'm meeting a friend on the bus."

We pull up to the bank and drag the boat back to the spot where it lives under a thicket of leaves. It's harder to do with the metal coated in mud and slime, but Beau makes it look easy.

"Thanks for the help," I say.

He ties the boat to a tree and makes sure the knot is good. When it rains, waters rise like a dam bursting, swallowing land. A boat will float away without a good knot.

"You're welcome," he says.

We walk the path back to the dividing line, over a carpet of leaves pressed flat into the ground by rains.

Beau pauses. "How about this? You ride with me to school and ride the bus home after school. Then you'll see me *and* your friend."

It's a good solution.

"Can I have your number? I'll text you when I'm getting ready to leave, and you can meet me out front, if you want." He watches me. "Do you want to, Willow?"

I pull my cell out of my pocket. "How about you give me your number?"

He rattles it off, and I send a one-word message.

Yes.

His phone chimes in his pocket, and an instant later, he pulls it out and reads the text. His look, heated and gleaming, makes me take two steps toward him.

"I don't trust your eyes," I say.

He grins. "You're smart not to, Willow Bell. Come to my house in the morning. I'll give you a ride, and maybe you'll consider telling me just a little bit more about yourself."

"You'll never get my soul," I warn, thinking of Gran's words. I smile because I know what she means. A girl could fall deep into a look like his, maybe lose parts of herself while there.

"I don't want your soul, Willow."

The sound of the front door slamming tells me that Gran is now outside, most likely watching us.

"All I really want," Beau says, taking a few steps backward on his way to his place, "is you."

L ater that night, under a star-speckled sky, I sit on my porch. There's no breeze to be felt, so my tank top sticks to me like gum. Even with my hair braided to one side and the sun having fallen beneath the horizon, I feel the lingering heat from the day. A nature song plays in the background, composed of frogs croaking, insects humming, and cicadas buzzing like a live electrical wire.

Each light in the house is off, due to everyone but me being in bed, fast asleep. I can't help that the swamp makes a night owl out of me. I like the calm of it all. I look forward to evenings alone, the moon my only friend. But I know a moment later that I'm not alone. In the distance, murmurs sound.

"I'm telling you, I saw it here."

I perk up at the sound of a female voice coming from the house next door. I wonder if it's Beau's sister.

"You're sure?"

I recognize the person responding, though I've only heard his timbre a handful of times.

"Beau, I saw it. It's over there."

From a window to the side of the house, a light turns on, voices drifting out. I catch sight of Beau exiting the front door and making his way outside.

"Did you find it?" the girl asks.

I still can't see her. What I do see clearly is Beau. He bends to the ground and retrieves a small creature.

"A squirrel." He holds the tiny thing up to the light.

"Do you think it fell from a nest?" she asks.

Beau looks skyward, to the tree that hangs overhead. "Probably. I need a flashlight."

I wait in silence, watching from my spot on the porch swing. A hand extends from the window, a flashlight gripped in pink-tipped fingers. Beau turns it on. Never does he shine it my way.

"There." He finds the nest, lit up by the flashlight beam. "I need you to hold the squirrel while I climb up on the roof."

"Not a chance." The girl remains in the room.

"Come on, Charlotte." I sense the frustration in his voice, but he remains calm. "I have to climb, and I can't do it one-handed. Once I'm on the roof, I'll take it from you and replace it in the nest. That easy. Help me out here. You don't want it to die, do you?"

My suspicion is right. The girl is his sister.

"You know I don't mind creatures. It's just that it's so *small*. What if I hurt it?"

This time, Beau's tone is kind. "You won't."

After a moment, an arm reaches back through the window to hold the squirrel. Beau hands it over and quickly begins climbing the side of the house until he's on the roof, stretching back down. He's gentle when taking the creature, careful to hold it close to his chest.

Who is this boy who rescues fallen animals?

He balances the flashlight between the crook of his arm and his ribs.

I don't dare swing. I don't want to call attention to myself. I want to watch from the shadows while a curious boy who claims to be wicked so gently rescues a tiny animal.

He places the squirrel in the nest and smiles down at the window.

"There. All finished."

When he makes his way back to the front door, he pauses and swivels toward my house. I inhale sharply. Don't dare to exhale. Under the porch light, Beau looks more like a painting than something real. I can't be sure, but I almost swear I see him grin. And then he's gone. Back inside his cabin. The window closes, and the voices are silenced.

Beau saved a baby swamp squirrel. His sister asked him to do it. They are nothing like the people Jorie spoke of. Still, Beau's reputation precedes him. I can't help but wonder why.

6

BEAU

GRANDPA CADWELL IS AN OLD MAN with a young soul. He thinks he can do all the things he used to do, and to some extent, that's true. But like the rest of us, he'll eventually die. If he keeps drinking whiskey the way he is now, he might die sooner rather than later.

"Grandpa," I say, joining him in the living room, "you can't drink whiskey straight at eleven a.m."

"Boy, I'm eighty years old. I can do whatever I want."

He takes another sip. Wrinkles crease his thin-as-paper skin. His hair is silver, and his wit is sharp. He coughs roughly and swallows it down with a gulp of whiskey.

I bring the paper to him and unfold it across the table. It's from last Sunday. That's how it works with us. We're a wide sky's throw away from town, and so no one will deliver this far. Each week, while picking up our mail from the post office box, I buy the paper, save it until the next Sunday, and give it to him bright and early with his morning coffee. Or in this case, whiskey. We pretend it's the paper from today and not last week. It's the ritual that he likes more than anything.

"It's been years since your parents passed," Grandpa says. "And still the town whispers about it when they think I'm not listening, wondering what exactly happened to them."

I don't like to be reminded that they're gone.

"Any trouble for you or Charlotte at school lately? People ask questions about your parents?" He inquires every few months, just to be sure nothing has changed.

"No," I answer.

Grandpa has legal custody of us. I never knew my grandma. She died in childbirth. Grandpa never did remarry.

Charlotte enters the room. "Morning."

"Charlotte," Grandpa says, nodding to her.

She takes a whiff of the air and smiles his way. "Whiskey, eh? I think I'll have a glass, too."

"Charlotte," I say. "You can't drink whiskey."

What I really mean is that she shouldn't. She smiles like she's going to anyway, but then she saunters past, into the kitchen. She begins making what she makes every Sunday morning: french toast and eggs. I peer out the window while she cooks, my insides eager at the prospect of Willow being there. I haven't seen her since Friday, two days ago.

"Are you looking for your dreadful little obsession?" Charlotte asks, smiling roguishly.

"Ah," Grandpa says. "I saw you with her. Virginia Bell's granddaughter, right?"

"Right," I confirm.

"She'll be a stubborn one," he warns. "Her grandmother is, too."

Grandpa doesn't often talk about the specific girls he

dated in his time. Stories, sure. Names, no. Except Old Lady Bell. She gave him hell. He loved every minute of it until she sent him packing. So he bought the land across from the parcel she'd inherited from her parents. Which wasn't supposed to be for sale, but that mattered none because Grandpa always gets what he wants. Except for Old Lady Bell. He never could get her back. Won't tell me how he lost her in the first place. Still, he reminds her every day that he exists. Even though she mostly refuses to acknowledge him.

I sit next to him on the couch. The air smells of cinnamon and sugar.

"Maybe that Bell girl will turn Beau down," Charlotte says.

I hope she doesn't.

My phone chimes in my pocket. I look down to see a message from Grant asking me to join him and Pax in town.

Give me two hours, I reply.

Charlotte sets plates on the counter and shuffles eggs onto them. She makes quick work of the french toast, sprinkling cinnamon over a dusting of powdered sugar. I walk to the kitchen and take the canister to add more sugar to mine, like always.

"Do you think Willow's aware of the target on her back?" Charlotte asks.

So she does, in fact, know her name.

"Who said she has a target?"

"Your eyes say so, boy. And you know it."

I take the first bite of breakfast. It's sickly sweet. Just the way I like it.

"Let's say you're right," I reply. "So what?"

"So I just wonder if she knows, that's all."

"That I'm interested in her?" I ask. "Sure hope so."

"You always have known how to be just cunning enough to get what you want, haven't you?"

I take her compliment and swallow it down with the rest of my breakfast.

The mall is more than an hour away, but Grant insists on getting a new phone, and on Pax and me joining him.

"Took you long enough," Grant says with a smile when I arrive.

Pax waits next to him, but the two couldn't look more opposite. Grant is stringy with curly red hair and a smattering of freckles, while Pax is linebacker built with brown hair like carpet falling down over most of his face.

"Was having breakfast with my sister and grandpa," I say.

"And how is that sister of yours?" Grant asks slyly.

"Still not interested in you."

Pax grins and leads the way toward the huge looming sign for the electronics store. Inside, it's lit like a beacon. Displays advertise sales. A squeaky guy welcomes us and takes down Grant's name to put him on the wait list for assistance. Looks like we have time to kill.

I watch the way Pax stares longingly at new phones he can't afford, even though his is always having problems. I wish I could help him, but we budget the little bit we have as it is.

Since Grant's parents are a bit better off, he wastes no time going to the wall rack of cases and eyeing each one.

"What do you think of this?" he asks, taking one down.

Pax tries not to laugh. "Is that pink?"

His Southern accent is so thick that most people don't understand him unless they're from around here or unless he speaks slowly and enunciates. Even then, it's still questionable.

"It's salmon colored," Grant says.

"So, pink?" Pax teases.

Grant places the pink case back on the rack.

"What about this one?" he asks.

It doesn't look much better. It has tiny foxes stamped into it.

"Man, you have money to buy a new case and *these* are the options you pick?"

Pax's voice is lighthearted, but his look tells me he's envious.

"Fine, what do you think about these tablets?" Grant asks, changing course.

I pull up one of the screens and begin playing a game while we wait. Grant and Pax go back and forth about which company makes the best product.

A girl walks by with hair as black as space. For a moment, I think it's Willow, but then she turns and I see that I'm mistaken. She smiles at me, and Grant takes advantage of the situation by trying to talk to her himself.

"You mind?" he asks me.

"Not at all." I lean against the wall and watch as he approaches the girl.

She looks uncomfortable. He looks ecstatic.

"You think she'll turn him down?" Pax asks, laughter in his tone.

"Definitely. He has thirty seconds, tops, before she does."

I'm wrong. It takes less time than that. Grant joins

us once again with a scowl.

"Shut up," he says to my amused expression.

The girl disappears into the crowd, and I think of Willow. I find myself looking forward to tomorrow, to driving her to school, to getting her alone again. I want to know her better.

"Some of us don't have it as easy as you," Grant says.

Willow's been different, a challenge. That, and Grant knows nothing of my past.

So I reply, "I don't always have it as easy as you think."

7

WILLOW

"**W**ILLOW," SAYS A VOICE that flips me upside down, topsy-turvy like a carnival ride I don't want to get off. My breaths quicken, fluttering with a false promise of flight.

"Beau Cadwell," I reply as I step up to his house on Monday morning, wearing a blush of rose on my face.

He's standing out front, hip cocked against the doorframe, hands in his pockets.

Beau watches me.

"What are you staring at?" I ask playfully.

"A beautiful girl," he says. "Who lives next door but makes me feel like she's a thousand miles away. Tell me what you're thinking."

He takes his hands out of his pockets. Touches my arm softly. He's so gentle, so careful, in complete contrast to what I've heard of his wicked ways, that I am momentarily stunned. Heat lands on my cheeks and tumbles down. His fingertips, only the smallest portion of Beau, the faintest points of pressure, deliver shocks, and I finally understand what it means to be out of control in my own body. This is the thought that finally snaps me out of it.

"Do you think Samantha would mind you touching me like this?" I ask.

Is she real? Does he not like her like he claims? Is he lying again? I can't tell if he's a harmless flirt, or if he really does mean something by it.

"Maybe I don't care if she does," he says.

"Maybe I do," I say.

Which is, of course, a mistake. I notice a second too late. Beau laughs, and I like the sound, though I'm not sure if I want to. But I *am* sure that he now knows that I'm drawn to him, and that I care if he has a girlfriend who he plans to hurt.

I turn away, go to his old four-wheel-drive truck, and hop inside. I know it's his truck because I've seen him leave in it before. Not that I watch him. Okay, maybe I sometimes do. It's how I also know that the old man drives a Volkswagen. I caught a brief glimpse of him getting into it the other day. And I assume the small red hatchback parked under the tree belongs to Beau's sister.

The orange exterior of the truck matches the rust that eats away at the interior bottom of the door. The seats are worn to threads in parts and showing their inside cushion in others. Beau hops in the driver's side and reaches into the small backseat.

"Can you hop out for a second?" he asks.

I'm not sure what he's planning, but I oblige. He places a soft blanket over the spot where I was sitting to cover the holes.

"Better?" he asks.

"Sure." I sit back down.

He starts the engine. It coughs and sputters like it has something stuck in its throat before roaring to life.

Without a word, he begins driving the thirty minutes it takes to get to school. The sky leads a blue, blue path out of the bog, and my thoughts trail behind.

It's not until we're moments from the school that he finally speaks. "I'll break up with her today. Would you like that?"

"No," I say. "You shouldn't end a relationship because someone new comes along."

"A relationship?" He laughs.

"Or whatever you want to call it. Either way, it should be ended because you want it to be, flat out," I reply.

"I do want it over."

"Because of me?"

"Or because of how annoying it is that she wants to hang out every single day," he says.

"Maybe she likes you a lot."

"Or maybe it's because she always steals my food when we go out to eat. She can order anything. Doesn't need to eat mine," he says.

I see where he's going with this. "Are even one of those possibilities the truth?"

"No," he says.

I look into his eyes. Hold his stare. "Is that the truth?"

"No."

"Are you ever going to tell me the truth?"

"No," he answers, pulling up to the school.

"Did you just tell the truth now?"

"Yes."

I think maybe, for once, Beau *did* tell me a truth. And actually, his truth might be scarier than his lies.

"Will you ride with me every day, Willow?"

"Why should I do that?" My insides jump at the thought of spending a half hour every school day so near to Beau, smelling the scent that is deliciously him. Like bonfires and mud.

"Because I want you to," he says. Problem solved.

"Maybe I want to think about it." I open my door to a parking lot of students shuffling toward classes. Some stop to stare. Soon, others do, too.

"Will it help if I tell you that I'm definitely not gonna be with Samantha anymore? The real reason is because I didn't want to be with her anyway. Now you come along, and I think maybe we can be friends. Or more than friends. If you'll let me, I'll see you after school. I'll meet you on the swamp path, and we'll go on all the boat rides and walks and whatever it is you like. And you'll tell me the things you want. And I'll hope that I'm one of them."

I don't have time to react because a girl comes into focus, angry face, tears welling.

"What are you doing, Beau?" she asks.

Her hands shake. She is beautiful. Long golden locks that fall to her waist. A slender face and frame. Cheeks and nose rosy like she's trying her damnedest not to cry.

It hits me who she must be.

Beau stills. "Why, hello, Samantha."

8

BEAU

I WAIT, A LONG PAUSE like a person taking his last breath, trying to decide what to do. Willow looks like she's attempting to figure me out. It also appears as though she feels bad for Samantha.

Samantha is on the verge of tears. Her lip trembles. She bites it to keep her composure. Then repeats herself.

"What are you doing?"

Her voice is barely a whisper now.

"Samantha, this is my new neighbor, Willow," I say. It would have been easier if she hadn't seen us arrive together. There's nothing to Willow and me—we *are* only friends—but I can see how Samantha might think something else. "Willow, this is Samantha."

I hate that the entire school is watching. This would be so much easier without a crowd. Samantha doesn't deserve a public breakup.

"Samantha," Willow says, voice strong. "So you *are* real."

Willow thought my riddles might not be true. That maybe I wasn't involved.

"Real?" Samantha asks, confused.

Willow sends me a hardened glance. She doesn't seem to care for the way the situation is unfolding, either. She offers Samantha a look of sympathy. It's unnerving, how none of my schoolmates seems to care that the bell will ring soon. No one moves or offers privacy.

I spot Grant trying to peer over the crowd. He's standing next to Pax, who has no problem seeing the situation unfold.

"Willow, would you mind if I meet up with you later?" I hate to see her go, but I have something to take care of first.

Willow nods and disappears into the crowd.

"Beau?" Samantha says my name, trying to pull my attention back. She's looking at me, hopeful.

"Want to take a walk?" It's the only way to get her away from the crowd.

"Okay," she replies.

Her anxiety shows in the fidgeting of her fingers, the slight tremor that she can't quite hide. I wonder if she, too, feels that it hasn't been working, this thing between us.

"We've been together almost a month now," she says as we escape the onlookers.

I suspect she knows what I mean to say to her, that our time is over.

"We were never really together," I reply. "Not officially." My voice is soft, meant to lessen the blow.

"What about the times we shared at my house?"

"I remember."

We make our way around the rear of the school, where only a few stragglers ever venture, leaving the crowd behind. I keep quiet as we pass two smokers leaning against a wall. They pay us no mind, more concerned with putting out their cigarettes and hurrying through the back entrance before the bell rings.

"Go ahead, Beau," she says when we pass them. "It seems you want to say something, so do it."

"I'm sorry." I really am. I don't mean to hurt her, it's just that I don't get close to people, which she's known from the beginning. We were never meant to be anything more than casual, though it seems to have developed into more for her. "I don't think it's working out."

She hides her face behind a blond blanket of hair. I almost reach for her. Not because I want her but because it would be nice, for once, to not be so unyielding.

"Are you sure this is what you want?" Her tone is sad, but there is a look of understanding when she meets my eyes.

"Yes."

She sighs and blinks several times quickly. "I kind of thought we were good together."

Shows how much I know about girls. I figured she understood that we are two worlds apart.

"Do you honestly think it's working, Samantha?" I ask. "We haven't spoken as much lately. We lead different lives. We don't have any of the same friends. You live on the other side of town, and school is the only real time we spend together, unless I make the trip to your place."

"I think it *could* work." She reaches for the door, opening it and glancing inside to make sure we're still alone.

A blast of cool air-conditioning hits both of us, ruffling our clothes and hair. We have a ways to walk to get to class, and we will likely be late, but it's better than the entire school witnessing our breakup.

"Maybe, occasionally, I should head to your place."

But even as she says it, she cringes. I don't hold it against her. The swamp isn't for everyone. It takes a certain person to be happy in such a quiet, eerie place.

"We both know you don't mean that," I say with a small grin.

I nod toward Samantha's outfit, a beautiful flowery dress and heels. Her hair and makeup are perfect. I can't help thinking about how quickly it would melt off in the swamp heat. Her clothes would be dirty in an instant, and her heels would never work.

"I have some shorts and T-shirts," she replies, a small smile in her voice. "That would be okay for the swamp, right?"

"Sure. But it's not just the clothes. You don't like the swamp. It scares you. You told me that from the start. And I don't want you to pretend to like it for me. You should never have to pretend for someone else."

We take the hall to the front of the school, where classroom doors are shutting, the final bell ringing.

"Maybe you're right. But I could still make more of an effort."

"It's probably best to let it go," I reply.

She'll find a guy more suited for her, I'm certain of it.

Samantha doesn't protest. She simply bites her lip and offers one more look.

"Goodbye, Beau."

"Man, did you hear?" Pax asks as he meets me for lunch in the library lounge. "Samantha left early today. Did that have anything to do with you?"

It's odd to hear of her early departure, considering that she seemed fine when I last saw her. Maybe a little disappointed overall about our breakup but not too upset. I frown, thinking back over it. I can't find any reason she'd need to leave school because of me. Unless it upset her more than she let on.

"Maybe. We broke up."

"Sorry to hear that. How'd it go?"

"Not too bad. She was nice about it."

"That's a relief."

"Maybe she's sick." I think over possibilities for her early release. "Who knows?"

Pax studies my unsure expression. "The thing is, I overheard one of her friends saying that Samantha was upset about a guy."

I sigh, knowing it's too big a coincidence to be anyone other than me. "Maybe she didn't take the breakup as well as I thought."

I feel a big hand settle on my shoulder. Pax grins goofily.

"Don't worry about it. She'll move on. They always do." He pats my back roughly before stretching both arms out and leaning back in his chair. "Good spot here, by the way."

Our school thought by adding several areas with comfortable chairs, and even more spaces between shelves with beanbags set right on the ground for people to sink into, that they would entice students to read more. What they've really done is made the library less of a quiet area and more of a designated separate cafeteria, since most people try to snag a room to eat in. The students not eating are either listening to music, earbuds in, or on the computers, surfing social media. A few do choose to read.

Pax brushes his mop of hair from his eyes and fills out the seat, making it look small under him. A second later, Grant arrives.

"Thanks for getting a spot," he says. "I heard about you and Samantha."

"Yeah," I reply, not wanting to go into the details.

Grant empties a sack on the table. Out falls a chocolate bar, bag of chips, pretzel, can of soda, greasy hamburger wrapped in yellow foil, and a pickle—the only healthy thing in there—which he promptly hands to Pax because it's his favorite, and because we know he sometimes doesn't have money for lunch, since his mom was laid off earlier this year.

I toss a turkey-bacon sandwich Pax's way and play it off like I hadn't planned on eating much.

"Not too hungry," I say.

I fool no one, but Pax takes the sandwich and eats.

"Thanks, man," he says between bites.

"So what's up with the new girl?" Grant asks. "She's your neighbor, I hear."

"She is, but I don't know much about her yet," I say.

I'm counting on that "yet," even though a small warning flares in the back of my mind, cautioning Willow may be different than the others, evidenced by how she doesn't demand my time—or much of anything from me, really—yet still I can't seem to get enough of her. By now, with other girls, a date is usually expected. Not with Willow. What she expects is for me to know that she carries a knife in the bog, smiles at gators, and hails from Southern blood that goes back as far and deep as the swamp itself.

Sandwich now gone, Pax eyes my orange. I toss it to

him. I'll eat extra when I get home.

"You lucky son of a bitch," Grant says. "What I would give to have a neighbor like her. All I have is the old man who calls me 'damn kid' and the lady who always forgets to lock her chickens up, so I'm constantly tripping over them in our yard."

I laugh. He's not kidding about the chickens. From the few times I've been to his place, I can attest that they're everywhere.

"Now that you're free, you gonna ask her out?" Grant asks.

"I'm thinking about it."

"Good luck with that," Grant replies.

"She have any friends?" Pax asks.

"Maybe. Why don't you ask her?"

Pax actually has had a couple of girlfriends, mostly ones who have approached him, though he's not with anyone at the moment.

I eat hush puppies dipped in buttery mashed potatoes and wash them down with a can of soda.

"I wish I had your life," Grant says.

He doesn't realize—because I hardly talk about more than school, girls, and mindless things with my friends— that the truth is, he wouldn't want my life.

Not if he saw the dark parts of it.

9

WILLOW

"I HEARD HE BROKE UP with that girl, Jorie," I say.
I haven't spoken to him since. It's been four days. I
needed time to process what it meant that Beau really did
have a girlfriend when he was looking at me like maybe
he wanted to be more than friends. He was involved with
someone else, and I'm not sure that I like the fact that
he was interested in me at the same time.

"He did, and I have a feeling that you might not be
too upset about it," Jorie replies, being her truthful self.
That's part of why I like her. "He's free now. And deny
it all you want, you're happy he's free."

Jorie lies on my bed with the elegance of a person
who is completely at ease. Like she's been here a
thousand and one times—throwing her shoes in the
corner, sprawled out on her back, watching me pace
the small area that houses a twin bed, an aged wooden
dresser painted pink, and a desk made from recycled
shutters. I circle the distressed hardwood floor, my feet
padding across a plum rug before connecting with warm
wood again.

"It's more that I wish he didn't have a girlfriend to begin with. I don't like the idea of him hurting Samantha's feelings. They were together for however long."

"Probably no more than a couple of weeks," Jorie interjects. "That's the longest he'll hold onto a girl."

I consider her words, but I don't know what to make of them. I think of the night he saved the fallen squirrel, showing a soft part of himself that I doubt many see. I want to give Beau a chance, to get to know him better. Reason warns me to be careful. Would he only want me for a couple of weeks?

But then the reminder of his soft touch on my skin severs all tension in my limbs. Warmth seeps into my cheeks and neck. I'm surprised by the want that worms into my bones. I can't erase the hope that he touches me again, that he shows me the softer side of himself, and that he locks his meanness away.

I stop pacing and sink into the mattress next to Jorie to think about how lucky I am to have made a friend quickly. How equally lucky I am that she doesn't mind my riding with Beau in the mornings and leaving her alone on the bus. How she doesn't seem to mind my talking things out with her.

"What do you think he wants from me?" I ask.

Jorie laughs wildly. When she does, I can't help but stop to stare at how her mouth stretches wide. It's contagious. Only I don't feel like laughing right now.

"Do you really want me to answer that?" she asks.

"Of course."

"He wants you to fall for his wicked ways and, consequently, him. He's no good for you, but I understand if you decide to give him a try. I know it's hard to fight the pull."

He does have a pull. *What's with that?*

"Maybe it's not as straightforward as that. There's a possibility that he genuinely wants to know me. But it's hard to tell because he almost never gives me direct answers. I try to learn about him, and he runs circles around me. The truth is that the more I get to know him, the less I know him."

"You will never win with him, Willow."

"I don't want to win. I want to know why he's so difficult to figure out. It's hard not to think about him."

"Think about who?" Gran says, surprising us in the doorway.

"No one," I blurt. Which is the wrong thing to say because it only makes Gran suspicious.

"Not again." Gran holds tightly to her cane. "I know you are *not* talking about the boy next door."

I sigh. "He's not *that* bad."

"He *is* that bad. Now you and your friend come downstairs for cookies and milk and don't even think about inviting him to join you."

I laugh and try to picture it. Beau at our kitchen table, reaching for a cookie while Gran throws a Bible at him, yelling curses at his sinful heart.

"Got it." I almost invite him over just to enjoy the show.

"By the way, Gran, this is my friend Jorie. Jorie, this is my gran," I say, making introductions.

"Pleasure to meet you, Jorie," she says kindly. Then proceeds to go right back to speaking about Beau.

She gives me one of her warning stares.

"You shouldn't be meeting him out there, either, Willow Mae." She points to the window, toward the dividing path.

"Mom and Dad said it's fine for me to hang out with him," I say.

"What do they know?" Gran huffs, leaning heavily on the doorframe. "They're too busy studying vultures."

Gran doesn't let up with her penetrating stare. She may be mostly rounded, but her eyes are sharp as tacks.

"Herons," I correct.

"Who cares?" Gran says. "They think it wouldn't hurt for you to have a little fun, but they're wrong."

I look at Jorie apologetically. I love Gran. I'm proud to be hers. But sometimes she goes off on fits, and who knows when this one will end. But Jorie doesn't look freaked out or bored. She looks interested.

"Just listen to me and keep a wide mile between you, you hear?"

"Okay," I answer.

I don't mean it.

She knows I don't mean it.

We're at odds.

"Did you hear that?" I ask.

With Gran's loud downstairs television and her hurling warnings at me upstairs, it's hard to notice much else, but I pick up on it.

"There," I say. "I think someone's at the door."

"Have mercy on his soul if it's the boy next door." Gran turns and walks down the hall.

Bang. Bang. Bang. The sound is louder as we descend the steps. There's definitely someone at the door. I only hope for Beau's sake that it isn't him. He's got to be smarter than that.

Gran opens the screen. "What in the hell's so important that you need to break down my door?" she says over the television volume.

A police officer stands there, hand on his gun, looking us over. He's quiet for a heartbeat, long enough for my thoughts to run wild.

I immediately think of nothing good. Fear freezes my feet to the ground. I can't move. I can't breathe.

"What happened?" I ask. "Where are Mom and Dad? Are they okay?"

"Couldn't tell you," the officer replies. "I'm not here about your parents. But if you'd turn down the volume, I'd like to ask you a few questions."

Relief courses through me. There is no bad news to deliver. I calm my racing heart.

Gran hobbles to the television and shuts it off. It's an old thing, the type with a turn dial and an antenna V-ing at the top. We wanted to buy her a new one, but Gran insists hers works just fine if you can see past the static. My room, thankfully, has a new flat screen.

We all take a seat at the kitchen table where Gran offers him every meal under the sun. Eggs and bacon? She can whip it up quickly. Lemon chicken and green beans? It should be done in twenty minutes. Why she expects him to stay that long, I don't know. Maybe leftover lasagna? Would take just a moment to heat. On and on. Each time, the officer declines.

I look at his badge. Deputy Clarke. I can't help but wonder why he would venture into the swamp.

Deputy Clarke flips a page in his notebook and pulls out a pen. "Have you noticed anything strange around the swamp lately?"

Strange things happen all the time. For instance, just the other day, I saw a gator trying to eat a bobcat. They'll go after just about anything. Nearly got its eyes clawed out for such an attempt. The officer will have to narrow it down if he means for us to know what he's talking about.

"Sure have." Gran goes to the fridge. "Good-for-nothin' neighbors next door. That's what's strange here."

The officer nods. "Why do you say that?"

"Do you know he thinks he has the right to tell me whether or not I can feed the gators?"

"Um," the officer says, taken aback. "You're not actually supposed to feed the gators, ma'am."

"Lord have mercy," Gran says. "Not you, too."

The officer turns to us. "Do you girls live here?"

"I do," I reply. "With my parents and my gran. This is my friend Jorie."

"I see," the officer says. "Have you two noticed anything off?"

"Not really," I answer.

Maybe Beau is a little off. Maybe I am, too.

"Do you know someone named Nicole Star?"

"No," Jorie and I say in unison.

"What school do you go to?"

We answer each of his questions. Name. Birthdate. Parents' names. He pauses and looks up at us.

"You sure you don't know her? You attend the same school. Maybe I could show you a picture?"

"Sure," I say.

His hand emerges from his pocket with a crinkle of paper. He slides a photo across the table to Jorie and me. We both gasp. I would know her face anywhere.

"Samantha," I whisper.

"Samantha?" the officer repeats. "Her name is—" He pauses. "Wait. Let me double-check her middle name."

He shuffles through his notebook.

"Right. Okay." He looks up. "I suppose you're correct. Her name is Nicole Samantha Star. Did she go by Samantha? Were you friends?"

"Were?" I say at the same time that Jorie says, "No."

"Do you know anything about her being in the swamp last night?" he asks.

"No," we say in unison.

"But she used to go out with the boy next door," I offer.

"I already questioned him on that." The officer picks the photo back up off the table and returns it to his pocket. "He didn't see her last night. Any chance you did?"

"No," I reply. "Why?"

"Because," the officer says, "the swamp was the last place she was known to be heading before—"

He leaves his sentence half hanging like a broken shutter.

"Before what?" I ask, curious.

What does he want with the ex-girlfriend of the boy next door, and what does that have to do with us?

"You and the Cadwell family are the only people out this deep in the swamp proper," the officer says. "These are the farthest waters before there's no more houses. I thought maybe you might have seen her? Known if she was with anyone? Talked to her at all? Her parents say she never ventures to the swamp."

I can think of one reason she'd want to come to the swamp. My gut-deep reaction tells me she meant to be here, and that she meant for Beau to know about her visit. Does it have something to do with their breakup? Or maybe they got back together? What I can't understand is what the officer has to do with anything.

"Why don't you ask Samantha these things?" Gran says, shuffling around the kitchen, squirting juices on the chicken she's preparing so it doesn't dry out. I hope she doesn't mean for the officer to stay awhile. She sets a plate of cookies and a pitcher of milk on the table with three glasses.

"I can't ask her," he says.

"Why not?"

"Because," the officer says, "that's what I'm trying to investigate."

"Her disappearance?" Gran asks, eyeing Mr. Cadwell's house.

"Not her disappearance."

Gran stops shuffling.

My eyes snap to his.

"What I'm investigating is her death."

10
BEAU

COME MONDAY MORNING, the entire school is abuzz with the news of one of their own. Slain, the officers are saying. The words "killed," "murdered," "dead" don't belong in our school.

I can't help but notice how girls won't hold my stare, how people shrink away from me. The hall parts swiftly and drastically, making me tense. They suspect me. They must if they fear my very presence. I catch a whisper here, another there.

He dated her.

Do you think he hurt her?

He probably wanted her out of the way so he could go after the new girl.

Do they honestly believe I'd kill a girl?

I zone in on Willow, dark-as-sin hair plummeting down her back. I want to go to her. I want to know why she won't talk to me ever since I called things off with Samantha.

The school's eyes are on me, following my every move. I had a feeling this might happen. Samantha was linked to me before she died, after all.

"Willow's not looking your way," Pax says with a small grin. "Must be driving you crazy."

It is, if I'm being honest. But I'm not honest often, so I keep my response to myself.

"When was the last time a girl didn't say yes to you right away?" Grant holds back a laugh.

They're having fun messing with me. For all the times I've joked with them, I deserve it.

"I didn't technically ask her anything, so she can't actually say yes."

I try to dig myself out of the hole, but it's no use.

"Have you taken her out yet?"

"You already know the answer," I reply.

Pax actually laughs out loud, turning heads.

"You guys are assholes," I mutter, but I'm grinning, too.

I grab books from my locker and take off toward Willow. Pax and Grant follow.

She spots me, but the flood of students delays my approach. I push through, thanks mostly to Pax's size muscling a path. When I get near, I see a guy has stopped to talk to her. She smiles at something he says. He extends a cup to her, and I notice the logo of the local tea company.

"He brought her tea?" Grant asks.

I wait for her reaction. She takes it like he's handing her gold and drinks immediately. So she likes tea. I'll keep that in mind. I wonder what else she likes besides boat rides in the mire, cursing, and tea from strangers.

"Want to go out sometime?" I catch the guy saying.

"Sure," Willow replies.

A bell rings, warning that we have a minute to get to class.

"Ouch." Pax watches the exchange, offering me a look that says he's sorry I have to see it.

"Man, I can't look anymore. It's too painful," Grant jokes as he slaps me on the back.

"I can't be late again." Pax eyes the other end of the building where he and Grant have class.

I couldn't care less about being late.

"Don't worry about it, man. It's just one date. Doesn't mean anything," Pax says. "See you at lunch."

He heads off with Grant.

Willow pulls a cell phone from her pocket to quickly program his number. It lights up with a text. Around us, students hurry to class, me standing snap-still like a pillar in the middle of the crowd, watching Willow.

"She said yes to someone else," comes a whisper.

I turn toward the voice.

Charlotte.

She's looking her usual self.

"Never thought I'd see the day," she says quietly, "when my little brother stands around watching another guy ask out the girl he's interested in. Sure you're not losing your touch?"

"I'm older than you, remember?"

She laughs, and the noise is something like what I'd imagine sea sirens would sound like moments before they drown their victims.

My attention returns to Willow and the guy who has short, dark dreadlocks. Willow looks right at me as she takes a big swallow of her tea from the guy who now has her number and the promise of a date.

He turns to leave just as the final bell screeches like a banshee through the corridor.

"We'll talk later," Charlotte says, making for her class.

I wait only a moment, enough for Charlotte and the guy to be gone, before I approach Willow.

"I didn't realize caffeine was the way to get a date." I flash a grin.

"Maybe I don't want to go out with you, Beau," she says. "Maybe I want to go out with Brody."

"Is that his name?"

"Or maybe I want to go out with the other guy who invited me on Friday for pizza. I happen to like pizza."

Two guys now? Maybe Charlotte's right. Perhaps I *am* losing my edge. No, on second thought, that can't be it.

"Or maybe I want to walk away from you and never speak to you again," she says.

"How does it feel, Beau? To hear nothing but riddles? Do you like it? Maybe one of those is true. Or maybe none at all. You figure it out."

Maybe it's the fact that no one challenges me, perhaps that's why I'm completely stuck, my words gone. I think, though, that I do like her riddles. I think I appreciate that she has a backbone and that she stands up to me. But it's hard to tell because nothing like this has happened before.

"I will meet you on the path today," Willow says as the late bell rings. "And you will answer every question I have about Samantha and how all this happened."

So that's why she seems upset.

She walks away.

"Wait," I say.

But she's already gone.

• • •

had nothing to do with Samantha's death," I say as Willow stands next to me under a weeping tree.

The fact is that I have no idea what happened to Samantha, not that Willow believes me. I wonder if she would if I told her that Samantha's death haunted me all last night, woke me from my dreams, drenched in a sweat so thick it felt as though I'd brought the bog inside with me. I'm the reason she visited the swamp, even though I'm not the reason she never left. I try to speak my feelings to Willow, but the words stick to my tongue, mixing with nausea. I can't help but feel guilty.

Samantha died on her way to see me. I didn't want her to come. Told her so myself. It seems Pax was right in what he'd overheard. Samantha did leave school early because she was upset. She sent a text that night, wanting to stop by to tell me how much our breakup hurt her, hoping I might change my mind and give it another shot. My response was a firm *no*. She even called to try to talk about it, wanting to visit me in person. I didn't see how her coming to my house would change anything. We were still two very different people. Done and over.

She never did make it to my property, and as far as I knew then, she wasn't coming in the first place. I thought my *no* was enough of a response. How was I to know that she'd take it upon herself to come anyway? I never imagined she'd drive to the swamp even though I told her not to come. She'd only ever been to my house once. Had she gotten lost, took a wrong turn, couldn't remember the exact way, and instead ended up somewhere she didn't mean to be, where someone evil took advantage?

"I'm telling the truth," I say.

I throw a quick glance at Willow's house. So far, so good. Old Lady Bell hasn't come out.

Her eyes slant. "Are not."

"Am, too."

"Liar," she challenges.

"I am a liar," I admit, swallowing down my trepidation. "Just not about this."

The sun trades off with the moon. There's nothing like a night in the bog. Cicadas buzz so loudly that I swear they've found a way into my eardrums.

"Trust me this time." I practically have to yell.

Willow laughs. "Trust you? That's rich."

I see her point.

"Look, all I know is that Samantha was upset. She called and asked if she could come over. I said no. I never should have let her come the one time I did. Usually we went to her house."

Willow's eyes narrow further.

"That's not the point," I say. "Point is, I said 'no,' and that was the end of it."

"Yet still, she ended up here."

I nod. "She must have come anyway. I didn't know. I never saw her. Ask my family. I was with them all night."

Willow looks me directly in the eyes. "See, right now I think you might be telling the truth, but maybe not."

"I am." I might be mean sometimes, but not mean enough to kill.

Willow shifts, and a spider crawls dangerously close to her arm. She pays it no mind.

"Fine, let's say I believe you," Willow says. "That really only leaves more questions like: who would do such a thing?"

"Believe me, I'd like to know."

Because that means Willow's family and my family aren't the only ones out here.

11

WILLOW

I DON'T SPEAK A SYLLABLE for nearly two hours. I know because that's the amount of time I've spent walking, rowing, climbing the swamplands, seeking relief from being stuck indoors, and thinking about the dead girl. My parents keep me company, searching for elusive birds that apparently, for whatever godforsaken reason, need complete quiet to show their faces.

As soon as Mom heard about the murder, she insisted we have a day together, picking me up directly from school to do so. Probably mostly to make herself feel better for leaving me alone so much. Dad, having questioned me about Beau's connection to the victim, doesn't seem convinced that my hanging out with Beau is a good idea, no matter how many times I tell him that the police cleared him of any wrongdoing and that Beau has an alibi. I don't blame Dad for looking out. He only means to keep me safe. Mom believes in the police findings, thankfully. If there were reason to doubt, she'd insist I don't see Beau again. But instead, she encourages me to keep close to a friend.

"I don't think the birds are coming," I say, glancing at my mother.

"They'll come," she insists. "You just haven't taught your patience how to wait yet."

How much longer could it possibly take? It's a couple of hours until dusk, the sun angling overhead, pressing down on us with blazing rays. I wonder if more birds come out at night like many of the other swamp creatures.

We're sitting in a grassy spot that snakes insist on taking from us. I keep having to warn them off with a long stick. So far only one of the three has been venomous.

"My patience is perfectly fine," I argue.

I almost never argue with Mom. She knows instantly that something is up.

"What has that boy done now?" she asks with an all-knowing grin.

Dad glances at us but notices the keep-out sign attached to my forehead, so he says nothing.

I can't talk to Dad about boys.

Mom is another story.

I lower my voice. "He had a girlfriend."

"But he doesn't anymore?"

"Right."

"And this is a problem because…?"

"Because," I say, sighing, "there's a chance that he might have broken up with her for me. I hung out with him, thinking the girlfriend rumors were false. It's so hard to tell with him. He doesn't always come right out and say things directly. But it was true—they *were* together. We didn't do anything, he and I, but still. What if I unintentionally played a part in their breakup? She came to the swamp to see Beau. I can't help feeling guilty for that."

Mom sighs, gently patting my hand. "Sweetheart, you can't make decisions for someone else. What's done is done. Try not to worry too much about the specifics. It's horrible, yes. But it's not your fault. You're experimenting. Creating memories. As long as you're safe about it, it's not a bad thing."

Mom is all about experimenting. It took her nearly all the years she's been married to Dad for Gran to warm up to her free spirit. Gran likes structure and boundaries. I do, too. I also like seeing how far they stretch.

"That's not how I wanted to start things with a boy," I say.

Maybe I'm a bit of a romantic.

"But you like him," Mom counters.

"I like a lot of things. Doesn't mean they're good for me."

"So don't keep him forever. Maybe just for a little while."

Mom is the kind of parent who hands the reins to me and lets me figure out how to steer. I appreciate her leniency, even if sometimes I crave more direct advice.

"So what you're saying is that I should go for it?" I ask.

Dad cuts in, although it might cost him his tongue. He promised not to interfere with boy issues. That's what Mom is for.

"I'm not sure I like this plan," he says.

"Do I need to tell your daughter some of the adventures we had at her age?"

They dated in high school. Broke up. Connected again after college. Once Mom was finished with her own experimenting.

Dad's face goes scarlet. "Absolutely not."

Mom smiles and kisses him so hard that he forgets

what he was saying. I turn around and try not to hear whatever it is they're doing that I'm going to pretend they're not doing.

"We're supposed to be quiet for the birds!" I yell.

They pull apart and laugh. We go back to not speaking. The entire time, I try to focus on the scenery and not on Beau.

It takes every filament of my being to succeed. When a bird finally lands on a low-hanging branch, Mom and Dad scribble reports in their trusty pocket notebooks. Mom hands a notebook and pencil to me, encouraging me to draw the bird. Since any reprieve is welcome, I get lost in the scratch of lead on paper, in the act of directing my attention to such an infinitesimal process, looking up every few seconds to commit another feature to memory. A shimmery blue wing. A sharp, quizzical look reflected in a beady black eye. A creature perched for viewing. My sketch is messy but surprisingly good.

"Impressive, sweetheart." Mom looks over my shoulder at the drawing. "I should bring you along for every observation. Do you want to stay longer and wait for the next bird?"

I love my parents, but I will die of boredom if I have to stay much longer. When I glance back up, the bird is gone.

"I have a date, remember?"

Mom leans in to me. "I remember. Are you sure that's the date you really want to be on, though?"

Somehow, Mom knows it's Beau I truly crave, not Brody. And since I have no intention of lying to her, I remain silent. My lack of response hangs in the air, and Mom seems to watch it float by.

"Do you think it's wrong for me to go on a date when

I have feelings for someone else?" I ask. Not that Beau and I are an item. I just wonder if I should go through with my plans tonight.

"No, it's not wrong. Go have fun. Who knows, you might actually enjoy yourself tonight. Maybe you'll like Brody more than you like Beau," she says.

Maybe she's right.

Even still, when I turn to leave to head back home, when I look up at the sky and try to make shapes of the clouds, it's Beau's face I see.

I'm not sure that going on a date with Brody is smart, especially since I can't stop thinking about Beau. But here I am. Brody seems much more likely to be boyfriend material. It's worth a shot.

Our double date begins just as the sun slips down the sky. Brody's friend Yin accompanies Jorie. I hope he's as nice as Brody. But just in case, if things turn sour, Jorie and I can leave together. No awkward goodbyes and fake excuses.

Keeping pace a step ahead of us, leading us through town to a shop that boasts a miniature golf course out back, are our dates. Seven dollars each to get in. Jorie and I offer to pay, but the boys insist that they've got it.

I wonder if Beau would pay for me. My gut tells me that he wouldn't. Maybe because he sees me as an equal who can take care of myself, or maybe because he doesn't have as many kind bones in his body as I'd like to give him credit for.

"They've known each other all their lives," Jorie says.

"Their parents co-own the general store in town."

Our dates have been best friends longer than I've been friends with anyone.

"Think we'll still be close, you and me, years down the road?" I ask.

Jorie's smile could light the entire town. "Definitely. One day we'll look back at this night and talk about how I beat you in miniature golf."

"Hey!" I laugh. "You don't know for sure you'll win."

A lady with a poof of hair held together by what appears to be an entire can of hairspray offers me a red-handled club and golf ball and Jorie a purple one.

"Here you go, sweetheart. Golf course is right out the back. Come on in for refreshments if you get thirsty. Cooler's on the side wall over there. I might even give y'all free slushes, since it's dead around here. Our little secret, though. Can't have every customer wantin' one."

She winks and offers Brody the green club and ball and Yin the blue one.

"Thanks." I drop a dollar into the tip jar.

It's quiet as we step outside. A beautiful breeze slides among the buildings and cools the heat, which is maybe why no one else is here. There's a storm on the horizon. The chalk-white moon spills over the course. Small stringed lights line each numbered section, reminding me of Christmastime, helping to ease my nerves.

"I can keep score if you want." Brody places a miniature pad and pencil into his shirt pocket and flashes me a warm smile. I like his smile. It's honest and genuine and nice. Unlike Beau's wicked grins.

"That'd be great, thanks." I tuck a loose strand of hair behind my ear and force down the nerves that lodge in my throat.

"Who wants to go first?" Brody asks.

They are opposites, Beau and Brody. Where Beau is wild and mysterious and sharp around the edges, Brody is smooth and kind, with soft eyes that match his gently smiling mouth, which quirks to one side with my assessment. His skin is beautifully dark, such a contrast to my own. His gaze fixes on me, calm and unflappable.

"Me!" Jorie says, showing a competitive side. "Y'all better be ready to buy me ice cream when I win."

That was the deal. The winning duo buys.

"Are you any good at this?" I ask Brody.

"You'll see." He winks.

Turns out Brody *is* good. Really good. He gets a hole in one right off the bat.

"How did you do that?" I cringe at the score he's recording for me. Okay, so I'm not the best golfer.

"There's not much else to do around here," he replies.

Which is true. The town is basically a row of shops that sell clothes, knickknacks, candy, ice cream, and coffee. Miniature golf is the only attraction. Which explains why both Jorie and Yin are good at it, too.

"We're gonna lose," I warn Brody.

He laughs and bumps my shoulder playfully. "It's okay, I don't mind. I'm just glad you're here."

Maybe I could go out with Brody again. It's easy to talk to him. And he seems like a good guy. For a moment, I honestly do forget about Beau.

"Yes!" Jorie yells when she sinks the ball in only two shots at a super-twisty hole.

It's my turn. It takes me eight tries to get the ball in the tiny cup.

"I forget. How does it feel to lose?" Yin jokes with Brody.

"It's my fault. Brody is really good." I'm bringing him down, but I honestly don't know how to do any better.

"I know." Yin smiles to let me know he's only teasing. "But there's just not enough chances for me to rub it in his face that he's losing."

"Because I normally beat you." Brody laughs. I'm drawn to the deep sound.

"I like peach ice cream," Jorie says. "In case you were wondering which to buy me."

"Oh, shut up." I grin.

"Are you even trying out there?" Jorie nudges my arm with her elbow.

"Would you believe me if I said I was?"

We walk to the next hole, enough space between us and the boys for Jorie to lower her voice so as to not be heard by anyone but me. "He's watching you."

I look up to see Brody's eyes on me.

"He's nice," I say.

"Better than Beau."

A sudden image of Beau's face flickers across my mind, a camera lens going in and out of focus. First, a sparkling-clear Beau with sweat dripping from his temples, standing under a one-thousand-degree swamp sun. Then a blurry Brody, obscured by low-reaching fog that begins to spread like steam over the golf course. Then Beau, mouthing my name, as though calling me to him. Then Brody edging closer to me.

"Yes, better than Beau." I think twice. "At being nice with people's hearts, I suppose, but maybe not better in other ways."

"Such as?"

I wonder if I should admit the truth. That I'm thinking of Beau even now. That I am comparing him to Brody.

"Such as keeping my interest."

"You're bored with Brody?"

"No. It's just that Beau won't let me be. Even when he's not around, I can't erase him from my mind."

"Well, at least Brody isn't tied to a dead girl. That ought to help ease your mind."

I cringe and fumble with the putter in my hand. "Is that fair?"

Jorie shrugs. "Maybe."

The wind catches her white dress and wraps it around her body. Her striped hair is decorated with a pink headband, and I think about how beautiful she looks. She put more effort into tonight than I did. I glance down at my jeans and cream top. My hair is in a messy ponytail, and I didn't bother with makeup. If it hadn't been for Beau taking up so much of my thoughts, I might have concentrated more on preparing for my date with Brody.

"Let's just have fun," Jorie says. "We've got three more holes, and then you can buy me ice cream."

She runs up to knock the ball into the hole, which she does in four tries. It takes Yin four tries, too.

Brody joins me. "The trick is to hit it to the left. There's another hole there that acts as a tunnel straight to the final hole. It'll pop out right by it. You can get it in two tries."

I take his advice and make it in two tries, much to my astonishment. I raise my hands in victory, a broad grin on my face. Even so, there's nothing I can do that will push us ahead of Jorie and Yin. Not even the fact that Brody makes a hole in one five times.

"Knew it," Jorie says with a smile.

"Fine, I'll buy you peach ice cream," I say.

We turn the clubs back in and make it to the sweet

shop just as the first raindrops begin to fall. The sky rolls with thunderclaps and purple waves of clouds. I picture Beau standing under it all.

No.

That's not what I should be picturing.

Brody slowly drapes a tentative arm around me, waiting for my reaction. And since I don't want to think about Beau tonight, I lean in to Brody to tell him it's okay, that I like him, because I honestly do. Simultaneously, I act as though I'm not at all thinking about another boy.

If only I were oblivious to my own lies.

12

BEAU

THE BOG STRETCHES on forever, and my curiosity goes with it. Charlotte and Grandpa sit in the boat with me, each of us wondering the same thing.

Who's creeping through our swamp?

No one has permission to be on our land. Old Lady Bell has given no one authorization to be on hers, either. We have a trespasser on our hands. A murderer, more like it. Finding them, if they're still here, is now our number one priority.

Just out of reach, a snapping turtle surfaces. Its spiky shell is covered in green fuzz, and its head is as large as my fist, tipped with a beak-like jaw. Its milky eyes and size tell me that it's old, and it's easily one hundred pounds. One of the bigger ones I've seen but certainly not the biggest.

"Mom's favorite," Charlotte whispers.

But then her face goes blank, as though she didn't mean to say the words. It's too late. I'm already remembering her.

I watch, transfixed, just barely nine years old, as Mom wrangles an alligator snapping turtle into the open for Charlotte and me to see. She's huffing and panting and completely out of breath. Her brown hair is plastered to her face, and she's lying atop the thing like she's wrestled an actual alligator, pushing all her weight on it to keep it still. Dad pins down the head, the most dangerous part because it has a mouth that can snap off fingers.

"Look at it," Mom says, in awe.

She's covered in muck from the turtle, which looks as though it's been submerged for a while. Unlucky, he surfaced for a breath right near the shore. Of course Mom and Dad took the opportunity to jump in the water and fight it onto land. This one is a male, I can tell from sheer size.

"Must be at least one hundred and fifty pounds." Mom huffs.

I feel as though I'm looking at a dinosaur with its prehistoric wrinkled skin and massive shell.

I glance at Mom. She's smiling.

"Well, come on," she says to me. "Give it a touch."

"It's going to storm," Charlotte says, whipping me out of my memories.

Above us, a grumpy sky glares down, threatening to spill. We don't mind, though. A little rain won't deter us from finding a killer.

"You sure you didn't do it?" Charlotte asks.

I rock the boat so she almost falls in the water with the gators.

"Told you a hundred times, didn't I? I'm no murderer."

"But you're the one who was sleeping with the enemy," Charlotte says. "Oh, no, wait. That was Samantha. She was the one sleeping with the enemy."

Cruel of her to make jokes about a dead girl who isn't here to defend herself. Even crueler of her to think of me as the enemy, a murderer. After all we've been through, and owing to the fact that she is my sister, you'd think she'd give me more credit. I'm not that evil.

"I might not have liked her anymore, but I didn't kill her," I argue.

Some people say Charlotte and I argue too much, but they don't understand our way of communicating.

"'Course you didn't," she purrs. "You don't have it in you."

"And you do?" I ask.

She shrugs. "Wouldn't you like to know?"

From the moment the news broke of Samantha's death, reporters have labeled it the "Mangroves Murder." Since that's technically where they found Samantha, slumped over a mangrove like a play prop. Body bruised, especially her neck.

"Did *you* kill Samantha, Charlotte?"

I look at her long fingers and wonder if they could possibly choke the life out of someone. That's not the official report, of course. Cause of death requires a detailed autopsy, and a toxicology will take weeks. I say it only because that's the word around town.

Strangled.

Charlotte crosses her legs and frowns at the sky. "Would I be on this boat searching for a killer if I had?"

I consider it. "Maybe if you didn't want anyone to know you did it."

She smiles. "There's an idea."

Thinking of my sister as someone who could harm another is so crazy that the thought doesn't linger. I don't really think she did it. Plus, she has no reason to.

"Charlotte, quit toying with your brother." Grandpa's words end with a sharp cough. He struggles to catch his breath, and I swear I hear him mumble something about his damn allergies. "We both know he wouldn't hurt the girl."

Grandpa's right, I wouldn't harm her. But someone did.

I wonder if Samantha fought back. She came this far out to see me, that much is clear, but why not stick to the roads? They found her in deep waters. She must have taken a boat, whether voluntarily or not. Guilt kicks me in the stomach, leaving a lingering impression. If only she hadn't attempted to come see me, she might still be alive.

The only people in these parts are Charlotte, Grandpa, and me. The Bell family, too, mind you. None of them would have murdered her, though.

"Grandpa," I say, mostly out of obligation, "did you kill her?"

But I don't think he did. Not one ounce of belief backs my inquisition. Grandpa wouldn't do it.

Grandpa's face remains impassive. His only answer is a haunting hum, filling the bog.

Police never found a clue. At least that they've told us. No witnesses.

I try to imagine a girl dropped into an unfamiliar landscape, dying. It's a difficult thing to think about. But something doesn't add up. She should have been on the roads, not in a boat in the swamp a half mile north of the property. She knew my address, even if she wasn't entirely familiar with the area. Why veer off track?

I slap a mosquito on my arm and another on my neck.

The oar I'm holding is smeared with greenish-black

algae, looking as though I've dipped it into a vat of mold. I place it in the water again, wondering if we can ever claim this swamp back, or if it'll always be tainted by the damn killer. I try to keep my exterior hard as a swamp rock, but inside I feel the change brought about by the murder. The bog isn't as free of worry as it used to be.

Grandpa takes us under a cluster of trees so thick that I have to duck to avoid branches clawing me.

It's getting dark. Light bleeds from the sky, overtaken by an army of clouds that swell like a bloated belly splotched with welts. I hold back a shiver when I feel the air change direction and brush a million cool fingers over my skin. It, like us, is picking up speed.

The boat hits a shallow part of the swamp, and we have to stick our oars into the mud and push hard, maneuvering so as to not get stuck. A few thrusts and we make it out, where the water depth drops off again, allowing us an easier ride.

The boat rocks, stirred up by the wind. But at the last minute, the storm changes direction and misses us. My stare swipes over the shore. Leaves are tossed into the air before swirling back down. I don't know what I'm looking for—any kind of clue, really.

Though we've rowed for hours, spreading across the swamp's surface like algae, we find nothing strange in nature.

No one is here.

Or else someone is, and they camouflage so well that not even trained eyes can spot them.

A chill tiptoes up my spine. Unease squeezes a tight fist around my stomach, and I have to remind myself to keep calm. It's the only way to gain an advantage over the killer. It'll do no good to hole up inside the cabin and wait for him to strike again.

We search well into the night. I shine a flashlight and catch the reflection of fox eyes, frog eyes, raccoon eyes. Never anything else.

It drizzles. The clouds smear themselves over the moon. Stars glint in the sky like the tips of a million blades. The night is heavy with humidity so thick that I feel as though I'm breathing in air straight from a heater vent.

"Call it a night?" Grandpa takes a bite out of his second packed sandwich. This one is peanut butter and jelly. "It's been hours."

I eat mine, too.

I've had plenty of water. But I still feel parched.

"I suppose," I say. "Maybe we can search again tomorrow. And the night after that. And the night after that. Until we find him."

"Or maybe someone else will find the killer first," Charlotte says, steering us back home.

I'm not expecting company the next morning. Through an open window, I spot a car sitting in our driveway. I don't immediately recognize it, black from top to bottom. When a man steps out, I know almost instantly that he's a cop. The folder. The pen. The look of authority. Like he's come to take notes on our family.

"We have a visitor," I say, alerting Grandpa and Charlotte.

Grandpa opens the door before the officer has a chance to knock. It's nearly time for us to go to school.

"Can I help you?" he asks.

"I'm here to ask for your cooperation in our ongoing case regarding Nicole Samantha Star." The cop glances purposefully at me. "I'm a detective with the police force. Mind coming into the station, all of you? Just routine stuff."

The way his gaze cuts the air in half and lands on me tells me that I'm his main concern. His look is weighted by suspicion.

"Sure," I say, letting my family know I have no problem answering his questions. I guess school will have to wait. I hope Willow won't mind my not driving her. "I'll go to the station."

After all, I have nothing to hide.

The officer gives Grandpa the address. "One hundred and third Avenue. Two-story brick. You know the place?"

I send a quick text to Willow saying I can't drive her, and I receive a response a few seconds later saying *Okay*.

"I know it, yes," Grandpa replies and goes to retrieve his car keys.

"Ride with me," he says to Charlotte and me.

The drive to the station takes twenty minutes, but it takes no time at all for the police to separate me from my family. The room they place me in smells like the rose air freshener they've plugged into the wall. There's a table, a water bottle, and a notepad. A detective walks in. Not the man from the house. This one is lanky, with a thin mustache.

"I'm Officer Cordova. Mind if I ask you a few questions, Beau?"

"Not at all," I say casually.

He shuts the door behind him. I lean in my chair and stare at the double-paned glass. Wonder who's looking back. Officer Cordova takes out a pen and readies it, along with a recorder. He presses play.

"As you know, there's been a murder in the swamp," he says. He waits, as though I might have something to add. Since he didn't technically ask a question, I keep quiet.

"Wonderful young girl. Such a tragedy. Been talking with her family and friends lately. What we can't figure out is who would do such thing."

I stare at Officer Cordova. I watch the way his eyes scrutinize me, assessing.

"Do you happen to know anyone who would do this to Samantha, as she was known, especially by those she was closest to, which I hear includes you?"

"Don't know a thing about it, Officer," I say. "Couldn't point you to anyone."

"Hmm," he says. "No one at all? Any help you can give us would be much appreciated."

"No one," I say.

"You mind telling me about your relationship with Samantha, then?"

I cross my arms and prop my feet up on the table with a comfortable ease that I force on the outside. Inside, I feel as though this small room can't contain all my nervousness. Do they really think I did it?

"Sure. I wouldn't call it much of a relationship, though. We sometimes saw each other."

"Romantically?"

"Yes."

My eyes slide to the window again. I wonder if the person—or people—behind it is taking notes like the officer in front of me. My fingers *tap, tap, tap* on the chair. Even though the detective's eyes fall to my movement and notice the crack in my armor, I can't seem to control my unease. I need to get out of this room. I don't want to talk about a dead girl. Especially not with a detective who thinks I'm the one responsible.

"For how long?"

"A few weeks."

The officer sets down his pen. "You seem pretty casual about it, Beau."

"I didn't have feelings for her anymore, if that's what you're hinting at."

I don't want to go into the fact that I don't have feelings for any of the girls I date outside of finding them interesting and having fun. I am honest with each girl, so it's not like I'm hiding anything. They know I don't develop attachments. Still, I *do* care if one of them is murdered. How could I not?

"Did she do anything to anger you? Did you fight often?"

"No and no."

The officer slowly loses his friendly facade, his tone sharpening to a point.

"Listen, Beau. I'm going to be straight with you. I know you and Samantha were involved, which you've admitted. I also know it was more than casual for her. And I know that she had contact with you the night she died."

I'm pretty sure I understand where he's headed, but I let him take his time getting there.

"She sent a text asking to come to your house. You replied with a firm 'no.' She then resorted to calling. You answered, declining her visit. Yet somehow, she ended up near your cabin anyhow. Want to tell me how that happened?"

"I wouldn't know."

I've gone over the possibilities myself, but I've come up with nothing. The officer surely knows more specifics than I do.

"I'm going to need the details of your interaction with Samantha on her final night."

"You already know," I reply. "You just said them. She sent a text, and then called. I'd broken up with her at school that afternoon. She initially seemed fine about the breakup but left school early. Apparently, she was more upset than I had realized. She wanted to come over. I said 'no.' End of story."

"Your whereabouts, Mr. Cadwell?"

The detective no longer bothers to call me by my first name, nor does he bother to make me feel comfortable. He leans into my personal space, hovering. It's overwhelming, the white sterile walls, harsh tones, and what I imagine are too many eyes staring from behind the glass. I want to leave.

"I was home with my family. You can ask them yourself, if you'd like."

"There was never a time you were alone?" he asks.

"Not until about two a.m., when I finally went to my own room to sleep."

I know good and well that Samantha's death occurred around midnight. The police said so themselves the following day when they visited the swamp and questioned my family, needing to know where we all were at exactly that time.

"Did you see or speak to Samantha after her phone call?" he asks.

"No."

He's nearing the end of his rope. I wasn't with Samantha at the right time. I have an alibi. I know his words before he speaks them.

"Okay, then, Mr. Cadwell. That's all for now."

Whether he suspects me anymore or not, I don't care. The important thing is that I answered his questions, and he has nothing to charge me with. I leave as quickly as I arrived.

In the car, Grandpa tells me that they questioned him and Charlotte.

"Damn police, never minding their own business. Just because we live out this way doesn't mean nothing," Grandpa says.

"Well, Beau *did* date her," Charlotte says.

"Doesn't mean I killed her," I reply.

"Then who did?" Grandpa asks.

I wonder if Grandpa doubts me like the others, or if he simply means to make conversation. I watch the marsh slowly come back into view—stagnant green water between slices of trees.

"That's what we need to find out," I reply.

"More searching?" Charlotte asks.

"Exactly," I say.

It's already lunchtime. I text an apology to Willow as we near the school and ask if we can eat together.

"See you later," I say to Grandpa as he pulls up to the front doors.

Charlotte hops out first and takes off without me. I shut the door and offer Grandpa a final wave just as my phone chimes with a message from Willow, accepting my offer to have lunch together beneath the shade of a maple tree.

. . .

"Sorry I couldn't drive you this morning." I sit in the shade, relishing the heat on my skin. "The police showed up, wanting to question me."

Willow takes a bite out of a turkey sandwich. "It's okay. I rode the bus."

She doesn't seem upset, which is a relief.

"They let me go easily enough," I explain.

"Of course they did. You have an alibi. You didn't murder that poor girl, but that doesn't stop the rest of the school from suspecting you. Who knows…maybe the police have questioned others. I'm sure, if they did, many of them mentioned your connection to her. They thrive on gossip, and you haven't exactly given them much reason to believe you're innocent. It wouldn't hurt for you to be a little kinder. I know you have it in you. Why do you show a softer side to me that you won't allow them access to?"

Because you're different. "No reason. Maybe you're wrong. Maybe there is no softer side."

"I'm not wrong."

When her hand stretches out to brush mine, I lose all train of thought.

"You, Beau, are not as dark as you want people to believe, and you know it."

She lets go of my hand and reaches for an apple, taking a bite.

"You are capable of being wrong, you know." I watch the way her mouth sinks into the fruit, leaving a wet sheen of juice across her lips.

"Not about this."

Her confidence is reassuring. I grin at her, lost in the moment. I notice the little things: the sun on her toes, reflecting off her peach-painted nails, which I can see because she wears flip-flops today; her hair blowing in the slight breeze; the little gap between her teeth as she smiles.

"What's their plan for finding the real killer?" she asks.

I frown. "I don't know. I guess they'll analyze evidence in their lab. Maybe search the swamp more thoroughly. I will, too."

I stay true to my word. I search and search the bog as the weeks pass. One, two, and then three. I'm frustrated and tired of eating packed sandwiches. My schoolwork suffers because I'm spending every hour outside the halls—where students give me a wide berth and accusatory stares—combing through the swamp. The only exception being the few stolen moments I spend in dreams, with friends, or with Willow, who, thankfully, has been riding to school with me.

She's the only one who makes me feel sane, aside from my family, Pax, and Grant. Everyone else looks at me as though I'm already guilty, their stares eating me up inside.

"It's no use." Though I say the words aloud, I don't completely believe them. I can't seem to stop looking. Even now, I'm looking.

I shine my light over and over and over again. I see trees and water and grass and creatures but nothing out of the ordinary. The swamp current rolls into our boat, rocking us. The air is humming with gnats, smelling earthy and dank, a reminder that rain has recently visited.

"We're missing something." Charlotte's brows pinch in concentration.

She is better at this than I am. Her focus allows her to not give up easily. The look she bestows tells me that I better not dare give up, either. Maybe she's toying with me. That would be just like Charlotte to do, to have a secret and then hang it up right in front of me, as big as the moon but just out of reach.

Maybe she knows more than she says. I didn't think it was possible at first, but now I wonder. With her elusiveness, it's hard not to suspect that she's up to something.

"Where's the killer, Charlotte? Do you know anything about the murder? Have you discovered any new details?"

Her brows relax. Her face transforms into a smile that is both intimidating and terrifying.

"Isn't that the million-dollar question?"

I don't know why she chooses to be so poisonous. Actually, I'm lying. I do know *why*, what I don't know is *how* she does it for so long. I hardly ever see moments of weakness in her. Even I have occasional moments. It's not normal, the strength of her resolve. One day she decided she would never love another soul. And then she lived up to her own promise, tenfold. People are scared of her, and I can't say I blame them.

"Charlotte?" I say her name softly.

I hardly ever do things softly, but for her, my only sister, I show a glimpse of the real me.

She regards me curiously. "Yes, little brother?"

I catch a grin before it fully forms.

"I'm glad you're here with me." The words are out before I can second-guess them. "Today. At school. At home. We make a good team."

I almost believe she wants to smile. Her pink lips begin to align into something genuine—a reminder of good memories—not backed by a razor-sharp tongue.

"If you say so." She turns to the swamp, not allowing me access to her expression.

I have no idea if my words affect her at all, but I hope they do. I want her to know she can trust me.

"You'd tell me if you knew something, wouldn't you?" I ask.

I can almost touch the stretch of silence between us.

"Perhaps."

"That's not an answer."

I don't understand why she insists on wearing a cloak of elusiveness with me.

"It's as good an answer as you'll get."

Since she won't turn around, since she insists on facing forward, the wind tells me her reply instead.

"Answer me the right way." I'll push her until she caves if I have to, but I can't keep sitting in the boat wondering if she's hiding information. "Would you tell me if you knew something more? Do you actually know something more?"

Finally, she offers me a solid answer.

"Yes, I'd tell you." Her voice comes out sounding like bells, but they are the type of bells I'd imagine would signal a warning of something bad to come. "Sadly, I don't know anything."

The thing is, I'm not sure if she's lying.

13

WILLOW

"**I** MIGHT HAVE TO EAT you alive," Beau says, but I think he means to say, "Good morning."

He stares at my dress, yellow as a bursting sunflower. Beau can't stop looking at me, and it thins the invisible cloud of worry around him. I need him to know I'm here, even when whispers trail him like a ghost, calling forth suspicion. He is connected to the victim, but I don't believe he's a murderer. I suppose I want him to know that he can let go of the tension that draws all his muscles tight, the guilt hanging off his shoulders, brought forth simply because he's an unfortunate link. His smile is sly, but I see it, the uncertainty, as though he expects that any day now, I will cross the dividing line to stand with those who think of him as guilty.

"Let's not go to school today," he says.

I have every intention of going to school. I decide to tease him a little. Lighten the mood.

"Fine, I suppose I should let another boy drive me."

I swear I hear something similar to a growl escape his lips.

"Who? Brody?"

I haven't had another date with Brody. We went out that one night. Had a good time. Maybe I'll do it again. Or maybe not. His second date invitation is open-ended, my choice to make.

"Or maybe I'll take the bus instead."

Beau bites his bottom lip and opens the truck door for me. "Hop in."

His hair is a tousled mess. His jeans fit just so, and his shirt is the lightest shade of gray.

"Not again." I glance out the truck window and notice Gran hobbling down the steps, a disapproving grimace carved into her expression. "Better go."

"Still isn't fond of me driving you to school, I see." Beau tries to hide a grin.

"She's warming up to the idea," I reply.

He arches a brow, gets in, and puts the truck in reverse.

"That's considered 'warming up' how?" he asks, pointing at Gran.

"Well, she hasn't forbidden me to see you yet, has she?" I ask.

Beau laughs and drives us to school. He tries not to stare at me and fails.

"Beau." I smile at the way my lips curve around his name, enjoying the easy shape of each letter. "I'm gonna stitch your eyes to the road."

But I don't actually need to. He trains his stare ahead the whole rest of the way there.

Two guys approach us as we arrive at school. I recognize them as the ones I sometimes see Beau with in the halls but have never officially been introduced to, mainly because my time spent with Beau is split between the ride to school and the bog.

"Hey, you must be Willow," says the smaller of the two, a boy with bright, curly red hair. "I'm Grant, Beau's friend."

"Hi," I say.

"Pax," says the other, bigger one.

"So when did you and Beau start going out?" Grant asks.

"We're not going out," I correct him.

"Oh yeah?" Beau says, as though he's challenging me.

With a gleam in his eyes, Beau leans toward me. I know his exact intention. I lean away because he's not getting a first kiss from me like this. It's not easy to turn him down, but I'll be damned if our first kiss is based on a challenge, on Beau trying to prove something.

"Gonna have to do better than that," I say as we walk to the front doors.

I hear Grant's and Pax's deep laughs, but there's a more musical one, too. I turn around to see the source and come face-to-face with the most beautiful girl I've ever seen. Her hair is blacker than black, rippling in the breeze like a flock of feathers. Her skin is olive like Beau's, her makeup flawless. Her legs are ten thousand miles long. Maybe ten thousand and one. I recognize her from my first-period class, though I've never heard her utter a word until now. Still, I know who she is.

Beau frowns. "Go away."

"Sorry about him," I say. "He's allergic to manners."

She has a wicked, glinting stare.

"Stupid girl, I already know that." She smiles at Beau. "I know much more about my brother than you ever will."

She's the one I've heard of but never managed to see around the bog or at his cabin. I wonder how we've missed running into each other in the swamp all this time.

"Charming," Beau mumbles.

They look alike. They have similar features now that I see them standing side by side. Not to mention the same confidence, shoulders back. Feisty grins, though hers is painted pink. An air of strangeness, as though they both carry secrets around in their pockets like pennies.

"I'm Charlotte," she says.

I somehow hate her and want to be her at the same time.

"And you are Willow, of course," she continues.

"Hey, Charlotte." Grant smiles nervously. "You look nice. Haven't talked to you in a while."

She sighs and picks at her nails, as though bored. He waits for a response, but she doesn't bother.

"What have you been up to?" Grant shifts from foot to foot, seemingly out of his element.

"None of your business." There is no masking the annoyance in her tone. "And the reason you haven't talked to me in a while is because you are too nervous to get up the guts to ask me what you want to."

This time, when she looks up from her nails, she's smiling something evil.

"Go ahead." She motions with her hand for him to hurry. "Ask what it is you want to."

Grant fidgets, running a hand through his hair and over the back of his beet-red neck.

"I don't know what you mean."

"Yes, you do," she practically purrs. "You want to ask me out."

I feel bad for Grant. He swallows roughly, his head bobbing up and down in confirmation.

Charlotte reaches for Grant's shirt, running a finger slowly down it.

"I don't date my brother's friends," she whispers so close to his face that she could kiss him. "And especially not ones who don't have the courage to ask me themselves."

Her eyes dart to mine long enough for me to notice the mischief dancing in them.

"Maybe if you'd asked me outright, I'd reconsider. But probably not. You should save yourself time and ask out another girl." Her finger leaves Grant's shirt. "Word of advice? When you do ask someone out, make sure she's meek enough to accept your offer. Someone like…Willow, perhaps. She seems more the type of girl who would go for you."

I gasp, too shocked to form a reply. Her obvious insult is unprovoked and unnecessary. What does she have against me? Or Grant, for that matter?

"Charlotte." Beau's tone is edged with a warning.

She glances at her brother, holding his gaze, and then yawns. "Well, this party has been lovely, but I have better things to do. Later."

And I thought Beau was sometimes callous. I guess I now know it could be so much worse.

A rumored cause of death for seventeen-year-old Nicole Samantha Star is something I didn't expect to hear while lounging on a Saturday afternoon.

Heart attack.

How could a young girl like her have a heart attack in the middle of a bog with bruises stamped into her body?

Police stick to their guns that something foul happened,

especially since the toxicology came back inconclusive. She definitely didn't pass due to natural causes. According to a source quoted by the anchorwoman, the heart attack stemmed from attempted asphyxiation.

Otherwise known as murder.

Jorie sits in my living room with me, watching the static-broken news across the television. Both of us listen in stunned silence.

The anchorwoman poses questions:

Did young Samantha have dangerous enemies?

Was she involved in something sinister?

Drugs?

What kind of monster did this?

It's all anybody can talk about. I shut off the TV and stand up fast-like.

"Let's go outside," I say.

Gran is sleeping. Mom and Dad are at the library writing the dictionary on every single known living and dead variation of bird, or something equally as boring.

We open the screen door and step into hell. Everything blazes. The beginning of autumn in the swamp sticks to our skin like sap. Sucks the air from our lungs. Makes me want to chop off all my hair, hoping for a breeze.

Jorie pops her gum and walks beside me.

"Where should we go?" she asks as I send my parents a quick text to notify them that I'm in the bog with Jorie.

Marshy ground slurps at our boots. A funnel cloud of white gnats swarms, making me hold my breath and squint until we make it through.

"We could go for a walk," I say.

Twenty steps into our stroll and we both sit down under the shade of a tree, agreeing that a walk will surely kill us now. We can hardly keep our skin from melting off as it is.

"What about the mall?" I suggest, but I'm not into it.

I try to think of other places with air-conditioning.

"Or the movies," I say. "Or maybe the pizza place?"

"What about swimming?" Jorie asks.

Submerging myself in icy waters to cool off?

"A swim sounds perfect, actually," I reply.

It will take thirty minutes to drive to the public pool, but it's well worth it. We make our way back up the steps. I knock on Gran's bedroom door. No answer. I write her a note instead.

Gone to the pool with Jorie.

The simple truth. I know Gran. She won't be angry that I took off. She'll just be glad that Beau wasn't a part of my plan.

"Do you need to call your parents?" Jorie asks.

"No," I answer. "I'll probably be back before them. They live for their bird discoveries and the process of recording them. Which means long hours away. I'll just send a quick text saying that we decided on the pool instead of the swamp."

"Do you mind if I call mine, then?"

I show Jorie to the phone, which, thank the stars, Dad replaced when Gran wasn't looking. So now we have one piece of modern technology on the bottom floor.

Jorie calls her parents for approval while I send mine a quick message, get dressed in a suit, and throw a romper over it. I wedge sandal thongs between my toes and pull my hair into a high ponytail. I have my license but not my own car. My only option of transportation lies in swiping Mom's car keys from the counter, since she rode in Dad's truck. I check that the tank has enough to get us there. It does.

Jorie meets me outside. "Ready?"

I nod and open the car door just as Beau steps onto his porch.

"My parents are cool with me going, so we can stop by my house to grab my suit and some towels before…" Jorie trails off. "Girl, what are you staring at so hard?"

She doesn't have to ask twice. I don't even have to answer. Because just then, she sees, too.

"Good Lord. How does that boy get hotter every day?" Jorie fans herself.

She stares. I stare. The sun and the reptiles and the trees stare.

"Beats me," I reply.

Beau smiles, and I die right there in the grass.

He crooks a finger and signals for me to join him.

Something heats in my belly. I attempt to act relaxed, as though I see a thousand Beaus every day. No big deal.

"Be back in a second," I tell Jorie.

I walk to him.

"Hey," I say.

My voice is traitorous. Breathless.

"Hey." He winks.

I shudder. Suck in a breath. Try not to let a pool of heat overflow in my belly.

When he leans forward, I have an image of him kissing me, though he stops himself just a bit shy of actually doing so. As much as I've wished he would, he hasn't yet. He's been too distracted looking for a killer. On the few occasions I've seen him, we've done a lot of things…

Sailed through the mire.

Walked through the woods.

Talked under moss-eaten branches.

Never kissed.

But since I'm a lying liar, that's not entirely true. He has *tried* to kiss me. Twice. Both times, I've turned away. Don't ask me why. Perhaps I'm crazy. Or maybe I'm waiting for the right moment. Which doesn't happen to be in front of his house with no privacy. While his sister watches out the window and Jorie stands at my back.

"Where are you going?" he asks.

I look into his depthless eyes.

"The pool."

He knows which one. There's only one public pool. Everyone is bound to be there on this muggy Saturday.

Beau waits like he expects an invite. But he'll be waiting until he's nothing but bones because I'm not the type of girl who ditches her friend for a guy, no matter how hot he is. Or the type who makes her friend feel like a third wheel.

"Well," I say, placing a hand against the thin fabric of Beau's shirt, directly over his hard stomach, "guess I'll be going."

His sister smiles in the window.

"See you later, Beau."

"Maybe sooner than you think," he replies.

He saunters into the house like the bobcats that saunter through the swamp, giving me one last departing look.

"Come on." Jorie hops in the car. "I'll show you the way."

There are too many bends in the road—too many turns and streets with no names—for me to ever remember how to get to Jorie's house by heart. Her description includes "turn at the knobby tree, another left at the bush that looks like an arrow, over the creek, ten streets past the red house with a green roof." The directions only get more obscure the farther out of the woods we go.

We've long been off the main road—there's only one here, all others are dirt or pebbled—when we come to an especially bumpy road. The car knocks along stones and broken rocks. The shoulder is soft, and I worry about getting the tires stuck in mud, but we make it.

Jorie's property could never be considered anything but rural. Even though it's not quite as deep into the swamp as Gran's house, it's not in the city, either.

The first thing I notice about Jorie's house is the driveway. Mostly because she doesn't have one. Where a driveway should be is an archway cut out of the trees—a path scraped through the forest.

I bend to angle my head so that I can peer up and out of the windshield at the curling branches above us, thick with moss and leaves.

"Jorie, this is beautiful," I say.

And, if I'm being honest, a little terrifying. The light has trouble breaking through here, as though the trees have forbidden it to shine. I drive along slowly, taking in the scene around us. It's quiet here. The woods seem to know we're coming. The leaves have stopped chattering. There's only the slight whisper of the wind, and even that's hard to make out.

The path opens into a quaint clearing—nothing short of enchanting.

A stone cottage rests lazily in the shade, its roof slanted to the left side like a slouching shoulder. The bones of the structure are cracking, sending fractures through the stones, and the windows are shrouded in curtains, making it impossible to see inside.

"You want to come in?" Jorie asks.

Well, I certainly don't want to wait in unfamiliar woods alone. My mind plays tricks on me, making me think the smears of mud are moving, that the vines have come to life, that something sinister could be waiting around the next sickly tree. Usually, I'm comfortable in the swamp, but Jorie's house is far removed, and I don't know these woods.

"Sure." I follow her through the overgrown grass up to the front door, which swings open before we reach it.

"You must be Willow," a woman says.

She's Jorie's mother, I'm sure of it. Her skin is much darker than Jorie's, but her hair is similar. Behind her stands a man in an unassuming shirt and khaki shorts. Jorie's father. His skin is the shade of mine, and his hair is deep blond. He has kind blue eyes that smile at me from the doorway.

"I am," I reply.

"I'm Veronica," Jorie's mom says. "And my better half is Jameson. It's great to meet you. Your name is the usual around here. Nice to put a face to it."

"It's great to meet you, too."

Over the front door hangs a sign with their last name painted on it in block letters: LANGSTON. Around these parts, people tend to label their houses with personal information, like they want everyone to know just who the property belongs to.

Jorie gives her parents a wide smile as she brushes past and beckons me to follow.

"I'm just grabbing a suit," she says, heading toward the back of the cottage.

I eye the pot on the stove. Something that smells like heaven is bubbling and popping inside. I have no idea why Jorie likes Gran's cooking so much when clearly her parents know how to whip something up.

"Smells delicious," I say. I find myself wandering over to the pot.

"Jambalaya," Mr. Langston says. "My wife's recipe mixed with my Creole family recipe. Turns out, it's the perfect blend. Want some?"

"No!" Jorie calls from the back room, which seems to sit right behind the kitchen, from the sounds of it. "We're heading to the pool, remember?"

Mr. Langston chuckles. "Of course, honey, just trying to be polite."

Jorie reemerges in a textured bikini top and jean shorts with a towel flung over her shoulder.

"Save me a bowl for tonight?" she requests.

"We'll save one for Willow, too, if she's coming back," Mr. Langston replies.

"Great!" Jorie says. "See you later!"

She brushes a quick kiss on her mother's and father's cheeks before rushing out the door. I manage a wave, not nearly as inclined to leave so quickly. What a beautiful place to call home.

"You ready?" Jorie says as we slide into the car. "The pool is bound to be packed."

She hands me a bottle of lemon tea she grabbed from the fridge. I uncap it and relish the sweetness. Heat on my skin, smile on my face, we head to the pool.

14

BEAU

LEANING BACK IN A WARM lounge chair, I feel as though my skin has actual real Georgia sunshine living within it.

I glance at Willow, who hasn't spotted us yet.

"You've come to the pool because of her," Charlotte says. "She didn't invite you. Heard it myself through the open window."

"We would have come to the pool anyway, and you know it," I reply.

It's a Saturday routine of ours. I glance at Pax and Grant, who are attempting to talk to a group of girls. Well, mostly Grant is making a fool of himself. Nothing new.

Charlotte laughs. "Fine, fine. You're right. But the point is that you've been fixated on her, and that's unusual."

My sister's not wrong.

"She's not making it easy," Charlotte says. "Aren't you bored of it yet?"

"Not at all," I answer honestly.

Charlotte hasn't stopped harping on this.

"Do I need to remind you how worthless you are

with her around?"

My sister's comment stings worse than swamp yellow jackets. Still, I don't let on how much.

"No." I shift my gaze because someone has blocked my view of Willow.

"Like a sad little puppy, trotting behind. You used to always be grinning. Now I catch you looking like you're deep in thought, transfixed. Your friends are here, in case you've forgotten. Why aren't you over there talking to those girls with them?"

"Shut up, Charlotte," I growl.

"Maybe I'll warn her off, tell her some of the stories of all the girls you've made cry," Charlotte whispers.

I whip around. "You can go to hell."

"Oh, I'm sure I will," Charlotte coos. "But not just yet."

Her threat is empty, it seems, because she doesn't move a muscle.

"I don't actually need to tell her," she continues. "Looks like she might be mad enough without my warning."

I look up. In my distraction, I didn't notice that Willow had spotted us. She and that friend of hers approach.

"Are you following me, Beau?" Willow asks, hands on her hips.

I smirk. "Now why would I do that? Far as I remember, it's a free country. And by God, it's a hot one. Which, incidentally, the pool helps with."

It sounds almost as though my sister whispers, "Liar," but I can't be sure.

"Funny thing, you never mentioned you were coming when I told you my plans."

Willow looks edible with her angry scowl and red bikini.

"Did I need to inform you?" I ask, cocking my head to the side.

Her skin is bronzed by the sun and shines with oil. She's not as thin as some of the girls here, and I like that—the way her body curves and moves. Her hair sticks to her back, and there's not another girl more beautiful.

"Usually that's the sort of thing reserved for boyfriends and girlfriends," I say. It's mean of me, but as much as I want Willow around, I don't need her thinking I'm all that into her. Even though I am.

I've never actually wanted a girlfriend.

This shouldn't be an exception.

For a moment, the only sound between us is my hard exhalation of breath, then laughter, the spring of the diving board, and loud splashes join our silent conversation. Not once does Willow or I say what we actually mean.

I think she wants me here but won't admit it.

I know I need to see her, but I won't tell her that.

Our day is wrapped in false pretenses and tension, the illusion of control.

She huffs. "Fine, Beau. Enjoy your afternoon at the pool."

I wish she would've invited me herself. I also wish that I didn't want her to.

I watch her go. Her friend won't make eye contact with me.

Beside me, Charlotte beams. "You are such a fool."

"I'm five seconds from drowning you in that pool if you don't shut it."

A guy approaches Charlotte.

"Maybe I'll ruin your chances here," I hiss.

Charlotte laughs. "Go ahead. Unlike you, I don't care.

There are many more to choose from."

Frustration laces through my thoughts. Charlotte can so easily dismiss them all. I used to be able to do that, too. Until Willow. I have a weakness, and my sister knows it.

The guy reaches the foot of her chair. He's nervous but brave when he introduces himself, wondering if she wants to go for a swim. She tells him she'd love to. I'm relieved to see her go.

Now I can eye Willow in peace.

Willow takes a few steps into the Olympic-size pool. A group of guys rest their arms on the edge of a corner near her. One sits atop the ledge.

I can't make out their words, but a couple of guys have approached. Jorie seems to enjoy the attention, and it doesn't look like Willow is opposed to it, either.

My blood suddenly feels as though it's boiling. *Damn this sun.*

I can't look away. Willow smiles. Laughs at something one of them says. I worry she might like him, and that pisses me off. I don't want those guys talking to her. She's driving me crazy, and I don't like it one bit.

I know the emotion I'm experiencing, though I've never actually felt it before. Well, maybe a bit the day in the hall when Willow agreed to a date with someone else. I'm definitely sensing it now. Disbelief punches my heart. Anger swarms, clouding my vision. I want to be allergic to this feeling, to stay as far as possible from it, to remain cold and neutral, but I can't push it away. I don't like it. I've seen it on other people's faces. Never on my own.

Jealousy.

I have to put a stop to it right away.

I glance at the girl near me who won't take her eyes off my face. And then I give her a full heart-stopping smile. She takes it as an invitation to join me. I don't object.

She tells me her name. Blah, blah. I don't care.

I glance at Willow, who is watching me back. I pretend to pay better attention to the girl in front of me. What was her name again? She moves in closer.

Five minutes pass. The girl continues to prattle on.

Ten minutes. Charlotte returns and begins talking to her.

I have to get Willow out of my mind.

The guy Charlotte met is part of the same group of friends as the girl next to me.

Twenty minutes. Charlotte invites them all to the house. There's four total. I don't catch their names because I'm too busy thinking of Willow.

I don't want to let the words burst free. *Go out with me, Willow. A real date. I'll show you that I can be nice.*

I'm dangerously close to speaking this out loud.

Damn, Willow. Somehow, she snuck into my mind. Maybe I will actually ask her out. Soon.

15
WILLOW

MY DREAMS ARE STRANGLING me, choking the very air from my lungs. I have somehow gone back a few hours to the pool, the scene replaying in haunting clarity. Beau leaves with a group of people, one of them being the girl who seemed to like him. I wonder if he likes her, too. The scene shifts. From my porch, I watch all six of them lounge in chairs off the side of his cabin, soaking up the sun until it falls from the sky. Jealousy burns, singeing my insides.

Creak.

A sound wakes me from my slumber. My eyes crack open enough to see a figure in my room. I sit up quickly, and then remember that Jorie spent the night. She stands by my window, arms leaning against the edge. At first, I think she must have sleepwalked, but then I notice her open, alert eyes.

"You okay?" I ask.

She startles. "Yeah, sorry to wake you."

I pull back my tangled covers and join her. "Why are you up?"

"Nightmare," Jorie says, trembling. "I had a dream that Beau came for me next, that he was the killer."

I peer outside, drawn to the moon shining off Beau's roof, making it look like a waxed, slippery thing. Stars claw holes above. Something howls a nighttime lullaby.

The front door opens, and the pool girl exits with Beau at her side. I don't know what happened between them, only that she obviously isn't staying the night. Why is he spending time with her in the first place? Did they do more than talk? Charlotte and the other three friends follow her.

They get in a car and leave, headlight glare swallowed by the shadows of the trees. Charlotte and Beau stay. I glace at the clock. It's two minutes past midnight. The car vanishes from sight. Beau turns toward my house and tilts his head like he means to find my top-floor window. Darkness cloaks the room, making it impossible for him to see me. Still, I feel his gaze.

"Come on," Jorie says, draping an arm over my shoulder. "Let's get back to sleep."

Though I thought it'd be hard to fall asleep while thinking of Beau, I somehow managed to rest a couple of hours ago. I can only hope for the same now.

Beau doesn't move from his front porch. The image of him burns my mind as I close the curtains, and slink back to bed. My sleep is not peaceful. It feels as though Beau's stare has followed me through the window and into my dreams.

• • •

The news of another murder stuns my family at breakfast Sunday morning.

"A serial killer?" Mom asks, dipping her bread in runny yolk.

"It's a Mangroves Murder, so I suppose," Dad replies with an uneasy look.

I can hardly eat my breakfast. Partially because of the news and partially because I tossed and turned all night, waking up more tired than when I fell asleep.

Jorie eats next to me, peering at the police officer in our kitchen. Neither of us heard anything strange. No telltale noises. No outsiders in the mire aside from Beau and Charlotte's guests. Nothing.

Now, blue-and-red lights pierce the windows. Cops park in our yard. They take boats out, searching the swamp for clues.

The Mangroves Murderer has struck again.

Same details: reported missing by parents. Found bruised and strangled alone in the bog. Only my family and the Cadwells for miles and miles. But one detail is different. This girl was killed earlier in the night, around ten o'clock instead of at midnight like the other victim.

Both were high school students. I didn't know this one, a girl named Julie Lore. I study the picture the officer has placed on our kitchen table. It's disturbing, to say the least, to be looking at a dead girl who was once so alive. Her short brown hair is pinned to one side by a flower clip. Her thin lips sparkle with gloss. The life still shines in her doe eyes, which stare right into the camera.

"Did you see her at your neighbor's house at any point in time?" the officer asks.

"No," I answer. All I saw was the girl from last night, who doesn't happen to be the one in the picture.

"No," Jorie echoes. She absentmindedly rubs the hem of her pink shirt, which matches nice-like with her pink-and-white-striped pajama bottoms.

"You sure you didn't see anything at all, not even the smallest clue?"

"Nothing," we reply.

"Did you know that the girl was once involved with the Cadwell boy?"

"Of course she was." I wince because that's jealousy talking. "He's involved with a lot of girls. So that's no real surprise."

The officer makes a note on his pad before pulling out a card. "Call if anything comes up, if you suddenly remember anything unusual, if something seems odd to you."

"Will do," Dad says, taking the card.

When the officer leaves, Dad turns to me. "I'm not sure I want you hanging out with that boy alone anymore."

"He didn't kill anyone," I say. "He and his family have been out looking for the killer, too. I've seen them. Plus, I know for sure he wasn't the one."

"How do you know that?" Dad asks.

"Because until about midnight, there were guests at his house," I say. "He couldn't have been out in the mire when he was home with them."

"In that case," Mom says, "maybe you're better off being with him or Jorie when you're in the swamp. I don't want you going out alone. I think you ought to stay in the waters close to the house."

Thankfully, Mom understands that I can't be cooped up all day, that I need to get out sometimes. I know she wouldn't be able to handle staying indoors constantly, either.

I nod. "Okay."

This morning is as good as any for a large pitcher of sweet iced tea, and since I need something mechanical to do, I begin banging in the cabinets for tea packets. I always do mechanical things when upset to distract my mind—cleaning, laundry, studying. Today, tea.

"What are you doing, honey?" Mom asks.

"Making tea."

Mom nods like this makes perfect sense. Hopefully I can distract my mind from the murders.

I find the tea bags. When the water begins to boil like bubbles coming to the swamp surface, I drop the tea bags in and wait. I make sure to double steep it. My hand is extra heavy when adding sugar, the way Gran taught me. I line up five clear glasses and fill them with ice that practically topples over the rim because that's the right way to make Southern tea, thank you very much.

Tea pours smoothly from the pot to a pitcher, and then into the glasses. I stop halfway to add more ice when the boiling tea melts the towers I made. I hand out the glasses and take a seat again, placing a sliced lemon in the center of the table.

I take a refreshing sip. The tea washes away my worries, and I pretend for a moment that I've not heard of a single murder. That everything is normal. Perfectly normal.

The chill of the murders returns to me at night when I'm alone in my bed. I leave the window open. The curtain billows like a ghost on a breeze. Warm air pools around my body, braiding through my hair and attempting to slide beneath my sheets. The sky is filled with broken clouds, and the ground is filled with eyes I can't see, creatures that peer into the dark. I wonder if the killer is one of them. I suppress a shiver.

I walk to the window in nothing but my pajama shorts and a tank top. I spot Beau's cabin in the darkness easily enough. I make for the stairs and out the front doors. I need to feel humidity on my skin, a splintered deck beneath my feet.

It's past midnight. No one is awake but me, the crickets, and the stars. I stick close to the front door, just in case. I don't dare wander with a murderer on the loose.

The creak of a door makes me squint into the darkness. Beau steps out on his porch, the moonlight catching in his hair. Shadows cloak me. He shouldn't know I'm here, but somehow he does.

Beau cuts across the path and stops at the dividing line.

"Willow," he says.

I make not a sound.

"Are you still riding with me tomorrow?"

I don't know if anything happened between him and the girl from the pool, and he must understand that the situation doesn't look good from my point of view.

"I think I want to ride with Jorie," I reply.

The wind picks up, this time carrying Beau's final words. "Are you mad?"

Disappointed, maybe.

"No. I just want to see my friend."

Jorie will have advice for me. I'm not ready to talk it out with Beau yet.

16
BEAU

IT'S BEEN DAYS SINCE Charlotte invited the group to our house.

"You miss her, don't you?" Charlotte asks, knowing full well.

"A little," I admit.

I scan the school hallway for Willow. She's been riding the bus with Jorie. Something tells me she got the wrong impression about the pool girl and me.

My sister sighs heavily and leans against a corner by the water fountain, watching me warily. Her looks of disappointment at my inevitable attachment to the next-door neighbor are many. I am half surprised she's managed to bite her tongue.

"What can I do to help?"

I nearly choke on the gum I'm chewing. Charlotte is offering to help? That's unlike her.

"You want to help?" I ask cautiously.

"Sure." She shrugs. "I invited the pool girl and her friends to our house thinking that it was a step in the right direction, but then you went and just *talked* to her.

Nothing more. I thought you were trying to get over Willow. A little advice: you're doing it wrong."

It seems like Charlotte means to say that I'll get over Willow if I start something romantic with another girl.

"Who said I needed to get over Willow?"

She laughs. "Please, let's pretend for one minute that I'm not offended by your assumption that I don't see what's happening here. You're falling for her, but I'll act as though this conversation never happened if it makes you feel better."

"You are terrible at advice," I grumble.

Students pass us, but Charlotte is an expert at not being heard when she doesn't want to be. Her voice is low enough for only my ears.

"Let's try again," she says. "How can I help? You need a different distraction, since you're too hung up on Willow, even though we're pretending you aren't. Join a sport or something. Maybe check out some after-school clubs and activities."

I frown. "None of that sounds like me."

Charlotte taps her nails against the fountain. "And this isn't you, either."

"I think I'll try to figure it out on my own."

"So you're saying you don't want my help?"

Though I'm exasperated, I feel the beginnings of a smile. "Charlotte, you make no sense, but thank you for trying."

She eyes a guy walking by like a cat eyes a mouse.

"No problem. I'm here for you anytime."

There it is, the thing that I think she means for me to see above all.

She's got my back.

Odd as Charlotte sometimes is, she is still my sister, and she cares.

I have the urge to say something more to my twin, like how at the moment she reminds me of Mom. She looks too much like her, but that's not really what I mean. More than anything, Charlotte's *acting* like Mom. Compassionate. Trying to dole out advice and comfort.

I catch sight of Willow. Electricity zaps my bones. Natural rays of light shine in on her from the large window she stands beside, and she looks as though she's been draped in gold.

More faces blur past, but only one, aside from Willow, catches my attention. I spot my best friend, a head taller than the rest of them. He shoulders his way through until making it to my side.

"Willow still won't talk to you, huh?" Pax steps next to me and nudges my shoulder. To my sister, he offers a small smile. "Have you tried making it up to her?"

Pax and Grant witnessed the advances of the pool girl firsthand that day.

"She won't let me within ten feet. Every time I try, she is suddenly busy hurrying to class or racing back to her own front door. I'm pretty sure she has the wrong impression about what happened."

"Maybe she needs time."

"Maybe I need to hear her voice because I miss it too much." I don't mean to say the words aloud.

Pax shifts uncomfortably. My sister inhales sharply. This is not a topic we broach so openly. We joke. We have fun. We don't free-fall off a cliff of emotions.

"Sorry." I try to grin but have a feeling it comes out more like a grimace. "I haven't slept much. I think the swamp murders are getting to me."

"It's okay." Pax's voice is forcibly light. "On both counts. It's okay if you—" He looks around to make sure no one else hears, Charlotte being the exception. Down the hall, Grant makes his way to us. "If you actually care. You're allowed to do that, you know. Like the law of gravity or something. Jump enough and eventually you'll fall. It's inevitable."

"What's inevitable?" Grant asks, offering a friendly fist bump. He notices Charlotte and pauses. I wonder if he's remembering their run-in last time, when Charlotte insulted him. She must feel bad because she actually speaks to him nicely.

"Hi, Grant," she says.

He's too stunned to respond.

"Your terrible taste in shirts is what's inevitable," Pax jokes, easing the tension.

I watch Willow. Her eyes skate to me record-fast, like she knows I'm looking. She glances back down at the textbook she's thumbing through to pass the time. Her eyes find me again. I can't decide if they're more full of anger or want. I hold her stare for several heartbeats, each one quickening the longer she maintains contact. We are in a staring contest, seeing who will break first.

"What's wrong with this shirt?" Grant pinches the unfortunate fabric between his fingertips. It seems to be a mash-up of street graphics—a graffiti wall in the background, a record table in the forefront with a cat spinning music.

"What's not wrong with it?" Charlotte says jokingly.

Grant appears flustered to have Charlotte speaking directly to him. His cheeks grow bright, and he shifts from foot to foot. I notice because he's in front of me, like a sharpened image, Willow in the background, a bit blurry around the edges.

I tune out the conversation and focus instead on

Willow's gaze. I imagine touching the rope that ties the two of us together. I can't stand another day of this, being shut out by her.

I take one step toward her. She takes one step back. Grant moves out of my way. The crowd parts for me now that I am more visible, out from behind my friends. People whisper as though they think I can't hear them. It's not hard to figure out what they're doing, labeling me as a suspect even though I've been cleared.

"Willow," I say.

For one moment, I think she'll respond to me.

But no. She walks in the other direction, as far away as possible.

I don't see Willow again for another week, except in school, where she breezes past. I hope that she will give me a chance to make things right and to explain what happened, or more that *nothing* did happen. Charlotte's right. I never did anything with the pool girl. I couldn't, not while knowing how I feel about Willow.

Tonight, she swings on her porch, oblivious to me exiting my cabin. I don't stop until I'm nearly at Willow's porch. She looks up and startles.

"What are you doing here?" she asks.

"I miss you."

"Why would you do that?" She stops swinging. "There's obviously nothing going on with you and me."

My breath hitches. "Do you want there to be something between us?"

The rickety screen door bumps against the frame.

"I don't know. The answer to that depends on a lot. You had a group over to your house, including a girl who seemed to be into you."

"Doesn't mean I was into her."

I probably should have made that clear from the beginning.

She searches my eyes. "Do you like her? Is that why she was there?"

She doesn't know that Charlotte invited the girl, not me.

"It was my sister's idea to have everyone over, not mine. I didn't want the girl there. Not when I feel the way I do about you. That's what I wanted to tell you before."

Willow seems to exhale the tension in her shoulders.

"I didn't realize," she says.

She thought I liked another girl.

"I only want you, Willow." The truth comes out. It's time she heard it anyhow. "Will you ride with me tomorrow?"

Driving to school with Willow beside me has become my norm, and I miss her there, changing the radio station, chatting about little things, hair blowing in the wind.

"Maybe." She takes a step toward the door.

I wait for more, but what I get is one last glance, and a tiny smile, before she slips inside, leaving me alone with only the bog for company.

Hopefully tomorrow morning, she'll be waiting at my truck.

17

WILLOW

I DECIDED TO RIDE to school with Beau again today.

"Willow," he says as I enter his truck. "I want you to know how sorry I am about the pool situation. I know I explained it to you, but this is the first time you're riding with me again, and, well…I'm really happy about that. I apologize that the situation looked like more than it was."

I bite back a smile. It's odd to hear Beau nervous, to witness him apologizing, but I'm glad he is.

"So." He starts the engine and lets it stutter to life as he watches me. "Are we good?"

I nod. "Yeah, we're good."

The ride is uneventful, and before I know it, we're entering the front doors of school and walking down the crowded hall. I make my way to homeroom, with Beau on my mind.

"I get to drive you again regularly, right?" he asks, just to be sure.

I pause outside the class.

"Yeah, and I'll keep taking the bus home."

He reaches for me, softly running his hand down the sensitive underside of my forearm.

"Good. I'll see you tomorrow morning, then," he says before slipping off down the hall, carried away in a sea of bodies.

I can't seem to rid my thoughts of him all day. I was wrong about the pool girl. Beau never wanted her. A thrill of excitement passes through me, and I can't wipe the grin from my face.

As soon as classes end and the bus drops me back off, I spot something waiting by the front door steps. A bouquet of white flowers. I push open the screen and place them in a vase on the counter.

"Who are they from?" Gran asks, turning to greet me. She spills a little salt on the counter as she seasons the soup she's cooking.

There's a single notecard in the center with a name scrawled across.

"Beau," I reply plainly.

I don't have to look at her to know that she's scowling.

"I thought he was out of the picture." She hobbles up to the bouquet and inhales deeply. "Smells beautiful. Charming just like that grandpa of his, I see. Go figure."

"What do you know about his grandpa?" She has my attention.

"None of your damn business," she says, no malice to her words but also no invitation to discuss the subject any further.

That's fine. I don't want to talk about Beau's flowers with her, either. I'd rather enjoy them.

She walks off shaking her head. If only I knew why she thought Beau being anything like his grandpa was a bad thing.

That night, I sleep better than I have in days. The scent of roses lingers in my dreams.

"Thank you for the flowers," I say the next day as Beau walks with me through the front doors of school, all the way to my locker.

"You're welcome." He grins. "Hey, do you think you can meet me at the path when the sun slips away today?"

His eyes are fire, burning every inch of me.

"I might be able to do that."

I notice the way his teeth clamp together suddenly. I follow his line of sight.

Brody approaches with a smile. He already knows Beau and I are friends. He also knows that I'm not spoken for and not interested in being someone's girlfriend. *Unless that someone is Beau*, my mind tells me, but I tell my mind to go on and hush. Brody and I are friends, too.

"Hey, beautiful," Brody says.

I am stuck between the two of them, pinned down by differing stares. Brody's, sweet and relaxed. Beau's, intense and disarming.

"Hey, man." Brody offers a greeting to Beau.

Beau nods.

"Hi," I say. "How was your math test?"

Brody had complained about it the other day, worried that he might not pass. Since we exchanged numbers, I occasionally get texts from him, and we often see each other at school, too.

"I actually did okay." He shrugs.

Beau steps closer to me, and I try not to notice the

sorts of things he does, like shift to one hip, exhale near my ear, and whisper my name in a soft, tantalizing breath.

"So, I don't think the next one will be as bad, you know?" Brody is saying.

I try to act like I'm paying attention. "Right. Piece of cake. You'll do fine."

"Thanks," he says.

"Willow." Beau drawls my name out in that slight Southern accent of his, completely different from the way he just whispered my name, as though in a plea. "I'll see you tonight, okay?"

He shoots Brody a hard glance. One that doesn't go unnoticed. And then walks away. After an awkward heartbeat, with not much time to go before the bell rings, I say goodbye to Brody.

"Well, I'd better get to class."

Brody nods, but I notice the cautious look in his eyes. Like Beau, he walks away.

The worry that I've somehow created animosity between the two of them settles into my mind.

I decide to meet Beau like he requested. He pushes the boat off the embankment and hops inside just in time. We row achingly unhurried, careful to not miss an inch of the swamp. My eyes and flashlight go to everything. Mangroves twisting above the murky water. Trees swaying in the wind, moss like hair billowing.

I admire the sounds the water makes mixed with the buzzing of insects with wings and the chattering of insects without them. If it weren't for the mosquito spray slathered over my skin, I might be able to smell the fresh fungus that always accompanies the swamp at night.

"Why did you purposely give Brody a mean look today?" I blurt.

It's been eating away at me little by little the whole day.

"It wasn't mean," Beau says, but I hear his grin. "I'm sorry if I ruined something between you two."

I doubt he's actually sorry. In fact, I bet he knew exactly what he was doing. I shine a flashlight at his face to confirm, and he throws a hand up to block his eyes from being blinded.

"You liar," I retort.

He laughs.

"Besides, there's nothing between him and me. We're friends, that's all."

Just then something bumps the boat, and I look down to see a gator, ten feet, if I had to guess. It could easily flip us. I meet its eye and hope that it's one of the gators Gran feeds because the way she explains it, there's an understanding between her and them. She feeds them, and they don't eat us. So far, it's worked.

The gator moves past.

Good thing, too, because it would have been a shame to have to use the shotgun I brought.

"So the date you and Brody had…was it not serious?" Beau asks.

I'm not sure how he heard about the double date. "It was an evening playing golf, that's it. And it was before this."

I motion between the two of us.

"Willow." I love the light Southern accent that twines around each syllable of my name as he speaks it. "Do you plan to go on another date with him?"

"No."

Beau's smile reaches his eyes. I shine my light back on the spindly, bony trees that remind me of curling octopus limbs stretching toward the sky. Beau doesn't much care for talking anymore and that's fine, because neither do I. His smile stays put for a good, long while.

We wind through the bog for an hour, listening to the sounds of darkness until finally I fall asleep to them. I know because I feel someone rocking my shoulder.

I'm in the middle of dreaming about brown eyes and soft lips brushing mine.

"Willow," Beau says. "You stopped rowing."

I yawn. "That could be because I'm falling asleep."

I stretch and peer around. What I see makes me uneasy. Beau nudges my oar, reminding me to row again, so I do.

The part of the bog we've entered now allows more moonlight. Half of Beau's face is coated in it. A mist creeps over us. Hangs low like a fresh dusting of snow. There's something about this part of the swamp that has me on edge.

I look closer and realize why.

"Where are we?"

I've seen the whole swamp within miles of the property, which must mean we're far out. Seems impossible to know the *entire* bog, though. It's too big for that. One day you see grass, next day it's covered in swamp. One day there's water, next day portions are dried up. It's constantly changing.

"Deep swamp."

I remember Mom's request to stay close to the house. Panic makes my heart race.

"Do you know this place?" I glance around, committing the new scenery to memory.

"A little."

"I think we should go back," I say.

He nods. "Me, too."

I decide, as we prepare to turn around, that this is as good a time as any to ask him something that's been on my mind. I'm just tired enough to not sugarcoat anything.

"I have to ask you a question." I chew on my lip and gauge my next words, anxious to be voicing my concerns aloud, afraid that saying the words will make them more concrete. "How many enemies do you have?"

"Well, that's a loaded question." He mulls it over. "A few, I suppose. Older brothers and fathers who don't like that I hurt their daughters and sisters. Some of the girls themselves. None too obvious. I don't really know *that* many people. Why?"

"What if the killer has a vendetta against you?"

"That would explain a lot." His casual tone tells me he's wondered the same thing. "The victims are connected to me. But I don't see why someone would go that far. What have I done aside from breaking a few hearts?"

"It's weird, you being connected to them," I admit. "Awfully strange that you knew them both."

"I agree. Stranger still is this deep part of the swamp. Do you hear that?"

I strain my ears. "No. What is it you hear?"

I don't like the deadening quiet that descends on this portion of the mire.

"Beau?"

He has gone statue still. He does nothing but stare at me.

I wonder for the first time if maybe he really could

be the killer. His alibi is tight. But then why do I get the pinch in my stomach that tells me I don't know all the parts of him, that maybe he's hiding something? My heart is pounding too fast with unease. I'm almost certain he can hear it.

"Beau," I say again.

"Shh," he finally replies.

The mist curls around the branches, the boat, my neck. It feels too thick. Suffocating. The unknown too heavy.

Someone's here, Beau mouths.

Shock halts my thoughts, and I don't process his words at first.

We shut off our flashlights. On the edge of the bank I make out a thin shadow. One that doesn't fit the tree next to it.

I sit frozen. Beau, too. Neither of us rows. Neither breathes. The boat bumps the shore. The point gets lodged under a bulging tree root, and we still.

The shadow that could be anything doesn't move.

Something tickles my cheek. The shadow slowly peels itself away from the tree, and someone screams. I realize after a heartbeat that it's me.

The shadow runs. Beau takes off after it.

Fear chews on my heart, and I cannot move. I clutch the edge of the boat until my skin stretches white over bone. I gulp down breaths, trying to rein in my terror.

Not a second ago, I was looking at a murderer, my gut tells me. But since I'm not completely sure which form is Beau's and which belongs to the murderer, I can't risk using the shotgun.

I flip on my flashlight, but it's no use. I see nothing but marsh and forest. Beau is gone. The shadow is gone.

I jump out of the boat and attempt to stand on shaky

limbs. I walk toward the trees, afraid of what I'll find. Terrorizing fear forces me to imagine Beau in the worst ways.

In a heap at the base of a tree, like a pile of snarled roots.

A crushed windpipe, unable to breathe.

Eyes wide and staring, drained of life.

I shake my head and dislodge the creeping worry.

"Beau?" I call out, uncertainty shaking my voice.

The wind answers back, biting at my skin.

There is the sound of a shuffle, and I point my flashlight into the dark. My eyes are keen enough to catch a glimpse of something before it darts out of my beam. I follow the sounds. I don't know where I am. I don't know the path out of the trees. I don't know the path into them, either.

I walk, beam trembling, until branches brush my limbs, clothes, hair. Moonlight creeps in between leaves and lands in shafts on the ground. Mist distorts the light. The landscape is blurred at the edges, as though someone has smeared it.

I pause. Listen carefully. Something is coming. Footsteps pound behind me. I run. I don't turn around. Fear grinds my heart until tears burn my eyes.

I run and run and run. Until my lungs heave and my chest hurts and I can't see anything. I still run.

I will not be murdered in a swamp, damn it.

I will not let the killer win. But I know my time is running out. The stranger is gaining on me. I turn around to fight and arms wrap me up tight-like.

"Let me go!" I scream.

"Shh," comes Beau's soft voice. "It's me. Are you okay? Did he get you? Did he hurt you?"

I pull back and look at his face.

"Beau," I whisper.

He looks me over. Hugs me again. "He's gone. I couldn't catch him."

Beau walks me back to the boat. Somehow, he knows his way out of the forest. When we get to the edge where we first saw the shadow, I freeze. My flashlight catches an object at the base of a tree. I bend closer and pick it up.

A single earring.

Silver with a dangling green-amber stone that nearly matches the swamp's surface.

18

BEAU

POLICE CLAIM TO HAVE not found a match for the earring in either of the victims' homes, and no other girls have been reported missing. Who did the killer take the earring from, then?

"Do we need these?" Charlotte asks, holding up a bag of apples.

The closest local town—a strip of shops, blink and you'll miss it—is nearly deserted now. Rain falls in a thick mist. Most people don't venture out on damp days, but we decided to restock our supplies.

"Only if you plan to cook pie. Otherwise, no. You know I don't like apples plain," I reply.

"Suppose I could make pie," she replies. "Maybe invite Willow over and tell her all about you. Ask her why she bothers with you. That'd be fun, wouldn't it? Watching her squirm."

"Don't you dare," I warn. "I will never forgive you if you embarrass her or me."

We both go quiet as a woman passes.

"Listen to you, defending her," Charlotte mocks.

She places the apples in a cart and continues to shop the local mart. There are three lines with cash registers, but only one is open. The store is small enough that we make quick work of buying food supplies to last a month: our usual breads and vegetables, fruits and canned goods, snacks and meat. There's even an aisle for ethnic food, which we use in the recipes my mom left behind. What we don't use right away, we freeze.

The cashier, a girl I recognize from school, smiles at me.

"Hi, Beau," she says.

I peer into her eyes. "Hey."

She rings up the items slowly. Charlotte watches the girl.

"That'll be two hundred dollars and ten cents," the girl says.

I hand her cash. Her stare lingers, trailing my every movement.

"Have a good day now, you hear," she says.

"Let's grab a quick coffee to go." Charlotte heads for the exit.

We load the back of the truck with groceries. Rain dribbles beads of water on the plastic bags, making them squeak as they slide toward the back of the bed. I pull the bed cover tight so they don't get soaked. Never know with Southern storms. One minute mist, the next monsoon.

We pass shops, an assortment of small buildings crammed next to one another—general store, post office, ice-cream parlor, and more. The coffee shop sits at the end of the block.

The bell above the door chimes and a guy—college age—comes to the counter.

"Hi, Charlotte." He smiles ruefully.

Though he's older by a couple of years, he knows her.

"Hello," she purrs.

What I like most about the place is the smell. It's not just coffee. Sweet permeates the air—vanilla and mocha. The scents mingle, and I inhale deeply.

"I'll have a large coffee, extra sugar," I say.

Charlotte orders the same coffee she always does, one that's sure to be swimming with cream so thick that the drink turns nearly white. We take a seat at a wooden booth with red-and-tan-checkered seat cushions while we wait. The tables are made from local trees, and the reclaimed wooden wall hosts a variety of signs. The air is hot, reminding me of the swamp's warm surface after it rains.

"You're different lately," Charlotte says. "And I think it's time we both acknowledge that it's because of Willow. She has a hold on you."

"Not really," I reply, but that might not be entirely true.

"I think you more than like her."

"Do not."

"Do, too."

My twin knows me too well.

"Your point?" I ask.

She sighs, frustrated. "You have to be cautious. You've always been so careful to only have fun. What's changed now?"

It's hard to say what's different about me with Willow, why my insides twist in a good way around her. Somehow when I wasn't looking, between trying to keep her near but not too close, Willow quietly slipped past my mental guards. She filled my head with smiles and trust and shot straight through my every defense.

The barista brings us our coffee. Charlotte leaves a tip on the table and, on the way out the door, a warning in the air for me.

"Beau, don't forget what happened to Mom and Dad."

I could never forget. I slam shut the door to my thoughts for fear that I might crumple under the weight of the memory.

"Don't let it happen to you, too."

19

WILLOW

TRY AS HARD AS I CAN to erase the image of the silver earring from my mind as I reenter the swamp a couple of days later. This time with Jorie.

The damn gators here are thick as blankets over the water. When one snaps at my oar, I hit it square on the head with the wood. Then talk to it like any sane marsh person would do.

"Listen here, gator," I say. "We have to share this swamp, you and me both. Now, I don't go shooing you out of the water, and you have no right to do it to me, either."

Jorie looks at me as though she's watching a movie play out, a grin on her lips. The boat holding us rocks gently.

"I'm gonna put this oar back in the water, and if you bite at it one more time, so help me God."

I don't have backup oars, and rowing home with only one isn't an option.

"Plus," I say, getting a good look at the gator's tail. It's mangled at the end, missing a few knuckle-size notches. "Aren't you one of the regulars Gran feeds?"

I decide to go on and answer my own question.

"You are. I recognize you. Bite at this oar one more time, and I'll tell Gran to never feed you again. That is a promise."

The gator dips his head back under the water and swims away. I grin a little.

"Girl," Jorie says. "You are reasoning with the gators. I've never seen such a thing in all my life."

"Sometimes they listen," I say.

Jorie laughs.

Today we've decided to take a boat ride for the hell of it. Some days are like that. Not much else to do in the swamp, anyhow. Jorie holds out a flask, and I take a sip. I don't typically drink, but this evening is an exception. Jorie says sometimes you got to have ordinary fun. And so we are.

"You think the sun will set proper-like—big burning ball they always show on postcards and paintings—and give us a good show? Or is it going to break apart like mist and disappoint us?" I ask.

"Proper-like," she replies, leaning back against the metal edge of the boat.

"Sure hope so," I say, downing another sip of the bourbon. It burns like hell taking up residence in my throat.

"Where did you say you got this?" I ask, examining the flask that has reeds and a duck etched into it.

"From my poppa's stash. He won't notice it's missing. He doesn't drink enough to know the difference."

In that case, I take two sips.

"I'm glad we met," I say.

"You're just happy that you had someone to warn you about Beau before you got in too deep," she jokes.

I smile. "Maybe a little of that, too."

She knows what I really mean. The distance from town and people can get lonely. Family is wonderful, but without Jorie I'd be in this boat alone most likely—Beau can't always be around to join me—and I much prefer to share it with her.

"I'm glad to have someone near, too," she says. "All the others are either boys or not my age, and going into town every day to see friends gets old quick."

"Do you have other friends in town?" She hasn't introduced me, if so.

"I know people," she replies. "Acquaintances, mostly."

"Me, too. I never had close friends in Florida." The confession hurts more than I thought it would. "I saw people at school and at after-school activities. There was a group—four of us—who tried to meet up for bigger events like football games and spirit days. But I didn't do best-friend things, like share clothes or spend the night. I didn't even know where they lived, much less stay over with them."

"There are friends. And then there are *friends*." Jorie pops her gum loudly. "Some you invite to parties. Some you call when you're having the worst day. One you show your front to. The other has your back."

I think I know which type to label Jorie.

"You can always call me," she says softly.

A smile tucks its way into my cheeks. "You, too."

The sky turns bright orange, burning the horizon. We get the sunset we'd hoped for. Colors are reflected and smudged in the water, dripping through tree limbs, landing on leaves and the forest floor. The entire world seems to be on fire.

"Where's the rest of your family?" I ask.

"Gone." She watches the sun slip away.

"They never visit?"

"Not if they can help it."

I nod, knowing the feeling. "Reminds me of my family. I have cousins up north. Aunts and uncles all over. None of them likes the swamp much, mind you."

Jorie shrugs. "Sometimes family is what you make it. Mine is my momma and poppa and none of the extended relatives who happen to think we're strange for living so secluded."

"I suppose I'm glad Mom and Dad moved me to Florida for some time. Helped me to see the world outside. Turns out that I happen to love country roads, but leaving for a while let me see that. I might not ever leave again. Think you will one day?"

"I hope not."

We stay out on the water until I'm pretty sure I'm tipsy. Until the sky darkens and a creeping takes over the swamp. I remember the person Beau and I saw in the woods and decide now is as good a time as ever to go home.

Shadows begin clinging to the trees the farther the sun slides down the sky. A shiver racks my body of its own accord.

"Are you thinking about the girls, too?" Jorie asks.

"How did you know?"

"I can feel it sometimes, the sadness coming off the swamp. I think you feel it, too." She dips the oar gently into the water. "I think about the killer more than I should. I guess it's mostly because no one's been caught."

"Speaking of, I don't want him finding us out here," I tell her.

She nods, and we try hard to row back, the flask now empty. We nearly forget the way. My brain feels fuzzy like the outside of a peach. When we finally make it home, Mom and Dad are waiting up for us.

Mom leans in to kiss me on the forehead.

"Wanted to make sure you made it back safely before we go off to bed," she says.

Her nose crinkles. I know then that she smells the bourbon.

She whispers in my ear. "Say good night to your father and go upstairs to take a shower."

I think she means for my dad not to smell the alcohol. It's not like he would mind much, I don't think, but it's easier to do as Mom says.

"Night, Dad!" I call as Jorie and I take off toward the stairs.

"Night!" he responds.

Jorie and I disappear to my room.

"You're still planning to stay over, right?" I ask. No way she can drive home in her state.

"Yes, ma'am." She salutes me with a goofy smile.

Jorie grabs a change of clothes from her bag before heading to the shower. When water pounds on the other side of the wall, I pull open the curtains.

And find what I'm looking for.

Beau's truck is there.

Once I've showered and Jorie passes out, I make my way outside. A minute later, Beau's front door opens, and he walks across the dividing line.

"Willow," he drawls. "What are you doing out here alone?"

He risks coming onto Gran's property to take a seat next to me on the porch swing.

"Counting the stars," I say slow-like.

He eyes me. "You can't count the stars."

"I can try," I insist. "Now stop interrupting me. You'll make me lose track."

It's no use. Now that I've caught sight of him, I can't look away.

His hair blends darkly into the night. His shirt is deep green, maybe brown. Hard to tell with only the stars to go by. I feel the texture of his jeans rub up against my bare leg.

"Did you go into the bog without me today?" he asks.

"Sure did. Watched the sunset with my friend Jorie."

I don't know if it's the rocking of the swing or the alcohol, but everything spins softly like a slow carousel.

"You're beautiful," I say, though I mean to say not a word.

Beau grins. I think he assumes I'm joking. I lean in closer, pressing my upper body against his, feeling the strain of his well-sculpted muscles. He inhales sharply.

"What has gotten into you, Willow?"

His breath is warm against my skin, sending an ache stealing through my blood.

"I can't stop thinking about you," I reply. "You have a way of enchanting people. And even though some whisper in the school halls, suspicious of you and the deaths, I know you didn't kill those girls. You're mighty mean sometimes, but you're no killer."

I did wonder at first about Beau's innocence. How could I not? His sister seems mean enough that she just might lie about his being with her, the original alibi he holds so tightly to. Gran always is reminding me of the evil his grandfather totes around like a charm, so who's to say his grandfather wouldn't lie for Beau, too? They're family, after all. Blood before all else.

It doesn't help that the police are always talking about his involvement with the girls. But I saw him with the group from the pool. There's no way he could have been in two places at once. He has an alibi for them both—he was with his family when the first girl was killed, and he had company over when the second girl was murdered. And the same killer *did* murder her—the police said so. It couldn't have been Beau. Not the boy who looks at me with sharp eyes, who speaks in riddles, who touches me softly.

I forget for a moment that Jorie is in my room, that Gran sleeps down the hall, and that Mom and Dad have a room on the bottom floor just below mine. I forget everything because his stare forces me to.

"I wish you could come inside with me," I say.

His eyes turn absolutely electric. "I don't know, Willow. Your gran isn't a fan of mine, and I don't want to mess things up with you."

He takes my hand.

A howl sounds in the distance, and I imagine a coyote lifting his snout to the sky and letting loose the beautiful sound. Beau turns to the woods, listening to the wail.

"I suppose it doesn't matter anyway. I have company. Jorie is inside."

But under the stars, no one is here to see a thing. Beau could press his lips to mine and no one would know.

"You should kiss me, Beau," I say boldly.

I'm finally ready.

I reach a fingertip to his mouth and brush his bottom lip lightly. There's a hunger in his stare. It takes everything

I have to control the pleasure it gives me to see him so unhinged.

When I move my mouth nearer to him, he backs up. Stands and straightens his shirt.

"Why do you smell like bourbon?" he asks.

I smile and stand next to him, trying to pull him against me. "You shouldn't concern yourself with that."

The world wobbles, and Beau is there to steady me.

"Damn it, Willow. I'm not gonna do a thing now, you know that, don't you? Not if you've been drinking."

He mumbles something about giving him more credit than that.

My eyes droop, and I reach for the door to steady myself. He holds me against his chest and exhales deeply.

"I'll walk you to your room, mostly to make sure you get there all right, but that's it. Try to be quiet. The last thing I need is for Old Lady Bell to spot me in her house."

I laugh as he follows me inside, up the stairs, and to my bedroom door.

He pulls me in once more for a hug. I memorize the beat of his heart. It pounds me a lullaby even after he turns to leave, and I lie down and fall asleep.

20

BEAU

AFTER SCHOOL, WE DECIDE to walk the swamp trails. Willow is two paces in front of me. Her button-up shirt is loose, and her jeans are tight. Boots reach her knees, protecting her from snakes. Somehow she makes clunky knee-high boots look sexy.

"You're really planning on capturing frogs to eat?" I ask.

That's what we're doing out here. Frog hunting.

She throws me a backward glance, grinning to the sky and back. "Sure am."

"You've eaten frog legs before?"

Don't ask me why I'm grilling her on it. Guess I don't exactly see her as a frog leg type of girl.

"Sure have. Plenty of times. Boy, don't you know my gran?"

"'Course I do," I say. The trail here is narrow, and so I keep pace a step behind Willow. "Her I could see eating them, sure. But not you."

"Well, I do, and they're delicious," she says proudly.

When the path widens and mud slurps at our boots, I move beside her. A sack drapes over one of her shoulders, held there by a strap.

"How many frogs can you fit in there?" I ask.

"As many as I can find, I suppose," she says.

"I've never had frog legs," I tell her.

Her arm brushes mine, and I wonder if she wishes she could keep touching me like I wish I could keep touching her.

"You're welcome to come over and have dinner with us." She tries hard not to laugh, but it's no use because one pours out anyway. I imagine the horror that must be painted on my face.

"And put myself within five feet of Old Lady Bell? Never."

"How about I bring you some frog legs afterward, and you show me that cabin of yours?"

The fact that Willow just invited herself over doesn't escape me. She must know what she's boldly asking to walk into. She's already had a small dose of Charlotte, and she didn't like it then. She won't like it now, either, especially in Charlotte's domain.

"That sounds like a perfect plan."

We walk a faint path through bushes, across a spot where the ground begins to dry, and down a trail that has worn itself into the earth. Pebbles stick into the soles of our boots. The water sits so still that you'd think it was green ground. Willow and I know the difference, though. Throw a rock at it and the flat surface shatters, only to re-stitch itself again in seconds.

"There!" Willow dives at a frog, catching it with her bare hands.

She startles the frog next to it into hopping at me. I pin it down with my boot, and Willow throws it in the sack, too.

"More come out at night," she says.

But there's no way I'm *walking* through the swamp at night. Even Willow won't risk it.

An eerie wind creeps around the trees, howling. The branches groan and bend like creaking bones. The sky overhead darkens, and Willow smiles. Sometimes I wonder if the girl has any fear at all, but then I remember the night we saw the man in the woods, and I know for sure that she does, rare as it may be.

"We've got another hour, at most, before the swamp floods," I warn her.

I kind of like that she's smiling, as though I'm issuing her a challenge, when most people would have called it quits right then and there.

She moves through the forest ahead of the storm, catching frogs and demanding that I do the same. The waters sweep out into what looks like a lake. Over it, where the trees are sparse, I can see the gale clearly. We're running out of time. Blackness bites at the sky.

We push it until the last minute. Until we get twenty-three frogs. Until the wind whips Willow's hair around her head in a crazed frenzy and we're running for the property dividing line. Rain pelts us, warning us to get inside.

"Meet me here tonight," she says.

I lean in and kiss her on the cheek. "See you then."

Excitement punctures my every thought, and my heartbeat matches the patter of the now falling rain.

. . .

The rain never lets up. Willow meets me as promised with a bowl in one hand and an umbrella in the other. For a moment we stand under an anemic silver moon, watching lightning tear open the sky.

"Come on, then," I tell her, leading the way.

Tonight is quiet and cool in the swamp, save the rain that drains all noise. No stars can be seen. It's as though they've fallen from the sky.

Our raincoats and exposed skin are completely soaked by the time we make it to my front porch, but neither of us mind. Willow's hair is plastered to her face, and her eyes are wide as I open the cabin door.

"Wow," she whispers.

I stand stock-still as she takes in everything. The living room and kitchen, the den and fireplace. A hallway splits off to the side, where three rooms and a bathroom can be found.

She walks into the entryway and takes off her boots and socks. Her bare feet leave wet footprints on the wooden floor.

"Willow," I say in her ear. "Would you like some coffee?"

"Do you have tea?" she asks.

"I do." I take her raincoat from her and hang it on the rack.

Her purple dress, only slightly wet, hugs her in all the right places. I cannot tear my attention away. I feel my body's reaction to her bubbling to the surface, and I have to forcibly shove it down, to look somewhere else, anywhere else, besides her hypnotic eyes, her unbelievably intoxicating dress.

She goes straight to the den as I remove my coat and shoes.

"Make yourself comfortable," I say.

I go to the kitchen to make hot tea, and I watch Willow through the open doorway the entire time. Which is maybe why, with my eyes on her, I don't see Charlotte in the shadows.

"Well, well, well," she whispers.

I turn to find my sister leaning against the counter, watching me. I set down the bowl I took from Willow. I suspect it's frog legs.

Charlotte grins slyly. "You finally invited her over."

I grab tea from the shelf and heat a pot of water on the stove.

"She even has you doing her bidding in here," she says.

I sigh. "It's tea, Charlotte. Give it a rest. Besides, what happened to helping me? Willow's finally here. Don't be mean about it."

"I meant I'd help you *get over* her."

"I don't want to get over her. And I think Willow might be around more in the future, so don't mess this up for me."

My sister steps out of the shadows, and I catch sight of her vindictive smile.

"Well, by all means, I should say hello, then, shouldn't I?" she asks.

I step toward her as the water begins to boil and pop on the stovetop.

"If you go anywhere near her tonight, I will kill you," I warn.

It's an empty threat, and she knows it.

She laughs and walks to the stove to drop the tea bags in herself. "That's not very nice of you."

"What's your problem with her anyway?" I ask.

"Maybe," she says, losing the grin, "my problem is

with you, not her."

I brush her aside to steep the bags several times, and then take them out and add sugar. Charlotte sets two mugs in front of me.

"You're fixated on her. You're reminding me too much of Mom." And with an air of finality, she stalks out of the room.

I remind myself to think of Willow. Only Willow. Not my parents and the agony of their memory.

I wait for the *click* of Charlotte's bedroom door before joining Willow.

Instinct tells me that my sister will leave us be for the night. But just in case, I shut the door to the den, blocking out Charlotte and Grandpa.

A barricade for Willow and me.

21

WILLOW

TO CALL THE ROOM A DEN is an understatement. Or maybe it's the large fireplace against the wall, making it look bigger. Two chairs sit by the empty hearth, waiting for Beau and me to fill them. I go to the next wall and examine the books, running my fingers along each built-in shelf.

"What a beautiful room," I say.

One wall is occupied by a large bay window with a seat. Rain coats the pane like a wash of tears.

"It's my favorite," he replies.

He hands me a cup of tea.

"I put sugar in it."

Like he knows I'd want sugar. Well, he's right. I take a warming sip.

"It needs more next time," I say, stubborn, even though it has enough sugar. I don't want him thinking he knows me inside and out.

I sink into the chair and rest my bare feet on the edge of the fireplace. Beau watches me. More than once I see his eyes slip to my dress.

"You'll have to try the frog legs later. Warm up the butter, they're better that way," I say.

Having eaten quite a few myself, my belly is full to the brim. Nothing better than a full belly and a hot tea. Well, maybe Beau's eyes are better. Yes, maybe that.

"What happened last night?" he asks.

I'm partially glad Beau didn't kiss me, as much as I wanted him to then. Now that I see his den, and his hungry look, I realize there are better places for a first kiss with him.

"I think we both know what nearly happened," I reply.

"You almost kissed me," he says. "Was that the drink or you?"

"The last one," I admit.

He grins. "Really?"

"Well, you haven't had any more girls here," I retort.

"Is that why, then?" he questions.

"Might have something to do with it."

"Might it also have something to do with the fact that you've been interested since the first day you saw me on the path?" he asks.

It's a bold thing to say, but he's not wrong.

"It could have a lot to do with a lot of things," I answer.

He sets his tea on a side table and walks to the bookshelf, like he's searching for something. And I'll be damned if I don't follow.

His impossible shock of dark hair refuses to lie any one way.

"Why do you go through so many girls, Beau?"

It looks as though he's considering not answering me, but then he says, "I guess I don't ever want to get close to anyone again."

"Did you love a girl once?" I ask.

I hate the thought, but maybe that's why he is the way he is.

"No. Not yet anyway."

His face softens, and I think I might be hearing the truth.

"Who'd you love, then? Who did you love so much that you turned mean when you lost them?" Because there was someone, of that I'm sure.

He winces. I'm close to his demons. I risk getting closer by threading my fingers through his.

"You can tell me, you know. I won't repeat your secrets."

He takes a deep breath and considers me. "I lost my parents."

So people *were* right about his parents' passing.

"What happened to them?" Maybe it's rude to ask, but I can't help myself.

I see the slight shift in his expression, one that tells me he might trust me after all.

"One morning, same as every morning, my dad went for a daily run," he begins. "That was the last time I ever saw him. A car turned a bend. The driver was distracted with the radio. My dad never stood a chance. His injuries were too severe, and my mom had to pull the plug."

Beau runs a hand roughly through his hair and looks away from me.

"It was a death sentence for my mom, as well. She died a year later of a broken heart, though the official report states pneumonia. She was too lost to grief to ever recover. She didn't sleep right, eat right, and she got sick. It went to her lungs, and by the time she entered the hospital, it was too late," he continues, as though determined to get it all out now and then not talk about it again. "She died a few days after being admitted. My mom couldn't stand a world without my dad, and I suppose I never want to love someone that badly. I never want to lose someone like I lost my parents, because I don't think I could handle it a third time."

He rubs the roughened pad of his thumb over my palm in a slow trance, not bothering to hide the sadness that gets trapped in the corners of his eyes.

"So you won't get close to girls now?" I ask.

"To anyone, really. I can't let people in."

"You've let me in."

His gaze narrows. "Have I?"

I'd like to think so. He did just share his parents' story with me. No one in town or at our school knows what happened, as much as they speculate, but Beau trusted me, to my astonishment and delight. That says something.

"Then there's Charlotte. She's the same as me, scared to feel again. But don't ever tell her I told you."

Suddenly, I see Beau and his sister differently. I think of my parents, of what it'd be like to lose them, and I can hardly stand the thought.

"No wonder you're scared," I whisper.

"I'm not scared," he says. But he's lying.

"Are too. That's why you've never invited me over yourself. Bringing me here is different than bringing the other girls, isn't it?"

He's quiet, maybe even shocked. Finally, he finds his voice.

"You're right. You're so close now, too close. I've not been able to stop thinking about you since the day I saw you through the kitchen window. And then you went off with Brody."

He reaches for the nape of my neck and cups it gently.

"I can't promise to give you myself, the real me. And I can't promise to give you what you need or deserve, but I also can't stop wanting you."

All I can think about is his hand on my neck and his breath on my face.

"Promise me you'll try. That's all I ask."

My stomach feels as though it's been filled with moths beating their wings in sync with the pounding of my heart. I can taste the excitement in the air, his confession hanging between us.

Beau places his other hand on the shelf beside my head, clenching it tightly.

"Can't you see that I'm trying to hold up a wall all on my own?" His eyes convey the warning he speaks. "This is my defense, Willow. This is all I have left. If I let it down…what then?"

I take a deep breath and exhale each word slowly. "Then you have a chance to feel something real."

"Pain *is* real. Grief, too." His jaw clenches with the effort to hold himself together.

I wonder how heavy the wall must be and how long he's been holding it alone.

I nod. "You're right. But sometimes letting go is the best feeling of all."

"I'm not ready." He removes his hand from the shelf and runs his fingers through my hair.

I inhale sharply.

"Then at least create a crack big enough for me to slip through," I whisper. "Try to let me see the real you. I think…I think I have already…in pieces. Let me have more. Try, Beau. Promise you'll give it a shot. There's nothing here for me if you refuse to let me in."

"Fine," he agrees. "I swear."

And then, finally, his lips press onto mine. Softly at first, giving me time to change my mind. But that's not going to happen.

I drown in Beau's taste and kiss him back, harder than I intend, but I can't help it.

I run my fingers down his arms. His skin is hot, hot, hot, so hot. His hands travel to my hips. I break away for a moment, just to see his eyes. There is something dangerous about them. A wild abandon. Part happiness, part dragging me back. He kisses me again.

I can't think. I ache where his fingers make contact, like a scorching blueprint of his touch.

"Don't stop kissing me," he says. "Don't ever stop kissing me."

So I don't.

Maybe I've gone mad because it almost feels like too much. Way too much. He kisses me to the depths of the sea. He reaches into my soul, I swear he does. And maybe that's what Gran meant all along, but I don't care. I really don't.

I kiss him more. His hands slip to my legs, to the hem of my dress. His fingers are on a course to a place where no one has been, and that's what finally snaps me out of it.

"Beau," I say, half dazed. "I have to go."

Even though I want nothing more than to stay here.

"You have to—" He pulls back, looking incredulous. As though he can't be persuaded to believe what I've just said. "You have to what?"

"I have to go," I whisper. "It's late."

I kiss him one more time. Okay, three more times. And then I walk away on wobbly legs, back to the property dividing line and into the house across from the boy who finally let down his defenses.

22

BEAU

I DON'T WORRY THE NEXT day at school when I find Willow leaning against a locker, talking to Brody. Because I did what she asked: I tore down my walls for her. We have something good. And besides, Brody could never kiss her like I do. She could never want him like she wants me. So, with no doubt on my mind, I slink up to her side and wrap an arm around her waist. I kiss her right on the lips. In front of the school. In front of Brody. In front of my sister, no less. Willow kisses me back.

I pull away a moment later.

"Beau Cadwell," she says, flustered.

"Later." I wink and walk down the hall.

"Grandpa, are you all right?" I ask, watching the way he limps to the chair. He never used to limp, did he?

"Just my hip," he says, shooing off my unease.

"Should we just skip it tonight?" Charlotte asks.

Her eyebrows pinch together, as though she's concerned. I hold my breath and silently hope that Grandpa won't call off our hunt. We haven't looked for the intruder for several days, and that's too long for my liking.

"Don't be ridiculous," Grandpa says.

I exhale and pack our sandwiches. It's a relief to have another chance to attempt to clear my name, to rid the swamp of a killer, to keep trespassers off our property.

"And quit giving me that damn look. I don't need your pity," he adds.

Just like that, Grandpa is one hundred percent again.

We load the boat and stretch our muscles before taking off for a night in the bog. Moonlight leaps and dances in our wake. Sludgy water foams at the shore. A scattering of leaf litter floats on the surface like tiny stained spots. The swamp, rimmed with tall marsh grass, is a perfect place for someone to hide.

With the last fading bit of sun, night begins to wrap around me. I feel dampness on my skin, slick sweat at my hairline, and a rough metal seat underneath me.

Charlotte watches the trees.

"Did you see that?" she asks.

I peer at the spot she indicates, through narrow reeds, but I see nothing.

We float closer to the edge of the water. Plumes of gnats hang like a barrier between us and solid ground. That's when my beam catches sight of something.

"Look here," I say. "The branches are disturbed."

We know enough of the swamp to tell when a disturbance has been made by human or animal.

"Not animal," Charlotte comments.

We coast farther up.

"And here," Charlotte says. "The markings on that tree. What do you think they mean?"

Three lines are etched in, as though someone scraped a bag or pack against it.

We look for more signs, and we find them. Footprints. Broken branches. Someone has been here. The tracks are clearly fresh.

They can't be from Willow or her family. They were gathered in their living room, watching a movie, when we left. I saw through the open curtains.

No matter how hard we search for the next hour, nothing turns up but animal bones and alligator backs.

As we near home, and the sky has gone blue-black, Charlotte holds out her hand and whispers, "There's something out there." She leans forward, scanning the shore. "Something's close."

I eye the scenery, our property, Old Lady Bell's property. I see nothing unusual. Just the swamp under moonlight.

"What's there?" Grandpa asks.

"A shadow," Charlotte replies.

Either she's seeing things or her eyes pick up what mine cannot. I shine the flashlight around. Nothing. I swing the beam around more. My hand freezes. I suck in a breath. Charlotte locks onto my face. I think I see it, but it's too dark to know for sure. There are too many shadows.

"See something?" Grandpa whispers.

The swamp is deadly still.

"Maybe," I answer.

I have the very distinct feeling that someone is watching us.

23

WILLOW

THE WIZARD OF OZ plays on Gran's static television. She loves it and cannot be persuaded to watch anything modern. I pass the heaping bowl of popcorn to her. Gran grabs a handful and passes it back to me. I pretend not to notice when her hands shake and she drops kernels on the ground. Mom and Dad share a separate bowl.

"Willow, why do you not have a nice pair of sparkly shoes like that Dorothy?" Gran asks.

I look at her in horror. "Because that would be social suicide."

"That dress is nice, too," she says. "I have an old table-cloth with a similar pattern. I could sew it up pretty for you."

"You're kidding," I reply.

She doesn't confirm or deny it.

The movie ends, and Gran insists I help her clean the kitchen. I don't mind, though. I like time with her. And the truth is, Gran is getting too old to do it all, which is why we moved here in the first place—to help her keep the place tidy, make sure she's eating right, and to keep her from getting lonely in her old age. God forbid if something happened to her—like a fall—and no one was here to help.

"You still talking to that damn hellion next door?" Gran asks as I stand at the sink to soap the plates she hands me.

"Mother," Dad says from the doorway.

"Don't you start with me about the cursing or I'll say every bad word I can think of right here and now, and I won't be quiet about it."

Dad sighs but lets it go. I shoot him a smile, and he shrugs as if to say, *What are we going to do about her?*

Mom watches our interaction, attempting to hide a laugh behind her glass of sweet tea.

"His name is Beau," I tell Gran.

Beau admitted that his heart is guarded. He hurts girls' feelings before they ever have a chance to hurt his, and so he thinks he's safe from ever caring deeply. But there was heart in the way he touched me. In his lips on mine.

Gran frowns. "What the hell are you grinning about?"

It takes me a moment to find my voice. "Nothing."

"I'm taking your smile as a 'yes' to my previous question, Willow Mae. You're still seeing him. I know it. When will you listen to me? You don't know what you're getting yourself into."

Actually, I think I do.

"Tell me, then." I place the clean dishes on the rack. They leave water marks on the counter. "Tell me why you hate the Cadwells."

I need to hear what Gran has hiding in the cobwebs of her mind.

I pay careful attention to the wrinkles carved into her

face. How much time she's had and how much wisdom must have come from that time. I see them deepen slightly as she frowns.

"Tell me what it is about them that upsets you."

"That family has a pull, Willow. I know you feel it."

I do. I can't deny it. I feel it in my throat every time I see Beau, the way I can hardly swallow. I should tell Gran that I feel it, but I don't.

"Give me a good reason to walk away," I say.

"Tell me if you feel it," she replies, ignoring me.

"Did you feel it for Mr. Cadwell?" I ask. "That's what I've heard. I heard he broke your heart once, and now you hate to see him. You want me to hate Beau, too, don't you?"

Gran's face falls, and I instantly regret my words.

"Willow," Mom warns.

Gran hobbles up to me, so close that her nose nearly touches mine.

"Let me tell you something, girl," she says in a calculated tone. "You think you can handle what that boy will do to your heart, but you're wrong. You'll never be the same. Not ever."

And with that, Gran leaves the room, goes upstairs, and shuts her door.

Well, hell.

"She's just grumpy in her old age," Dad reassures me. He grabs a rag and begins wiping the table and counters. "She doesn't mean anything by it. Maybe you're right that Mr. Cadwell broke her heart once. It would explain a lot. Not that she's ever admitted so to me."

Mom stands at my back and wraps her arms around my waist. She rests her chin on my shoulder. "You can see the boy as long as you want. Don't listen to her."

I relax in Mom's arms the way I always do. The way

autumn brings colorful leaves and pumpkin spice and scarecrows. The way wreaths and lights and hot cocoa go with Christmastime. The way the swamp is always listening, a place to tell your problems and secrets. Mom's hugs are natural and warm, a part of everything I know.

I turn around and hug her back.

"Thanks," I whisper.

I finish the dishes. My eyes slip to the stairs. I can't help but wonder what exactly Gran is hiding from me. And what has her thinking I need protecting from Beau.

I finish cleaning the kitchen and begin to make my way upstairs to Gran's room. I find her at her desk, photo album open. She sighs when she sees me in the doorway.

"I'm sorry," I say.

She waves me in.

"If you want to know the answers, they're in here." She glances at the album.

I want to reach for it, but I'm not sure if I should, sensing that whatever is in there is deeply personal.

"Go on," she says, hand fluttering to the book. Her old fingers curl slightly, though she holds nothing in them. "Look already."

I sit on Gran's bed and open the book. Black-and-white photographs stare back at me, four to a page. I know right away that they're of a younger Gran. The first is of her—hair tied back with a bandanna, smirk on her face—standing in front of an old car. Well, possibly new then. Second is of Gran with a girlfriend, both their heads tilted back, laughing at who knows what. Third is of Gran at the pool. I smile. She was a knockout. Fourth is of her up a tree, a dog waiting at the roots.

I continue to flip through the pages, Gran in various places and poses, until I get to one that makes me stall.

"Yes," she says. "That's who you think it is."

"Mr. Cadwell?" I ask.

Beau's grandpa.

"You were right. We were an item," she says.

I trace a finger over the clear plastic that covers the aged photo. The corners have faded, and I'm afraid with enough time the entire square might erase completely.

Mr. Cadwell is handsome. Beyond handsome. Just like Beau.

I turn a page. And another. And another. His face is everywhere.

"There are several pictures of you and him together."

"Yes," Gran replies.

I swear she almost grins.

"He pursued me. Said I was the most beautiful creature he'd ever seen. Little ol' naive me believed him, too."

I flip to another page. Gran and Mr. Cadwell are in a boat in the bog. They look only a few years older than I am now.

"We stayed like that." Gran touches a picture of him. "Together from when we were seventeen until we were twenty-two, when I discovered the truth. All the cute notes he'd written me, the weekly wildflowers he'd left at my doorstep, the kisses he'd steal…he'd done the same for other girls. I was never the only one for him, though he'd later swear that he was young and dumb and that he *did* truly love me."

She stops there. Not another word.

"What did you do about it?"

She blinks back what I suspect is the beginning of decades worth of tears.

"I ended things that day, of course. Never looked back, except in memories. But it did something to me. I wasn't okay for years afterward. You have to understand that I thought I'd marry that man. I was completely convinced. And when you give such a big part of your heart away, you never do get it back."

I reach for Gran's hand and squeeze it lightly.

"That's why I'm warning you away from that grandson of his. He's Parker all over again. That I can promise. I've seen him interact with girls in town, heard the way he smooth talks them. Even his mannerisms mimic Parker's. It's best if you stay far away. Trust me."

I want badly to trust her. But then I think about Beau's grin. About his recent honesty. About his hunting for the murderer.

"He's not all bad, Gran," I say. "Just because he's somewhat like his grandpa doesn't mean he'll hurt me."

"Oh, my stubborn Willow. You don't understand what it's like to live with half a heart, never being able to truly trust one hundred percent again, never being able to love as deeply as you once did. It's a hard thing to know that you gave the best part of your heart to someone and that you'll never get it back. Every other lover afterward will suffer because of it. They might not know it, but your mind will sometimes revisit that burning, all-consuming feeling you once had, and anyone from then on will never receive anywhere near as intense a love from you."

I see it in her stare, how she's still not over him.

"You're going into this thing with Beau unguarded. You don't know what it's like to live with the memories of a love so strong that you wish you could feel something that good again, while understanding that you never truly will."

She shuts the album and locks me in place with her stare.

"You might not know the feeling yet, but keep this up with Beau and you will soon enough."

24

BEAU

TODAY, I HAVE A FEW quiet hours to myself.

The swamp welcomes me with a soft caress of wind and a water snake slithering past my boat. There's a purpose to my quick movements, each tug and pull as I row to the spot I picked out especially for Willow. I stretch my feet, careful to not kick the supplies I've brought, and secure the oars as I step out and drag the boat to land, wedging the nose in a fissure between two sturdy rocks. I tie it up good and sidestep a gator lounging near the water line, its scales wetly reflecting sunlight. It tracks my movements, blinking once before deciding I'm no threat.

I haven't yet told Willow what I'm doing or, more specifically, what I'm building.

Though the water sloshes over my shoes, I make sure to keep it off the supplies I carry from the boat. With each haul of heavy materials lugged dozens of yards through thin trails, I feel the heat. My arms shake with exertion, and I swipe at the sweat forming over my brows, threatening to drip into my eyes.

Birds keep me company, chirping loudly from tree to tree. Out of the corner of my eye, I watch the gator. Last thing I need is for it to sneak up on me, but it seems content to leave me be.

When all the supplies are finally loaded on land, I grab a hammer and nails and get to work. It'll take days, but I'm determined. It's the first time I've shown that I care like this. With every breath I take, I push aside the pinch in my chest, the warning that I've gone and done exactly what Willow requested of me.

I've allowed her close.

Still, I push on until it's time to go home. I need to meet up with Pax and Grant. I look over my creation, checking each section. A few more trips and a couple more days set aside, and it'll be finished. Willow is going to love it.

Hiking the town trails is nothing like the swamp. Here, the ground is solid and holds my weight without my boots sinking in. It's green, all right, but there are no vast waters, no alligators. All things I've grown accustomed to.

"It's hot," Grant complains, taking a seat on a fallen tree trunk. "Wish we'd brought water."

We've been hiking for an hour, tops, and he's already tired.

I lean against a tree and look skyward. Try not to think about the swamp and the murderer and the lies. Someone out there is going about his nights killing young girls and acting innocent. He must be good at disguise because otherwise he'd have been caught by now. Tracks aren't easy to cover, but somehow he has.

"…know what I mean?" Grant says.

He's been talking about something, and I haven't been listening. Not one bit.

Grant's waiting for an answer.

"What?" I say.

"You're not listening for shit. You thinking about that girlfriend of yours again?" he asks with a smile.

A spear of sunlight hits his red hair just right and sets it on fire with color.

"Not that I blame you," he continues. "I'd kill to snag the attention of the kind of girls you do."

I stare at him quizzically. "That's a strange choice of words."

Kill.

His face goes blank.

"You know what I mean, man," he says. "It's just that you're always gettin' the girls. They never even notice Pax or me with you around."

But what I notice is the way he begins to fidget. He scratches the back of his neck, his leg, his arm. He's nervous. What's he have to be nervous about?

I try to imagine him making his way through a tumbledown swamp—trees blocking paths, mud eating boots, rough trails and dead ends, snakes and gators. I hardly see him as the type of person who can handle navigating the bog. But then again, he could be a good actor. I've never thought of him as a possible suspect until now.

"You aren't seriously worried about me, are you?" he asks.

He must spot the suspicion on my face.

"I don't know," I say. "Where were you when all these murders happened?"

Pax gives a weak laugh, unsure if I'm serious.

"Come on, man," Grant says. "We've been friends for years. You know me better than that."

Do I? Do they really know me? Maybe in the ways I want them to. They don't know my past, though. They don't know what happened to my parents. They think I play girls for fun, but they don't realize that I have no choice. I'm guarded for good reason, or at least I used to be.

Grant's brown eyes squint at me from a few feet away.

"You've lost it, man. You really have. I wouldn't hurt anyone."

The wind blows and a tree branch leans toward me, brushing its long, leafy fingers over my shoulder. Sweat pools on my skin, the heat starving my body of liquid.

"He's only joking," Pax says.

But he's wrong. I'm not joking at all, and I think they both know that. On the one hand, they're my friends. On the other hand, how well can you ever actually know a person?

I'm not quite sure what to think, so I turn on my heel and start walking up a steep hill. Our destination isn't far. I like it for the small pond. Nothing but fish and turtles in it, but something about the water draws me.

It's our spot. The place where we goof around, talk nonsense. Mostly, I listen. And mostly, they rag on me about girls. There are things we don't talk about, too. Like how Grant is never happy with being himself, always wanting what others have. And we never mention Pax's mom getting laid off and the possibility of them losing everything. Another thing we don't talk about is me.

"I seriously hope you're joking," Grant says.

I don't bother with a response.

Everywhere I step, shafts of sunlight filter in like hundreds of flashlight beams. My jeans pick up dirt where they drag on the ground. I make my way through the overgrown maze of greenery, the few skeletal dead trees. Some of the trunks are browbeaten and moss-stained. I think I like those the best.

"Dude, you *were* joking, right?" Grant doesn't let it go. He catches up to me and begins to wipe dirt from his pants.

"Hard to say," I reply. My breath comes out labored as we hike the spike in landscape.

"Look, you're lucky, that's all. Wish I was."

"You're jealous of my life?"

He has both parents. A nice, if not a little ragged, home. Good grades. Friends. What more could he possibly want?

"Well, I wouldn't say... Actually, I guess if you put it that... Never mind. Point is that I'd never hurt anyone. Can't believe I even have to explain this to you." He huffs in frustration.

We approach the hardest part of the hike. A few more yards and we'll be at the top of the hill.

"I don't know why I'm defending myself," he says under his breath.

Pax mostly keeps quiet, as usual, a few paces behind. Twigs and leaves and rotten pieces of wood snap underfoot like wishbones.

"You know what's hard about being your wingman?" Grant asks.

"What?"

"The fact that it leaves no girls for us."

He motions to Pax like he's speaking for the both of them.

"You go through them so quickly, there's hardly any left," he says. "We obviously can't date the girls you have, and your sister is off-limits."

"I never said she's off-limits," I reply. "She makes her own decisions. If you're brave enough, go for it. And why can't you date the girls I once dated?"

"Guy code, man," Grant replies with a look that says I should know this. "We can't step where you have. That'd be wrong."

Pax stays strangely quiet, and I wonder if it's because he agrees.

"Why not?" I ask.

Grant sighs, exasperated. "It's the rules, don't you know this?"

I would never knowingly disrespect them or hit on a girl they genuinely like, and I figured that was silently understood and went both ways.

"I think that only applies if I'd actually liked the girl."

I haven't cared about a single one.

Until Willow.

"I still don't understand why *you* get them all, though," he says. "Not really fair to the rest of us."

Grant, for once, isn't smiling.

He's jealous. It's written all over his face. If the saying is true that jealousy makes some people act deranged, exactly how deranged is Grant willing to go? I find myself wondering again about him.

"You can have whoever you want. The only person I care about is Willow," I say. "And why have you been bringing up my past girls lately? Do you want a shot with them?"

Pax looks away from me, as though he doesn't want to be a part of our conversation. He only does that when he's not interested in having me read his expressions, which gives me an odd feeling.

"They won't give me a chance anyhow," Grant mumbles.

"Why not?"

Up close, I notice the way he tries to hide a grimace.

"I already tried, okay? That's why. That's how I know. And look, I'm sorry, I know it's wrong. I'm not supposed to date your exes. But I thought this one might have liked me. She always glanced my way in biology. So I tried. She shot me down. Said I remind her of you because we're friends. I can't get the girls you did, Beau," Grant says, envy thick in his tone.

"There are plenty of girls I haven't dated," I say.

The conversation makes me wonder if Grant secretly has something against me because of his own issues and chooses to use me as an excuse. My gut tells me he does, though it's not enough to ruin a friendship over, I suppose. Otherwise, what's he doing here?

"Your girlfriend is great," Grant says. "I wish I could get a girl like her. She's nice. Always smiling. She seems cool. That's all I meant by the whole thing."

"Okay," I reply.

I really can't see it anyway. Grant killing.

He could be something good or something bad, and I wouldn't know the difference. But if it is him, he can trust that I'll find out. I've made it my mission, after all, to catch the killer.

We're not quite to the spot yet, but I take a moment to pause. At the apex of the hill, I can see all the way down into the woods. This park is public, so there are a few other hikers quite a bit ahead of us. I spot an eagle at the topmost summit of a pine tree, the world at its feet.

I breathe deeply, relishing the balmy air, and blink against the bright light of the pooling sun.

"This view…" Pax says.

Yes, this view. It has nothing on the swamp, but it is definitely second best. Safer, too.

"Who do you think's doing it, Beau?" Pax asks.

It's on all our minds.

"I don't know," I answer honestly.

I think of all the people I know: Grandpa, Charlotte, Willow, Pax, and Grant. Since my mind is a dark place, I spin each of them as the face of the murderer. But they don't fit. Or maybe it's that I don't want them to fit. I don't want to know the person behind it, to look into their eyes and speak into their ears and share the same air as they do. I want it to be a face I've never seen, so I don't have to know what it means to have associated with someone who's fond of taking lives.

"They haven't got a single suspect," Pax says. "Aside from questioning and releasing you."

That means the killer is free.

To kill again.

"You have any thoughts about who might be behind the attacks?" Pax asks Grant.

My fingertips touch knobby bark. I inhale the scent of alpine.

"Not really," Grant replies.

The world around us is mostly still. Holding its breath and waiting.

"The killer could live miles from the crime scenes. He might be using the swamp, far from where he'd be implicated," I say. "Or maybe he's an outsider, camping out and taking lives."

"Or it could be someone we know," Pax replies.

"Or it could be a complete stranger who gets his rocks off on hurting others and is damn good at almost never leaving a trail." I roll thoughts around like dice. "Even though most of the whispers through town and school suggest I did it…I didn't, of course. Most don't believe me. Maybe it's someone who hates me."

Grant watches intently as Pax and I volley possibilities back and forth.

"Makes sense, because how could he be so good at knowing the swamp if he's a stranger?" Pax asks. "He'd have to be local to have a vendetta."

Solid point.

"Let's say he's local," I reply. "He must know how to keep far from my house and Willow's property. He's good at not being seen. That would mean he knows where Charlotte is. And where Willow is. How long do you think it'll take before he turns to one of them as his next victim?"

Pax ponders my question for a moment, not speaking.

"Don't ever leave them by themselves," he finally says. "Seems like the best solution."

"Guys." Grant grunts, clearly not a fan of our conversation. "You two are killing my mood. Let's talk about the party this weekend. Or for fuck's sake, *anything* that doesn't have to do with dead bodies."

It's a gruesome way to put it, but I buy in.

"Who's throwing the party this time?" I ask.

I choose the right words. Grant smiles and carries on about who, what, where, when. His long-winded talk goes on and on as we make our way down the hill and to our spot.

Pax looks my way, a strange expression passing over his face. I think he knows I'm only placating Grant. I think, for all his quietness, he also knows more than he says.

I'm just not sure what that means yet.

25

WILLOW

The air is as warm as lava. Yet I try not to shiver.

It's happened again.

They found another dead girl today.

I think about what it means as I sit by the fire, Beau by my side, his friends Grant and Pax across from us.

"It's unreal," I say, stoking the fire with a twig, earthen fingers playing in the embers, flicking them into the air to be swallowed by darkness.

Rocks circle the pit. Beau and I sit atop a blanket to keep the bugs off us.

"That makes three girls," Grant says.

"First Samantha," Beau chimes in. "Then Julie. Now Maggie. I knew them all."

By "knew them" he most likely means "dated them," but I try not to think about it.

"They say Samantha was on her way to see you," Pax says. "That Julie was hiking. And that Maggie had rented an airboat for a sunset ride and taken it out on the swamp."

I think back to the news reports this morning.

"The boy she was with, supposedly her boyfriend, was afraid of the woods, especially at night," I say. "Who wouldn't be? Who, besides locals, would voluntarily choose to come here knowing a killer is loose? Word has it that Maggie was an adrenaline junkie and dragged him with her. So the boyfriend stayed in the boat even when she didn't. She taunted him that if anything happened to her, it would be his fault because he wasn't there to protect her. Then the crazy girl laughed all the way into the woods. That's the last anyone ever heard of her."

They checked the boyfriend's handprints. Compared them to the ones left on Maggie's cold, blue body. Not a match.

"What a chickenshit, that boyfriend of hers," Beau says, wrapping an arm around me. "I would never leave you alone in the woods."

"That poor boy must feel destroyed now," I say. "She meant it as a joke, but it came true. Imagine, her death is now on him. Her own words."

Beau nods. "Parting words are nothing to mess with."

"You think he saw something but just doesn't want to say?" Pax asks, his hair flopping in front of his face like a mop.

"Possibly," Beau replies. "But then that'd mean that he's scared shitless. Too worried that the killer will come for him next, maybe?"

"What's the motive?" I ask.

I puzzle it out. Three girls. No witnesses. Same killer, according to the crime scenes. Signature throat bruises.

"Don't know," Beau replies. "Simply to kill?"

Part of me refuses to believe it because it's too ugly.

"Maybe the killer was linked to them in some way. They all go to our high school. All females. Something matches them up," Pax says.

"Maybe not," Beau counters. "Sometimes people are evil, plain and simple. No reason. No rhyme. Just devil evil."

"Maybe it is the devil," Grant says jokingly.

Mention of the dead girls, along with the dark night and too many shadows, begins to make my nerves spike. My heart beats a haunting tune. No one knows who the killer is. He could be out in the woods right now.

"Let's not talk about it anymore," I say, holding my arms tightly.

"She's getting scared," Grant replies. "Guess maybe she should be. She's the one dating you right now, Beau, and we all know how that's been turning out for your previous girlfriends."

"You ass," Beau says with a sharp glance at Grant.

I can't believe Grant's words. I also can't believe how true they ring. *I could be next.*

"Don't listen to him. I'll protect you, Willow Bell." Beau brushes my hair from my face. "I won't let anything happen to you."

"Well, we have to go," Pax says. "Grant wants to hit up Devon's party in town. He has the absurd idea that he might actually be able to get a girl's number without you there, Beau."

Grant punches Pax on the arm. "I will. You wait and see."

"You sure you don't want to come?" Pax asks Beau. "You're welcome to join, too, Willow."

Beau looks at me as he answers. "Nah, I'm good right here."

"Thanks anyway," I say.

All the lights of a party hold nothing to sitting under a blanket of stars.

Pax and Grant offer goodbyes on their way out.

"You sure you don't want to go?" I ask Beau as they start the car.

He grins. "Do you know what guys go to parties for?"

"Beer?"

"No. Girls. Beer is just an added bonus. And I have the only girl I want right next to me, so you do the math."

"You telling me that you stayed here to keep yourself out of trouble?"

I can't help the small smile that works its way across my face.

"Possibly."

He takes my hand and kisses the back of it softly.

"You want to come inside?"

I instantly picture his den filled with books and kisses.

"Yes," I say.

I try not to worry what will happen if I meet Mr. Cadwell face-to-face. The man in the photographs who changed Gran's life.

This time when Beau opens the front door, he gives me a tour. The living area. The kitchen. His room. He points to Charlotte's and Mr. Cadwell's rooms. I peer through the open doorways. They're perfectly cozy.

Beau grins. "You look nice tonight."

I'm wearing jeans, a shimmery top, and boots. My hair is wavy and down. Beau likes my hair down. He runs his fingers through it and makes me lean into him.

"Thanks. Where is everyone?" I ask.

He removes his hands from my hair and places them in his pockets. Then he leans casually against the wall, his eyes glinting.

"Charlotte took Grandpa into town," he says. "So it's just us."

I think I understand the look he gives me.

"Want a tea?" he asks.

I do. "Sure."

"I'll make some," Beau offers.

He walks to the kitchen and reaches toward a top shelf. He pulls down a canister, but there are no tea bags inside.

"We're out," he says. "There's more in the storage shed. We keep extra food supplies there. Give me a minute."

He grabs a key from a hook by the door before entering the side yard. From the bay window, I observe him as he unlocks the shed. Thanks to the outside lights, I can see him clearly. And because something draws me to this house, I look around more closely. Floorboards squeak in high-pitched protests as I bear down on them, making my way through the living room. Beau's place is clean. It doesn't look as lived in as Gran's or Jorie's house.

I venture into the hallway. Black-and-white photographs of old barn houses dot the wall. I wonder what their significance is, and then I think maybe they don't have one. Maybe they simply fill a spot where family photos should be.

I glance back outside, looking for Beau. He's disappeared into the shed.

At the end of the hall, I find a bathroom and step inside. I check my reflection, smoothing down stray strands of hair and adding a layer of gloss to my lips.

Out of the corner of my eye, I notice something glint from a jewelry box on the counter, the bottom of three drawers ajar. I edge closer, peer inside, and make out a garnet as red as blood attached to a silver chain and an emerald brighter than a flower stalk set in an old, tarnished broach. I admire a turquoise stone framed by an intricately carved ring, but suddenly my blood turns cold. There, just next to the ring, is a silver earring, a chunk of green-amber dangling down. I inhale sharply.

I know this earring. I found its match in the woods. Left there by the person in the cloak, who I happen to think is the Mangroves Murderer.

The door creaks behind me, and I spin around, nearly face-to-face with Beau.

"Everything okay?" he asks. "I heard you gasp."

"Beau." His name is barely a whisper on my lips. "Whose jewelry box is this?"

"Charlotte's." The smile drops from his face the moment he notices my expression.

"You're sure it's hers? She didn't have a friend over who accidentally left it? Or maybe your grandpa had a visitor who left this here?"

Beau shifts uncomfortably. "It's Charlotte's, I'm sure of it. It used to belong to my grandmother."

I slowly turn back to the box.

"Look inside," I say.

He steps up to the counter, peers at the jewelry, and stills.

"Is this what I think it is?" He pulls out the earring.

"You tell me."

I'm standing in the house of the girl who wore those earrings in the woods.

"The police were right," I say. "These didn't belong to one of the victims."

I brush past Beau and into the living room, trying to get to the front door.

"I'm afraid," I say, "that they instead belong to the killer."

Beau's sister could be the killer. I'm in her house. She

could return at any moment.

"Where are you going?" Beau asks.

"I'm leaving." *God, Gran is right, isn't she?* "I need to go."

I take a step away from Beau.

"There has to be another reason," he says. "Maybe Charlotte found the other earring. How do you know it's hers?"

"I…" *Well, actually…* "I don't."

Beau trails a finger down my arm, stopping at my fingers, which he winds his through.

"And how do you know she's not helping the investigation in some way?" he continues.

"I don't," I repeat. "But this is pretty damning evidence. Why didn't she take it to the police? Why didn't she tell anyone she found the earring?"

"Maybe she did, and we just don't know. Or maybe she didn't think anything of it. We never told her about the match, remember?"

"True," I say.

"Until we know something, let's not jump to conclusions. Let me talk to Charlotte. If she can't give me a good reason for the earring being here, I'll hand her over myself."

"You'll turn her in?" I ask skeptically. "Your own sister?"

"I will damn sure make certain she never hurts anyone again, if that's what you mean."

He watches me close-like. His penetrating gaze burns my blood right up. And there, in his stare, I find truth. If Charlotte is the killer, Beau will stop her.

26

BEAU

I HAVEN'T TALKED TO CHARLOTTE about the earring yet, and Willow's asked about it only once since she discovered the stone yesterday. She's agreed to give me time but not much. Soon, I'll need to confront my sister.

The truth is, I'm afraid to ask. I don't want her to be involved, or to know why Charlotte has the earring. It's too close to home. If it isn't hers, and I ask for an explanation, I just might strain the most solid bond I have with another person. Charlotte is mean, sure, but she's my sister. She's been with me the longest. She knows me the deepest.

Willow takes a seat with me under a pecan tree. We gather a few of the fallen nuts and break them open against a hard rock. Her small boat sits at the shore, tied to a tree. This part of the swamp is like our own private beach. Only instead of clear waters, we have green swamp. And instead of sand, we have dirt. The peacefulness is the same, though.

"Beau," Willow says. "Do you ever miss your parents?"

"Yes." I surprise myself by answering.

"Tell me about them?"

I don't think of them often. Well, that's a lie. I do think of them, but usually I push the thoughts away. This time, I let them come. And with each one, I feel it, the pang of grief, heavier than anything I've attempted to carry.

"My mom used to crochet everything. Scarves. Blankets. One year she knitted me the ugliest sweater out of all her scraps." I laugh at the memory. "I still have it."

I picture Mom's wavy black hair, her open smile. She smiled so much. Until she lost my dad. My dad is easier to remember. Maybe because his death was an accident. He didn't choose to leave us. He was a hardworking man, tender toward Mom and Charlotte, tough in a good way toward me.

"She shouldn't have died the way she did," I say with a grimace.

Willow must notice my frustration because she asks, "Are you mad at her for leaving you?"

"I suppose I am, yes. A little bit." I dig my fingers into my palm to distract from the pain in my chest. "I wonder sometimes why we weren't enough. Why she couldn't have tried harder."

There's a lump in my throat, and I can't talk past it for a full minute while I work to swallow it down.

"And your dad?" she pushes.

"My dad was a strong man, up until his last breath. We used to go fishing. I remember quiet times with him. Funny how he didn't have to say anything, but I heard so much in his silence."

Willow reaches for my hand.

"He had this thing he did where whenever he left to go somewhere—the store, work, out with buddies—he'd put me in charge, tell me to take care of the family. I do that now. I take care of Charlotte. I look out for her. Though she'd have my head if she heard me say that. She likes to think she looks out for herself, and I suppose she does to an extent."

"What about your grandma?" Willow asks.

"Died during childbirth, so I never knew her, but I hear she was nice to everyone. I guess Grandpa needed that after the hell your grandma gave him."

Willow offers a sharp look that makes me think I offended her. Maybe she knows more about it than I do. Or maybe she's just fiercely protective of family. Probably the latter.

"Don't you talk about my—" she begins, but I cut her off with a kiss.

When my lips touch Willow's, there's an instant sweetness and a bit of the lingering taste of pecans.

"Willow," I say, "I can't talk about my family anymore. Please understand."

Willow, because she's sweet like that, nods and doesn't mention another word about it. I breathe a sigh of relief, tension melting from my bones.

A hot breeze blows over our sweat-stained skin. Branches reach toward us. Leaves weave through and tangle in her hair. And soon, so do my hands.

I lean her back against moist earth and a rotten piece of log. She doesn't complain even one tiny bit. I brush dirt away from her sticky skin and kiss her again.

• • •

An hour later, Willow helps me drag the boat into the water. Our fishing gear weighs down one side, so I move the small tackle box opposite the rods.

"Do you fish often?" I ask.

It was Willow's idea to catch our own dinner, then cook it over an open flame afterward. It reminds me of my childhood.

"Not often, but enough to know what I'm doing," she replies.

We glide over the water with a smoothness that makes it feel as if we aren't on water at all. A cormorant suns itself on a branch, its wings spread wide, exposing black feathers, a long neck, and a hooked beak. Another torpedoes underwater for a meal. It surfaces near our boat to swallow a fish in a slick gulp, its head bobbing up and down like a buoy.

"Let's look for the next big opening," I say.

We need an opening like this one—minus the feeding birds—to drop our hooks. Channels don't offer the same opportunity to go home with a catch.

We find what we're looking for not long after. Willow baits a hook with a fake worm and casts her line. I haven't fished since my father died. It's been too hard to revisit his memory this way until now. Though my gut aches with the memory of him, I still remember the same stretch of muscle as I swing the rod. The same sound of line unraveling as it runs through the wind. The same *plop* as it hits the water.

"Perfect hot day," Willow says, closing her eyes for a moment, a tiny grin pulling at her face.

Already, out in the open, sun beating down on us, I feel the beginnings of a burn tingling across my skin. But we came here for a fish, and I'm not leaving without one.

I love what's happened today. For the first time since my parents' passing, I've purposely done something that reminds me of them. Maybe all I needed was for someone to ask me the way Willow did. To replace the pain with a new, good memory. My line tightens almost immediately. I wait a moment to let the nibbles turn into a real bite.

When the line yanks, I begin to reel in whatever is on the other end of my hook, hoping that it's a fish and not a turtle or crab.

"Look at that!" Willow says as I bring it in.

A white-gray catfish belly flops on the bottom of the metal boat. It's a small thing compared to some of the monsters under the depths, but it's big enough for the both of us. She admires my catch while handing me pliers to remove the hook. I'm careful to avoid the spine on its back, not wanting to get impaled.

When I get it off the hook, we head back to shore, where Willow starts a fire.

"I know we've gone over it," she says while adding leaves to the flames, "but I can't get those poor girls out of my mind."

"No one can, Willow."

"Have you talked to Charlotte about the earring yet?"

I wince, knowing I need to question my sister but dreading the moment I actually have to. "Not yet. I will soon."

She spears the fish with a sharp stick and cooks it over a wood blaze, scales and all.

"Do it, Beau." Her eyes find mine, and I see the conviction in them. "If you don't, I will."

I don't doubt her sincerity for a moment.

"I'll do it," I say.

I watch the fish on the spit, turning it over after

a minute to cook evenly on both sides. The smell of charred scales fills the air. Willow says nothing more of Charlotte, but still I feel the urgency of the situation settling between us.

"I keep trying to think of people who might have something against you, though I could be completely off track. Maybe it's all a terrible coincidence, your connection to the girls," she says. "I know Brody is jealous of you. But the murders started before he became jealous, so it couldn't be that, right? I could never see him harming anyone anyway. And speaking of jealous, Grant's envious of you, too."

Does she mean to label them as suspects?

"I know."

"Do you think Grant is imitating you? Maybe he's trying to go for the girls you dated."

I rotate the fish again over the flames as I consider her implications. It's not like I haven't thought the same thing myself.

"Maybe."

Willow's eyes widen, and she lets my answer sink in.

"And while we're naming people close to me, there's also my grandpa, but I don't think he did it. Charlotte, either. They are innocent, I'm sure. But like I said, I plan to talk to her about the earring soon."

"They," Willow says. "Oh my God, Beau. What if… what if more than one person is to blame? What if the killer has an accomplice? Or worse, if there's not just a single killer?"

"I hadn't thought of that."

What if she's right? What would that mean? How many people could possibly be acting together to kill innocent girls, and why?

"I suppose it's possible," I say.

"What about Pax?" she continues. "He's so big and quiet. That frightens me. What's going on in his mind?"

I pull the cooked fish from the stick and curse as it burns my fingertips. I drop it on a clean wood plank for Willow and me to share.

"Do me a favor, okay?" I say. "Don't stop being aware of your surroundings. Don't stop questioning people's innocence. We don't know who the killer is, and I don't want you caught off guard."

"I'll be careful," she says.

I believe her.

27

WILLOW

I AM FALLING FOR BEAU, and I'm not completely happy about it. My heart stutters each time I see his face and with every rumbling word he speaks. I daydream about him in class. I talk over things with Jorie, because I can't always figure him out on my own. It would be easier to fall for someone like Brody—soft smiles and plain to read. Beau is the opposite of plain. He knots my stomach and twists my thoughts and invades my dreams.

"It wasn't supposed to happen like this, Jorie," I say.

She doesn't even attempt to argue. She agrees completely.

"I asked him to let me in, and there's a possibility he listened. I'm not sure if he's ready for a relationship, but I think maybe I am."

"I've been tellin' you," Jorie says. "He's dangerous. Please hear me. Girls linked to him are showing up dead."

The wooden bench cuts into my legs, so I pull them up and cross them. Jorie unpacks her lunch and sits with me under the oak tree that shades us.

"Am I stupid to keep talking to him?" I ask, biting

into my apple.

"Maybe," she replies.

Jorie hands me a carrot stick, and I give her half a slice of my homemade banana nut bread with peach marmalade baked on top.

"He's not gonna let you go now. Not until he's good and ready. Girl, didn't I warn you?"

I smile. "You might have."

The courtyard is a pristine blanket of grass. Practically no one in the school eats inside, despite the heat. Jorie and I stretch out on the bench so no one gets the idea that they can join us. The earring settles on my mind, and it's hard to erase…or keep to myself.

"We found an earring in the woods. Right after we spotted the hooded stranger there."

Surprise colors her face. "A dead girl's earring?"

"That's what I thought at first, too, but the police said they don't have a match. As far as they know, it doesn't belong to one of the victims, and there aren't any new bodies."

I shudder at the thought of the possibility of a new fatality, another gone girl.

"We found its match," I say. "In Charlotte's jewelry box."

Jorie stops eating. She stares at me like she's waiting for the catch. There isn't one.

"You don't think Charlotte…?"

"I don't know what to think. Should I suspect her? Do you think it's crazy of me to?"

Jorie looks around the courtyard as though speaking of Charlotte will somehow conjure her up on the spot.

"I think the girl is strange, and I wouldn't rule her out," she replies.

Charlotte is nowhere in the crowd.

"Just be careful," Jorie warns. "I've seen the way she is. Mean. Stubborn. She doesn't have friends. Don't you think that's strange?"

"Yes," I admit.

"She's smart, as far as I know," Jorie continues. "I sit behind her in biology and she's always getting As on her papers and tests. She most definitely shouldn't be confused with dumb. There's a difference between book smart and street smart, of course, but she's both. There must be a reason she keeps to herself."

I remain quiet.

"She's not in any extracurricular groups. She doesn't play sports. She's hardly seen in town. No one knows a thing about her, except maybe that brother and grandpa of hers."

"Doesn't make a person a killer, to want to be alone," I say.

"No, but finding an earring match in her house sure does seem odd."

I'll give her that.

"Where are her parents?" Jorie asks.

I offer a noncommittal shrug.

"No parents. No friends. No social life. Suspicious."

Beau seems to think his sister is innocent.

Jorie cups her hands around her mouth like a megaphone and shouts, "Find something to do, won't you?"

I realize she's talking to a group of people who have made it their mission to stop and stare at me, passing quiet words among one another.

The girls scatter.

"They wouldn't quit staring," Jorie says.

Hell, they've been staring since Beau kissed me in the hall a few days ago. Different groups of them take turns watching me.

"Apparently Beau doesn't normally show affection?" I ask.

Jorie laughs. "Affection? Not even. More like claiming."

She adjusts the waist on her white skirt and pulls the hem of her shirt down to cover her slightly showing stomach. My skirt is long, black, and covering my sandaled feet. I fan my tight-fitting shirt in an attempt to stanch the sweat that threatens to drown me.

"He claimed you, girl, and you know it," Jorie says. "And no, he's never done that before. Why do you think all these damn people are staring now? They need to know why. Why you? Why the girl who is every bit as ordinary as them? No offense."

"None taken," I say.

She's right. I'm not model beautiful like Charlotte. I have absolutely nothing particularly astonishing about me. I could be the girl walking past us. Or the one laughing with her friends. Or the one reading, spread out on her back under the sun. I'm no different than Jorie or the next girl.

"They want to know why," Jorie says. "But there is no 'why,' and that confuses them more than anything. They're sheep. One whispers, and so the next one does, too. They begin their rumors as a herd. Then they add fuel until eventually it burns out and they get bored."

I hope that happens to be soon.

"Except none of them, bless their hearts, ever seems to get bored of Beau."

"Some of them must have moved on," I say.

"Of course they have. I'm just speaking for the

majority of his exes here. I think it must have something
to do with the way he ends things so abruptly. Maybe
they feel they never get closure? All of them swear he's
just fine one day and the next he's gone. You'd think
they'd learn."

She looks apologetically at me as she realizes her
slip-up. I'm the one with Beau now, and all I've realized
is that he makes a good friend. And that I love his lips
on mine.

"They expect him to be rid of you soon. They've
placed their bets on when and where and how. They'd
probably love to see it play out at school, sorry to say."

He pretends not to care for a very good reason. I
can't tell Jorie why I sympathize with him, so she isn't
necessarily wrong in her observations, but she doesn't
understand him on the inside.

"Let's not forget that he's involved in a murder
investigation, either," she continues. "There's reason to
worry."

"Do you think things are different for me?" I ask.
"I mean, I know he's been with other girls and that he
doesn't stay with them for long. But we were friends
first, which he doesn't normally do. And I don't believe
he killed the girls. His alibis are airtight."

"Are you sure you're friends?" Jorie asks. "Because
maybe he's using you for a purpose. No offense, but he's
Beau. This is what he does."

"I'm sure."

For the first time, I know Jorie is wrong. Beau is more
than he appears to be.

28

BEAU

THE NEWS OF ANOTHER dead girl isn't what shocks me the most. It's the fact that they didn't find her body for two days. She was too deep in the swamp, too far in the thick mangroves. Her body was bloated with water and infested with decay brought forth by the relentless Georgia sun. Word around is that her eyes were crawling with worms and her body was heavy with mosquito bites, looking like chicken pox. Luckily, a gator didn't get her. They tried, though. They colonized in the water like a leathery, scaly tarp, waiting for a good rain to wash her into the deeper waters where they could feed.

This time it was Jackie Wales, another girl from our high school who I'd known. We'd dated. A few times together, quickly over.

They say she was murdered late in the evening two nights ago. A shiver crawls up my spine.

"What's bothering you?" Grandpa asks.

He's on the couch, remote in hand, TV on, but watching me instead. Black circles rim his eyes.

"Nothing," I say as I take a seat at the window chair.

I stare at Willow's house.

"Don't lie to me," he says.

My lies are harder to tell when they're told to him. But I want to lie. I don't need him thinking I'm in deep with Willow. Already, he and Charlotte suspect I like her, as opposed to her filling a use for the time being. But unlike Charlotte, Grandpa doesn't mind my dating the next-door neighbor.

"Okay," I say, biting the bullet. "The murders aren't stopping. They obviously have something to do with me. Do you think Willow's safe?"

"I knew you cared too much," Charlotte says, coming into the room.

The earring still bothers me. I still haven't questioned her about it. Mostly because I don't believe Charlotte is the killer. Or maybe I don't want to believe it. Either way, I haven't had time with her until now.

"I don't want her to die, Charlotte. Why is that so hard to understand?"

"Because you've never cared enough to let your thoughts wander this far."

"There's never been a murderer until now," I say, exasperated.

She grabs pots from the shelves and cooking utensils from nails in the wall, then lays them on the counter along with a cutting board and knife. She goes to the fridge for meat and butter. From a wicker basket on our counter, she removes fresh vegetables. I join her in the kitchen to help prepare dinner.

Grandpa pulls himself off the couch and takes a seat on a barstool at the kitchen island, which is nothing more than a wooden table with storage underneath that I made myself, wheels on the bottom to roll it out of the way when we need more room.

I slide past Charlotte and begin chopping vegetables.

"I think you'd better keep an eye on her just in case," Grandpa says.

Sometimes, it hurts to look at Grandpa. He and Dad are far too similar. They have the same eyes, same slant of their cheekbones, equally strong jaws.

"Do you think the killer will target her next?" I ask.

He scratches the scruff on his face, thinking over my question, long and deep as is his way with things.

"I think these girls all have something in common. You, to be exact. Did you have messy breakups with each of them?"

"No." Matter of fact, I can't find a common thread. "For as many rumors as people spread about me, I didn't actually break all their hearts. Sometimes the girls wanted to split from me. Or we both decided it was time."

"So broken hearts aren't the motive," Charlotte says, seeming genuinely concerned.

"I've thought it over. None of the victims lived close to one another. They had no friends in common. They aren't all even in the same grade. I can't figure it out."

"Do you think someone's jealous?" Grandpa's voice sounds like Dad's. "Maybe a guy who wishes he could date the girls you have, but they've rejected him."

"Maybe." I pace the floor, trying to find the missing piece of the puzzle. Pax and Grant sometimes seem envious. But they're my friends. They wouldn't hurt innocent girls, would they? "If only I knew *why* the victims were targeted, I might be able to figure out if Willow is in the killer's sight."

"You're really worried about her, aren't you?"

The truth slips free. "Yes, Grandpa, I am. What if I

can't protect her?"

Charlotte and Grandpa have no reassurances for me, which tells me they're worried about the same thing.

Looking for the killer so far has done us no good. I want to stop him before he hurts another girl. I want answers.

Why was there an earring in Charlotte's room that matched the one dropped in the forest? Why is each dead girl someone I've known?

If it's me the killer is targeting, then why doesn't he just come for me instead?

Or maybe it's not a "he" at all.

I reach into my pocket and pull out the only evidence I've found so far.

"Charlotte." It's time I ask her about the earring. "Whose is this?"

I drop the green-amber onto the counter and watch her eyes hone in on the earring.

"Mine." Her tone sounds relieved, but that doesn't make any sense. "Where did you find it? I've been looking for it for a month."

Grandpa runs a finger over the smooth stone. A smile touches his face. "These used to belong to your grandmother."

"Which is why I was so worried when I lost one," Charlotte says. "You know I don't have much from her. Just the jewelry box."

"You lost the earring?" I can't keep the doubt from seeping into my words. "Any chance you lost it in the forest while running from me?"

Her eyebrows knit in confusion. "What are you talking about? I never wear these or even take them out of the house. They're too valuable, and I don't want to lose them, which is why I couldn't believe it when one went missing. I discovered it was gone the same day I came home to my window being open, when I could have sworn I'd shut it before we left. At first, I considered the idea of a robber. But why would they only take one earring?"

"So you thought you misplaced it instead?" I ask.

She shakes her head. "It doesn't make sense, right? A robber would have taken the pair, not just one, and would have likely taken more than just my earrings. Are you saying you found this in the woods after chasing someone?"

"That's exactly what I'm saying. Actually, the one I found in the woods is now in police custody. This is the one from your jewelry box, but they're a match. Why were they separated?" I lean against the counter and rub my temples, trying to make sense of the situation. "You're saying someone snuck in the house, took one earring, and fled to the forest. Why? Who would do such a thing?"

Grandpa clears his throat. "Answer that and you have your killer."

29

WILLOW

BEAU'S HANDPRINTS DON'T match the marks left on the dead girls. That's what I've learned this morning. Police took Beau in for more questioning, simple blood tests, and fingerprint analysis. I suppose they needed to be certain that his alibis weren't lies.

He's not the killer.

It's a relief, that's what it is.

They released him quick-like when they knew for certain that they had nothing on him. And now, here we are.

"Charlotte isn't the killer," he says. "The earrings are hers. Someone stole one of them from her."

His nostrils flare and his eyes twitch. Is he lying to me?

"I'm supposed to believe that she didn't lose it that day? That she isn't the person we saw in the woods?"

"I'm telling you it wasn't her."

"You sure about that?"

He smiles. "Absolutely positive."

"How do you know she's telling the truth?"

He rows gently, his long legs stretched out toward me. In the small boat, our feet touch.

"Talked to her last night. I can usually tell when she lies. Those are the times when she won't look me in the eyes, but she did last night. Nothing to worry about," he says. "Strange as Charlotte is, she wouldn't hurt anyone, I don't think."

This is the most Beau has ever tried to convince me of anything, and so I decide to trust him. The police have questioned Charlotte. They don't suspect her. Beau doesn't suspect her. Maybe I shouldn't, either. Yet still, I can't completely erase my doubt.

I try to shake the thought from my mind, promising myself I'll come back to it later. For now, I want to concentrate on Beau's surprise.

"Where is it you're taking me?" I ask.

"Just you wait," he says with a mischievous grin.

The bog gurgles beneath us as bubbles rise to the surface and pop, followed by a turtle head. The sun's rays scratch holes in the canopy, creating shafts of light that form a path through the water.

"You're up to something," I remark.

"Always," he replies.

We turn a bend. I look back, wondering how far exactly we've come. A mile, perhaps? Far enough away from home that no one will see us. But not too far that I have to worry about disobeying Mom's request to stay close to the house.

Up ahead, I make out a cluster of trees that juts out of the water. It takes me a second to realize it's an island.

Beau stops rowing, and the boat gently floats toward the shore. From beneath his seat, he pulls out a rope.

"What are we going to do on a small island, Beau?" I ask.

A smile slips through. I don't think I care what we do on the island as long as it involves Beau being there.

Beau does exactly as I suspect. He ties up the boat, places the oars securely inside, and helps me out and onto solid ground. I can see only a few feet into the trees, but I want to see more.

"Are we going in there?" I ask, hopeful.

"Would you like to?"

I answer by taking a step into the leaves. The sun retreats. Tree trunks line up like markers. Bushes dot the landscape.

I make my own trail. Beau follows.

The walk is littered with stones and broken twigs. Leaves rustle like crackly paper. The wind brushes my skin so lightly that it's almost a sigh. And then, only a few minutes later, I see the thing Beau wants me to see, sitting in the middle of it all.

"What is this?" I ask.

I bound over to it. Tree roots pop up from the ground like veiny scars intersecting a path. The crazy boy has made a platform for us out of wood, with four stilt legs beneath it digging into the ground. The wood is pine and smells like it, too. I run a finger along the edge, feeling where he smoothed it. It's newly made, I can tell by the flakes that pepper the forest floor like pencil shavings and the rich wood smell. Atop the platform are another four posts with a fifth in the center, and draped over that is a canopy of white fabric. It sways in the breeze like spider's silk.

"I wanted us to have a place to hang out," Beau replies. "Where we won't run into Old Lady Bell, Charlotte, or Grandpa, and where we can both be alone to relax."

His eyes roam the swamp around us.

The makeshift pavilion is smaller than my room, but still it's the most beautiful thing. Clear lights are strung around it, reminding me of fireflies. There is not enough space in my lungs for the quick breaths of excitement I find myself taking. I gasp at the beauty of it all.

"How did you get them to light up?" My question is filled with wonder.

"Battery powered," he says, his grin growing. "Wait till you see inside."

He helps me onto the platform that protects us from wandering critters below. It's easily five feet up. I try not to catch my feet on the lights.

Beau pulls back the drape. A small cluster of cushions sits on the ground, fronted by a tiny wooden table topped with freshly fallen leaves and sticks, reminding me of a bird's nest. A pink magnolia marks the middle, the source of the floral smell that sticks to the air.

"You did this?" I ask, mesmerized.

"All by myself," he says.

It's hard to imagine. Sure, I can see how Beau would bring the cushions and lights and tools to the island by boat, and how he could use the resources already here—the trees and stump for the table, the sticks and flower and leaves—to construct everything, but what I can't see is *why* Beau would go through the trouble. Isn't he the boy Jorie warned me about—the one who breaks hearts? Isn't he the one Gran swore was darker than the night? That Beau doesn't match the one standing before me, watching my reaction.

"I love it," I say.

And then I wrap my arms around this surprising boy and press my lips to his. It's daring. It's electricity zapping the air. It's him sighing into me.

Beau's fingers move to the hem of my shirt, to the base of my spine, where they tiptoe their way to other places. He holds me the way shadows hold darkness, so close that there is no space between us.

"Want to know a secret?" he whispers.

No matter how good Beau is with riddles, for one brief second, so quick I wonder if I imagined it, he is useless with hiding his emotions.

"I'm glad I met you, my beautiful Willow."

I know he means it the moment his lips touch mine. This time, he adds a hunger that has everything to do with the way our bodies fit together. Want sews itself under my skin. Longing makes my hands explore the planes of his back and the ripples of his stomach. Beau creates a heat in me that even the swamp can't compare to, and his eyes tell me that he feels it, too, even if his lips won't speak the words.

He trails kisses down my neck, making me break out in gooseflesh, despite the stifling air. When he slowly moves to the cushions, I follow. He picks up the magnolia and tucks it behind my ear.

"You are perfect, Willow," he whispers. "And I don't know what you've done to me, but please don't stop."

The note of desperation in his voice hooks me. He drapes an arm over my shoulder, and we lean back so that for the first time, I see the hanging lantern he's constructed out of vines. An artificial candle flickers inside.

Even over the strong aroma of the flower, I smell the scent that is deliciously Beau. Mud and swamp and a lingering whiff that reminds me of a bonfire at night. I could stay here with him all evening. Maybe I will.

He strokes my hair and watches my profile like he

doesn't give one damn that he's completely transparent. His riddles have, for the moment, been left in the bottom of the swamp. And I think I might like it that way. Now, I see a Beau more real than I imagined possible—a Beau not one person will believe exists—vulnerable and sweet.

Maybe still a little wicked with his grin.

30
BEAU

THE WIND MOANS A SONG that weaves through the trees—a long wail that accompanies us. Here, deep in the swamp, the air is shrouded by near darkness, like dense smoke that I can hardly see through.

It's been hours since I showed Willow the canopy. We're in a different part of the swamp now. She holds my hand, smelling sweetly of magnolias.

I try to make out the words of the wind song, as though they've been whispered into the air, but I can't. A groan here, a whine there. Nothing more. The leaves speak in cackling chatters, whispers that fade into the swampy night.

I'm looking for something. Listening for it, too. I hear it again, like the softest *click* of a camera, though I know it's a twig being stepped on. I edge closer to the sound, hoping the wind is kind enough to disguise my breathing. I don't intend for my presence to be made known to anyone but Willow.

The fog cocoons us. I can barely make out the sound of distant frogs. Here, the ground is higher. The water rests farther off and so does most of the danger from nighttime critters. Our boots protect us from any wandering snakes.

Another sound comes, this one a whisper, and I bet it's not the wind.

I catch something at the edge of my hearing, almost as a person does with their sight, if they look out of the corners of their eyes. Suddenly the sound—an almost whisper—breaks and disbands into the air again. The wind snatches it and rips it away in its grip. A second longer and I would have caught it.

I take tentative steps, deeper into the swamp forest. My sight dissolves completely. The trees swallow the moon in one gulp. In the darkness, I have to let go of Willow's hand and reach out my arms, fingertips at the ready to feel everything in front of me. My feet are unsure.

"Don't let go," Willow whispers.

"I have to," I reply. "Just stay close. Follow the sound of my feet. We need to be quiet. I can hardly hear it anymore."

A crunch. Closer this time.

Why would anyone be in the bog this late after sunset?

Even Willow and I didn't mean to be here. The fog cut short our ride home. No way to row and maneuver a boat when you can't see a thing. The boat is still attached to a tree. And we're waiting out the fog. I hope it clears soon.

I see something up ahead—a beam of moonlight too strong to be eaten by the night. Just outside of the moonlight is a rush of black. A cloth? The tail of a coat? I pick up my pace. I'm close. But I lose the noise. I stop to listen. My gaze darts through trees. I don't see movement anymore, so I wait.

Whoever is out here isn't using a flashlight. He is braving the moaning night and, for whatever reason, doesn't want to be seen. I can't help but wonder if it's the Mangroves Murderer.

A flash of silver appears. Too quick to decipher. Maybe I should have brought a weapon. The silver flashes again, this time closer. I turn to the left, the right.

"Willow, stay here." My words are whispered into her ear, a warning. "Someone's near. I'm going after them. Call for help."

"But—"

Her response is cut short by my swift kiss to her cheek. "Please, Willow. There's no time. Stay here. I need you to be safe."

And then I run. I run right at the sound until my body smacks into someone. We topple to the ground. I am stronger, and I pin his hands to the ground. A dagger clatters against a tree root. I can only hope that the person I've pinned down is alone.

The frame beneath me growls and struggles. It's thinner than I expected but strong nonetheless. A hood covers the head, face turned away. Hard ground bites at my knees, pressing pebbles into my skin. A slick sweat lines my brow, despite the cool air. I struggle to maintain my grasp. The person wriggles like a worm on a hook. I take a risk and quickly let go, long enough to grab the dagger and press it to the neck of the one beneath me. The person stills. I use my other hand to pull the penlight from my pocket. I shine it into the night.

The head turns toward me.

The hood falls away.

I realize instantly that the slip of black I saw wasn't a piece of fabric. It was a lock of hair. Tumbling black hair.

I nearly stumble backward. I know the face as well as I know the swamp.

"Charlotte?" I ask.

"You plannin' on dropping the blade, Beau?" She's careful to not move her neck.

"That depends on how you answer my next question," I reply.

She waits for me to ask. I stare into her face and wonder why she would be here. Why she would sneak out this late. Why she'd come alone. The dangers are more than I can name, and it's unlike her.

"Why are you here, Charlotte?"

Surely she wouldn't associate with a murderer. Surely she wouldn't *be* a murderer.

"Because he's here, and I need to find him," she whispers.

"Who?"

A blink of a second passes, the moment of it weighty.

"The killer."

I pull back so quickly that I stumble into a tree behind me. Charlotte sits up and rubs her neck, eyeing the blade still in my grasp.

"He's here," she says. "In the swamp. I saw him for sure."

"When?"

"Two nights ago," she says. "And then again tonight. He came to the edge of the trees, hood over his eyes. Stepped into a beam of moonlight, and then disappeared again, almost as though he wanted me to see him."

Charlotte sits up, brushing leaves from her clothes, and winces. Her hand is bleeding from the fall, dripping like paint on the ground. She inspects her palm slowly, wiping dirt from the superficial wound.

"But I doubt he's still here now, after the commotion we just made. Let's go home," she says. "I need to get this cleaned up."

I glance back and call Willow's name into the night, letting her know it's safe to come to me.

The sound of her footfalls nears until she stops beside us, huffing, mouth wide in shock at seeing Charlotte.

"You brought her," Charlotte says.

"Of course I brought her. None of us should be going into the woods alone. God, Charlotte. What did you think you'd do if you found the murderer? Do you honestly think you could take on someone like that alone? What is wrong with you?"

Willow grabs my arm and stands firm beside me, though I feel the slight tremor of her hand.

"I guess I wasn't thinking. I just saw him and took off, a gut reaction," she says.

Willow's eyes narrow in disbelief. "Your gut reaction is to go into the woods alone at night?"

Charlotte sneers. "No, you fool. My gut reaction is to find the murderer in order to save you, because something tells me you aren't exactly safe, since you're tied to Beau. Not that I'm doing it for you, of course. This is strictly for my brother."

Willow looks as though she doesn't know whether to be thankful or offended.

"He seems to have an obsession with you," Charlotte continues. "I'd hate to see him lose the only girl he's ever actually wanted to keep."

31

WILLOW

I'M TRYING MY HARDEST to concentrate on schoolwork and not on the memory of finding Charlotte in the woods last night.

Soft whispers float over my desk, and I lift my head.

"Wonder if she's connected…"

"Maybe the first victim…"

"No one's brought her up for a while…"

A group of girls is having a hurried conversation in hushed tones by the art table. I reach for my paintbrush and fake fruit, setting up my props and materials for today's assignment.

"Do you think she ended up like the others?"

"Possibly."

"Maybe he *did* do it."

"Maybe she's just really gone."

"But people are saying…"

"Ericka never came back…she just *disappeared.* People think she might have died."

Just then, one of the four girls glances up and notices me staring.

"Suppose you heard us," she says.

I nod, wondering if it's a bad thing that I did.

"You should be careful now that you're dating him," she warns.

Just like that, she looks away.

I drop the fake fruit on the white sheet propped up on my desk. Jorie sits beside me, watching the confrontation, if it could even be called that.

"Don't worry about her," Jorie says. "She's just jealous because she dated Beau once. Couldn't keep his interest past a week."

"Who's Ericka?" I ask.

The other students on each side of us perk up at the mention of her name.

"A girl who used to go to school here," Jorie explains. "She moved away quickly and people thought it was odd."

"Why was it odd?" I ask.

"Because she never said goodbye to anyone. She withdrew from classes. Didn't go to school for a few weeks. In a place as small as this, people notice. I'm telling you, it was nothing. But you know this town, always needing to have a story to spin."

"How do you know it was nothing?" I ask. "Those girls seemed to think it was suspicious."

"Listen, I used to tutor the girl in math. Her parents got another job offer, and they sold the house and moved. Only reason people even talk about it is because of what happened right before. Terrible coincidence."

I dip my brush in water, and then in paint, but I'm not paying much attention to the assignment.

"Didn't you used to hang out with Ericka?" the girl to my left says to Jorie. "I thought you were friends."

Jorie glances sharply at the girl, her eyes hard. "Not

your conversation."

"Were you?" I ask. "Friends with her, I mean?"

Jorie shrugs. "Sure. You could call us friends. I helped her out in math, and she sometimes brought me the most delicious chocolate chip cookies as a thank-you. We weren't enemies, but I wouldn't say we were close, either."

Maybe Jorie knew her well enough to understand more of the girl's story.

"What happened right before?" I ask.

Jorie is quiet for a moment. "Remember how I told you that Beau breaks hearts?"

I don't like where I suspect this is going.

"Well, word has it that Ericka and Beau dated. He's dated so many girls, it's hard to keep track. Mind you, he's not always public with the girls he sees, so who knows what went on behind closed doors."

"You telling me he hurt this girl?" I ask.

"That's what people think. That he hurt her feelings so badly, in fact, that she up and disappeared one day. Her whole family did. No one has seen her since. But like I said, her whole family didn't leave town for a breakup. Much as I don't like Beau, it's mighty hard to believe he caused a girl's disappearance, don't you think?"

"But those girls said that maybe she died," I say. "That maybe she is actually the first of the Mangroves Murderer's victims."

"Well, that's impossible. She wasn't found dead in the swamp, see?"

"That's true," I say.

Still, I wonder if she really did move away.

. . .

Gran shuffles around the kitchen, acting like she doesn't need a cane, holding onto the counters and chairs for support as she moves about.

"Set the table, will you?" she asks.

Mom and Dad discuss birds at the kitchen table. It's been confirmed that they did, in fact, discover a new species. They're thrilled. I'm not. Maybe because I miss them, and maybe because I'm jealous that they have so much love for each other and their profession that they don't mind being tied up in it. Though lately, they've been staying home more because of the murders. Even still, it's obvious they miss the field. As much as I like having them around, I can't wait for them to get back to what they love. And for the murderer to be found.

"Mind grabbing the gravy, too?" Gran says. "Can't have turkey and taters without gravy. Get the green beans while you're at it. I need to fetch the rolls from the oven."

"Sure," I answer.

There's something on my mind. Something I need to discuss with Gran. If anyone knows the truth, it's her. Gran always has a way of finding things out.

"Gran, do you think you could tell me about a teen girl named Ericka who disappeared?"

She sighs heavily. "Ericka Sprayer. I knew that story would eventually find its way to you, though I'd hoped it wouldn't."

"Why didn't you want me to know?"

Gran takes a seat in the living room and beckons me to do the same. My parents are too busy pointing at numerous pages in their journal to notice what Gran and I are discussing.

"Because there's no use in scarin' you. Some things

happen 'round here that folks don't talk much about, and this is one of them. That girl, she had it all. A family. A nice house in town. Friends. Up and left everything. Her parents got a job offer somewhere else, though most people don't believe that version of the story. No one ever heard from her again. Shame, I tell you."

My stomach churns with nerves. Something tells me that this girl has a part in the murders. How? I have no idea, but I suspect that she's connected.

"Well, 'course there are a few 'round here who can't leave well enough alone. The town librarian, for one. She went digging. Swear some people are born with the need to know, and some are born with gossiping mouths. Thankfully the librarian didn't tell many people, and the ones she did tell decided to keep quiet."

"Were you one of those people?"

She watches me with a sharp look.

"You seem to be the type who has to know. So I'll tell you, I will, but I want you to keep quiet, you hear?"

I swallow a lump in my throat and nod.

"I was one of them, yes. Saw the reports on the internet myself. That Sprayer girl didn't disappear. Neither did her family. They quietly sold their house and left. The reason they got positions elsewhere is because they *wanted* to move to help their daughter, you see. The girl was having trouble here. No one is quite sure why. What would make her as sad as she was? Word has it that her family had a history of depression. Secrets like those are normally carried to the grave around here, such a stigma attached. Shouldn't be, of course, but there you have it. Something upset her so badly that her parents thought it was in her best interest to leave town altogether."

"They moved?" I ask, not quite sure I understand.

"That's all? She's not dead?"

Gran closes her eyes slowly, and when she opens them, worry shines through.

"Now, I didn't say that," she whispers.

I don't understand, not at all.

"It didn't seem to matter that she moved across the country. The girl never recovered. She took her own life. So yes, she's gone."

I feel sick—my stomach churning like the swamp waters after high winds. There's something familiar about the way Gran gazes at me, as though she means to comfort with a single stare. Ericka's life is lost. I somehow feel the absence, even though I never knew her. I wish I could have helped. I wish someone—anyone—would've helped her. I wonder if she reached out in her pain, in her time of need. Was her family there for her?

"What happened?" I ask. "What would drive her to such a thing?"

"Like I said, so many rumors around here. Maybe depression. Maybe something personal. But some say she dated your boy, Beau."

"A lot of girls have," I say.

"Yes, but Beau's wicked ways could have spawned her actions. He is prone to upsetting girls."

Gran stands and nearly falls over. I catch her arm and wait for her trembling muscles to steady. She takes a minute and then walks back to the kitchen to pour herself a glass of tea. I pretend not to notice when she spills a few drops. Sensing that she's not done yet, I wait.

"I wouldn't doubt that Beau emotionally destroyed her," she says.

"If it's true that he dated her, and that she suffered emotionally and mentally, I wonder why she didn't say something to someone other than her parents. Wasn't there some way to help her?"

"Maybe," Gran replies. "Or maybe he hurt her heart too badly for healing, Willow Mae. And perhaps she never recovered."

32

BEAU

I EASE THE BOAT AROUND an eddy, through silt waters that have risen from the rain. Mangrove roots can no longer be seen. Everything is covered in a clear sheen of swamp like a thin wax coating.

Today, Willow and I have boated to the platform.

"Beau, I need to talk to you about something," Willow says, tying up the boat and splaying herself out on the wood. Not a care in the world about the mud and dirt and bugs below. I smile.

"Oh yeah? And what's that?"

I lie next to her, peering at the hanging lantern.

"There was a girl once," she says. "You knew her. I want to know what happened."

"Happened to who?" I ask.

I hardly see how telling Willow about a girl I once knew could be interesting to her, especially since all the girls I know, aside from Charlotte, are linked to me romantically.

"Her name was Ericka."

I stiffen.

"She disappeared one day and never came back. People are speculating that she's connected to the murders. What do you know about this?"

"You sure you don't want to talk about anything else?"

"Tell me, Beau."

I sigh, resigned.

"Okay, I dated her. It lasted"—I think back, trying to remember—"maybe a month? I called it off. I don't know anything about this connecting to the murders. The murders just started, and she left a while back."

Willow winds a lock of dark hair around her finger and then lets it go.

"What do you remember about her?"

Shit, that is not the right question to ask me. I remember the way she kissed me like she was dying to get more. But even these remembrances are distant, like a far-off sound, hard to make out.

"Willow, I really don't think—"

"Answer me."

I don't want her knowing this.

"I remember some times with her," I say tentatively.

"Doing what?"

"Willow." I groan.

She must know what she's asking of me.

"Say it," she demands.

"Fine. I remember private moments with her at her house when her parents were working. That's it. I hardly knew her."

She cringes.

"I'm sorry! I didn't want to tell you, but you insisted."

"Do you know why she left?"

"No idea."

"Do you happen to know that she missed weeks of

school after you broke things off with her?"

"Did she?"

"And then her family sold their house, packed up, and they were gone."

"What does this have to do with me?"

She rolls to her side to look me in the eyes.

"I heard she couldn't get over you, and that's why they left."

"Who told you that?"

Willow waves a hand around. "Oh, you know. People at school. Pretty much everyone knows your history with girls, and so they assume you were the reason."

I've honestly not thought of Ericka since she moved a year ago. Of course, I first heard the rumors that she left because of me, but I figured they were just that: rumors. Now, I wonder if they were true. My heart kicks up a notch as I think about what that means for me, that maybe my actions are to blame.

"You seemed to have broken her heart, and I wonder, Beau, if you know just how many girls you've hurt. And if you evcn care."

A wave of guilt makes me feel uneasy. "I hope I didn't have anything to do with it, and you know why I've been closed off. I'm working on that. I definitely don't want anyone to be hurt. I feel awful about these victims. I can't stand the thought of anyone else coming to harm. You believe me, right?"

"Yes, I believe you," she replies. "And plus, you just admitted that you care. Not in the exact words, but you've let down more defenses."

"Maybe you're right."

"You mean I am." She folds her arms and narrows her eyes at me.

"I mean maybe."

"Or I suppose I could be reading this all wrong."

Her eyes search me so thoroughly that I have the urge to look away.

"You're not."

"You and your damn riddles, Beau."

She leans into me like she's planning on kissing me. So I close the gap between us and kiss her.

"It's getting late," she says, pulling away. "We need to be on our way back."

I help her up and take the oars to row home.

We're a little ways down the swamp when I notice a hush fall over the trees, followed by a scraping through the brush.

"Someone's here," I whisper.

"How do you know?" Willow glances at the tall grass, which bends ever so slightly away from us, like it doesn't want to be bothered.

"The markings," I say. "They're everywhere."

A just-made scratch on a tree, sap oozing. An overturned leaf. Branches slightly askew.

I quickly dock the boat again, and we carefully get out and push through the grass. Thickets of trees begin to thin as we approach the edge of the swamp forest.

Is it my imagination, or did the trees move?

I hold a finger to my lips to signal Willow to be silent. Her eyes widen, and she stands dead still. My heart thrashes with anticipation, and I can hear Willow breathing wildly. Her eyes dart around, looking for something to settle on, trying to track the person we both know is near.

I take closer stock of the trees. A flicker of black. A small moan. A vestigial shadow.

I burst through the trees.

And nearly fall to my knees.

My legs wobble and threaten to give out.

There's a person hunched over, interested in something at the edge of a channel of water that separates the land. A cluster of mangroves nearly hides the stranger, who's wearing a black cloak, hood up.

"Hello?" I say.

I barely feel Willow as she lays a hand on my forearm.

The stranger spins around, holding the hood down so that all I catch is an angular chin draped in shadow. I've startled him. I now see why. Tall grass obscures part of what I'm witnessing, half hidden. The other half is unmistakably a pair of legs.

"God," Willow says, taking a step back.

"No," I say, taking a step forward.

The swamp separates me from the stranger.

The killer.

I take off running into the water. It drops off suddenly, and I am swimming, swimming, swimming as fast as I can. There's a gator near me. I can only hope that it won't mistake my sudden splashing movements for prey. I can't stop to think about anything.

I've nearly reached the mangroves when the killer runs.

I pull myself out of the water and glance at the legs, which lead to a body.

Her name is Michelle—a girl I once dated. Her neck is bruised, and her eyes are wide. And then she does something I don't expect her to do. She moves her fingers.

I need to find the killer.

And I need to help Michelle.

She looks as though she wants to say something. As

I approach, I have to hold onto my wits because what I see is horrific. Her throat is crushed. She's attempting to breathe in short raspy inhalations that get more desperate by the second.

I can already hear Willow in the background on her phone, trying through patchy reception to tell the police we need help.

I don't want to let the killer go, but I can no longer see him, and Michelle doesn't look as though she has long. I bend over her and set my hands on her chest, ready to begin CPR.

Michelle is dying. Right in front of me.

"I will find him," I whisper to her. "And he will pay for doing this to you and the others."

Her chest suddenly rises so roughly that her back arches off the ground in desperate attempts for air.

I begin chest compressions like they taught us in school. I can't remember if I'm doing it right, but I don't want to stop. I can't stop.

Suddenly, Michelle stills.

"Help her!" Willow screams as she draws near in the boat.

"I'm trying!"

I continue the compressions—one, two, three, four—until Willow erupts into a burst of sobs. Water drips from my wet hair onto Michelle's face, making it look as though she's crying.

I keep at it until the police show up and emergency workers take over. It seems like forever, too long, before they shock her with electric pads and push down on her chest, breathe into her mouth, and wait and wait and wait for Michelle to breathe on her own. She never does.

I reach for Willow and try to offer her comfort,

knowing all the while that my mind is elsewhere. We were so close to having a witness, someone to identify the killer. I could have caught the Mangroves Murderer. If I'd left Michelle, maybe he would have been stopped.

These girls are gone because of me. It's too hard to deny the connection. No matter what I do, I can't get them out of my head. Especially now that I just watched one die.

And her killer is still on the loose.

33

WILLOW

"PLEASE STATE YOUR NAME."

"Willow Mae Bell," I say.

"Do you have any idea where the killer went?" the police officer asks me.

I can't think. I can't remember. I keep seeing legs. Legs attached to a dead body.

"He ran off into the trees," I say, gesturing in the general direction.

"And you?" the cop asks Beau. "Do you remember which way he went, aside from 'into the trees'?"

"He seemed to be heading north," Beau replies.

The cop nods, more satisfied with Beau's answer than with mine.

"Can you describe him to me, miss?"

I remember in flashes, bursts of images like a digital camera in playback.

"Tall, maybe. Black coat. Hood over his face."

That's it. That's all I've got. I shiver from the memory, clutching my cardigan closer.

The police officer makes notes on his legal pad.

"You knew the victim?"

"A little." Beau shifts uncomfortably. "But we haven't talked in months. I haven't even seen her except for a few times in school. We're not exactly friends."

"And you?" the cop asks me.

"I didn't know her at all." I can't remember ever seeing her.

Bile rises, burning my throat, and I fear that I'll be sick.

Another officer approaches. The swamp is swarming with them like mud wasps buzzing everywhere. Looking for any sign of the Mangroves Murderer.

"This is Officer Keely," the cop says. "He will escort you both home. It's not safe in the swamp."

I can't help but look toward the body, laid out on the mangroves like a play doll. There's a sheet over her now. But I can still picture the girl's pleading face, her look of terror as she struggled to breathe. Suddenly, my stomach turns and I can't hold back. I bend over and lose my dinner. Beau is there with a comforting touch, rubbing my shoulder softly, holding back my hair.

"Ma'am," Officer Keely says when I'm done. "Best be getting you home."

Once we arrive back at our cabins, the officer leaves us be and returns to the swamp investigation. In his wake, another of his colleagues takes patrol at the dividing line, keeping watch over both our houses.

"Who would do this?" Beau asks as we enter his cabin. "And why is the timing different? The others took place late at night. This one happened in the early evening hours. It almost seems as though the killer is becoming more desperate."

"Or the killer is becoming sloppy," I say. "Either way, we were there, right there. Too close to the crime."

I've already checked in with Gran, who advised me to reconsider going to Beau's house. But I had to come here. I have to talk it out with someone, and seeing as how she doesn't want to discuss it, and as how Mom and Dad still have a forty-five-minute drive home until I can talk with them, Beau's place seems like the right decision.

Charlotte is waiting for us in the living room as we enter the cabin. Her stare is trained out the window, into the dark night. A candle flickers beside her, smelling heavily of spice.

"Is it true?" she asks. "Did you find a dead girl?"

"How did you know that?" Beau asks.

Charlotte stands and walks to the kitchen to retrieve a cup of coffee. She makes one for Beau and me as well, adding cream and sugar.

"I arrived home just afterward. The officer taking watch spoke with Grandpa and me. He told us."

As though hearing himself mentioned, Beau's grandpa walks into the room.

"Beau," he says, nodding a greeting. His eyes find me. "Virginia's granddaughter. Lord, you look just like her."

It's the first time I'm seeing him in the flesh up close, reclusive as he is.

"Thank you," I say proudly, taking a sip from the mug that warms my hands.

The coffee is sweet—enough sugar to zing my senses, a hint of vanilla flavoring.

"Why can't they find the killer?" Charlotte says. "He

can't have gone far in such short a time."

"Why would he do it?" Beau's words fade to a whisper. "Who has reason to kill innocent girls?"

Charlotte suddenly turns to me. "Do you have something to do with this, Willow?"

What? A shiver runs through me. How could she ask such a thing? Does she honestly think of me as a murderer, even after we've told her that we caught the killer in the act? Is she that inclined to think me guilty?

"I most certainly do not have *anything* to do with this," I say, disgusted. "Why would you think that?"

Charlotte sips her coffee and leans her elbows against the kitchen island.

"I don't know you. I don't know what you're capable of, and it doesn't hurt to ask. Plus, the murders didn't start until you arrived." She gives me a piercing look. "Let's say you're being honest," she continues. "If it wasn't you, and it wasn't me, and it wasn't Grandpa or Beau... Then who?"

"Knock it off, Charlotte," Beau says. "You know that Willow didn't kill anyone."

"Beau's right," Mr. Cadwell says. "I don't think she'd hurt a soul."

He doesn't know me well enough to say, but his faith in me is appreciated. I can't help but compare the wrinkled face in front of me to the smooth-skinned face in Gran's photo album. He looks older than I originally thought he was, and there's a wet sound to the way he breathes. This is the man Gran once loved. Perhaps still does.

"Where can the killer possibly be hiding that none of us can find him?" Mr. Cadwell asks, but his words turn into a barking cough. It takes him a full minute to catch his breath again.

None of us has a solid answer, so as it turns out, there's not much to discuss anyway.

Mr. Cadwell takes his coffee mug with him to one of the living room chairs, settling into it with shaky limbs.

Beau's fingers wrap around mine and, for once, I feel as though he needs my support, like I might just be the very thing holding him together.

Charlotte twirls a ring on her pointer finger. The stone matches the candy-red paint on her long nails.

Beyond the window, police lights blare a belated warning.

"Do you think they have any leads?" I wonder if they would tell us if they did.

"Aside from badgering Beau? No." Charlotte doesn't look at me when she speaks, but I feel her gaze when I glance away.

Though I've been too frightened to speak the words aloud, I finally voice something I've been thinking about lately, another option, albeit a dangerous one.

"Do you think I should try to lure the killer?" The words are out of my mouth so quickly I have no time to debate them. Anger flashes across Beau's face. I try to backpedal, to explain. "That's what everyone thinks, that the killer is after me next. I hear it in the halls. I know you think it, too, Beau. Even your friends wonder. It's a logical train of thought. My parents and Gran would kill me for even speaking like this, but maybe there's a chance to catch him if it seems as though I'm in the swamp alone. You could be nearby. Maybe we can trick him. I don't know what else to do."

"Are you crazy?" Beau's voice leaks with venom. "Have you lost your mind?"

"I wouldn't actually go alone. We'd just make the killer *think* I'm alone. Maybe then he'd come for me."

Beau shakes his head slowly, his eyes trained on me and me alone.

"Every day, Willow." He takes a deep, steadying breath. "Every single damn day, you are a target. Moving from my house to yours to the swamp to school. Lately, whenever I see you, I see them, the dead girls. I wonder if you'll be next. It drives me mad, and I can't stand it. You will *not* become an even bigger target. No way. I can't let…"

He trails off, and I wonder if he means to say anything else at all. Charlotte and Mr. Cadwell watch us silently with expressions I can't quite read.

"You can't let what?" I finally ask.

Beau leans closer to me, as though he intends to shut out the rest of the world.

"I can't let it *be* you. Not ever. I feel so much guilt over the girls who've died. But if something happened to you—I'd be lost."

I wonder if he cares that his family is hanging on his every word with their stares.

I open my mouth to protest. To comfort. To tell him it won't be me, even though that might be a lie.

"Don't." He holds up a hand. "Don't placate me, Willow. Just hear me, okay? Please. You are so full of light. You brighten the entire damn world, and I can't go back there." His voice lowers. "I can't go back to before. Cold emotions and distance. I need you."

When he leans in and kisses me, I am absolutely dizzy with pleasure. His words leave a tingle on my skin, a warmth that feels something like love. I forget about our audience. I know nothing of murders or danger or police.

There are only his lips on mine. His heart is beating so fast that I can't distinguish between it and my own. I don't remember what it is to know this world without Beau and these kisses and this fire, fire, fire.

I hope I never have to.

34

BEAU

"GRANDPA, MIND IF we talk?" I ask.

He turns toward me and sets down the book he's reading. His eyes are tired and the sun has only just risen.

"I figured you'd notice," Grandpa says.

I keep quiet to hear exactly what he means.

"Charlotte's already come to me, of course," he says. "The girl notices everything under the sun, that one."

I had actually meant to discuss a different strategy to find the killer. The police aren't doing a good enough job, and I can't seem to get the dying girl's face from last night out of my mind. It's haunting me, and I fear the only way to stop it is to find the killer. But now, the need to know what exactly Grandpa means pulls at me.

"Charlotte knows. Suppose you do, too."

"Sure," I lie.

His eyes narrow. "Damn."

And then he does an unexpected thing. He laughs good and loud. He laughs so hard that he coughs, which turns into a fit. He puts a hand to his mouth to stop it.

"Grandpa, you okay? You catch something?"

Finally, he stills and pulls his hand back.

His chin and palm are covered in bloody speckles.

"Well, hell," Grandpa says. "Here I thought you came to talk about me dying, when all along, you didn't know. I caught something, all right. A fatal lung cancer."

I stagger back a step.

Fatal.

I try to blink away the shock of his statement. Despite my best intentions to stay so carefully guarded, I'm going to lose another person in my life.

"But you've never smoked a day in your life." I don't know why I say it. It's just the first thing that comes to mind.

Panic surges through my veins. I wonder if the anguish I feel is reflected in my expression. I consider Grandpa closely. My stare goes again to the red flecks on his skin. Does it hurt to know he's dying?

"Don't be dense, boy. You don't have to smoke to get cancer. 'Course, you sure increase your odds if you do, but cancer handpicked me, and so here I am. For all my sins, seems like a mighty right way for me to go. Could have been worse."

I grab a towel from the side table and hand it to him.

"How much longer?" I ask. I don't want to know. But I can't *not* know.

"A week? Two? I don't know. Haven't eaten much. Can't keep most things down. Mind is going in and out. I'm tired, Beau. It's close to time."

"How long have you known?" I ask. My voice is steady, though my thoughts are not.

Grandpa is dying. I feel as though I am dying, too. And suddenly, the weight is too much. I take a seat, my head in my hands. I stiffen, fighting back the sobs that threaten to wreck me. Not again. Not Grandpa, too. I can't lose him, too.

"About six months. Went to the doctor in town. He sent me to the hospital. Know what it's like to get stuck with needles and poked a million times, feeling like a pesky porcupine went and put its quills in you? Well, it's about as awful as it sounds. Actually, worse."

"What about medicine?" I ask. "There must be something they can do."

Grandpa wheezes. "They offered treatments, sure. I'm not taking them, though. I want to die the right way. Here in my own home." He stops to catch his breath, which never seems to happen. "Let the swamp have me when it's over, will you? That's all I ask. Sink my ashes in the muddy gator water. Wouldn't want it any other way."

I came to talk to Grandpa about strategy, and now I'm taking an oath to respect his death.

"I'll do it, you know I will," I say. A pinch of anger rolls through me. "But were you ever going to tell me? Was I just supposed to wake up one morning to learn that you never will again?"

Anger gives way to sadness. I take a ragged, steadying breath and place a palm against my chest, over my heart, where it feels as though I'm being split in two.

Grandpa shrugs. "What would you have done, Beau? On the one hand, I suppose telling you lets you see it beforehand. But I wonder what good that does. Can't change a thing."

"It gives me a chance to say goodbye. That's more than I got from Dad and Mom."

"Then say it," he replies.

"Not now, you're not that close to being gone yet."

"Might as well be. The worst is comin'. Can't promise

I'll remember if you don't say it now."

"I'm not going to," I say, a note of finality in my tone.

It's not fair, none of it. I press two rough fingers to my lips to keep the goodbye from slipping out. Each breath feels as though it's sawing through my lungs, too painful to bear.

"Suit yourself. Maybe I can tell you something, though?" Grandpa requests. "I want you to know that I've only truly loved a few people in my life, and you happen to be one of them."

I'm silent. I'm stone, unmoving. The Cadwell family doesn't express emotions. It's not who we are, damn it. But I see it anyhow. It's written in the way my hands shake. In the way I open and close my mouth several times in indecision. I want to tell him how much he means to me, too.

Maybe I should be telling Grandpa that I love him, but I can't seem to pull the words out past the rock in my throat.

Grandpa wraps a blanket around his shoulders even though it's about a hundred degrees with the windows open. His eyes are getting heavier, drooping nearly closed, like even sitting here and staying awake is too much of an effort for him.

Charlotte rounds the corner. Grandpa takes shallow breaths, sounding wet like the slurp of mud tugging at boots.

"You've told him, then," she says.

Grandpa nods, saving his voice. Even the slightest sigh sends him trying to swallow down coughs. Now that I think about it, it makes sense. He's been weak, tired. Staying to his room. Off balance, maybe due to dizziness from not eating much. The cancer is swallowing him whole.

For once, Charlotte's face is somber.

"Now what?" she whispers.

"Now we wait," Grandpa says.

The end of his sentence hangs silent and invisible, but I say it in my mind anyway.

We wait...for his death.

35

WILLOW

A WATER MOCCASIN COILS and waits like a stump by the tree, but I see it good and clear, even though it mostly blends into the dirt.

"Watch your step," I tell Jorie.

We pass the snake without incident. Occasionally they give chase, but not today.

"How about that tree?" Jorie asks.

The weeping willow is clear of snakes, and so we take a seat under its hanging limbs. I place the picnic basket between us and get to work opening its contents. Down the way, a gator suns himself, side-eyeing us. I can tell by the way he hardly moves that he's cold from the water, needing warmth to reenergize him. It's the ones that have been out in the heat for hours that you need to worry about. They're faster than fast and feisty, too.

"What've you got?" she asks.

"Ham, egg, and cheese sandwiches with grapes, melon, and sweet tea."

I unzip a baggie and take a bite of a sandwich. Gran made them just the way I like—thick honey-cured ham sprinkled with brown sugar, salty eggs, cheese melted into a crispy croissant shell. Suddenly, I'm hungrier than I was a minute ago.

"Sweet Lord," Jorie says as she sinks her teeth into a sandwich. "Your gran sure knows her way around the kitchen."

It takes all of a minute for us to finish our sandwiches. I eat mine so fast that I forget to get out the mason jars to pour Jorie and me some tea. The mason jars are already packed with ice, lids screwed on tight. The ice has only just barely melted in the heat. I drink the water that's collected on the bottom of my jar, and then fill it with tea. Sugar shocks my senses in the best way.

With several gulps in me, my mind finally casts off the last dregs of sleep. I get a feeling sort of like my bones fit right in a place like this. The trees, the murky water, the creatures, all of them are a constant in my life now, and I wonder how I lived anywhere else.

"You ever get the feeling you're meant to be somewhere?" I ask Jorie. "Like here, in this swamp? Does it ever call to you?"

She nods. "It does. It always has. My family and me, we've visited other places, sure. But I can't handle being away for more than a week. I get homesick."

Home. That's what the swamp has become to me. I'm sure of it. This place has completely claimed me.

"The swamp gives me a sinking feeling in my bones, but in a good way," I say.

"I know just what you mean," she replies. "It's as though you are chained to a place but somehow totally free."

"Exactly. I never did feel that when we lived in Florida, or in another part of Georgia for that matter. But then again, I never did live in the swamp proper, so there you go."

Jorie sips her tea, crunching on a piece of ice. Today her hair is pulled up into a messy bun and her lips are painted a deep brown that goes perfect with her skin.

"You know, it nearly makes me sick to separate myself from this place," she says. "Where else can I get fresh gator tail, or frog legs, or catfish that tastes just right?"

"You think after high school finishes that you'll go off to college? Or will you stay close?"

There is no college close by, which makes me question what I want to do. And considering that we have only a couple of months left of senior year, I need to make a decision.

"Haven't decided yet." Jorie reaches a thin hand into the wicker basket and pushes aside the flannel towel to grab a bundle of grapes.

"My mom asked me today if I had applied," I say.

"What'd you tell her?"

"The truth. I haven't applied anywhere." I don't tell Jorie that Beau, his family, and the murderer have occupied my mind and time. "But I might. Suppose it can't hurt to take classes a few days a week at the community college. It'll be a long drive, but I'm sure I want to stay in the swamp. Maybe I can even take some of the courses online."

"There're people who will tell you to get the hell out of the swamp while you can, b'fore you get stuck, but I happen to like being stuck," she says, popping a grape into her mouth. "Seems better than having wandering feet, always taking you places, never laying down roots."

It feels good to know that someone else understands. The swamp is both of our homes.

"Whatever happened to Brody?" Jorie asks, out of the blue.

I shrug. "We're friends. Nothing more."

"Brody's nice," she says. "You know you'll never make a nice boy out of Beau."

"I don't think I want a nice boy," I reply honestly. "I think when you find the boy who makes you feel like you're wearing your skin backward, who turns you inside out and heats your blood and sets you on fire with want, it doesn't much matter."

Jorie sighs heavily. "I just want you to be happy. I don't think there's a chance that Beau *won't* hurt you. You're setting yourself up for it."

Maybe I am, but I can't stop now.

"You're a good friend, Jorie," I say. "You really are."

Something flashes in her eyes, an emotion gone too quickly for me to name it.

"I'm still gonna warn you away from him. You know that, right? I probably always will."

"Because you think he's dangerous," I say.

"Because I know he breaks hearts, and you aren't set up to handle something like that."

"What's that supposed to mean, that I'm not set up?"

I try to keep the edge out of my voice, but for a second there it sounded like she was saying I'm not strong.

"Don't take it the wrong way." She lays a gentle hand on my arm. "You know I care what happens to you, and I think you're getting in deep with Beau. At first, I figured you'd be like the rest. He'd use you and toss you aside, because that's what he does. But it's been different with you. He's not backing off right away. I think it'll make everything harder when he finally does."

"So you're trying to tell me that I shouldn't see him anymore? That I should end things with him?"

"Better you breaking it off with him than him hurting you."

Isn't that the exact philosophy that made Beau so guarded in the first place? The one that kept him from opening up and truly feeling something deep? I don't want that kind of darkness. I prefer to feel emotions, even if they do hurt. I want to love and be loved. The risk is worth it to me. It will always be worth it.

"Says who?" I ask. "If you're happy with a person, why end it?"

"Because you won't be happy for long."

"But I'm happy now."

Jorie leans back into the tree, taking her touch with her. "I'm just saying that you are my friend, and as your friend, I want to encourage you to be happy and healthy."

"And Beau's not healthy?"

I'm getting defensive. I can't seem to help it.

"He's Beau, Willow. What do you expect? He uses girls. You are filling a use for him now, but what about later?"

She's wrong. I'm more than a spot to fill.

"Stop," I say. "Please."

She frowns. "See how much you like him now? See how much it pains you to think about splitting from him? Imagine how much worse it'd be in another month or two."

This was supposed to be a nice breakfast. Sit in the swamp and watch the sun take steps up the sky until it is as high as it can go. My best friend wasn't supposed to discourage me from being with the boy who makes me feel more alive than ever.

"Willow, listen. I just don't want to see you wrecked like the others."

I look steadily at Jorie. At her messy hair and wide eyes and relaxed body, legs crossed at the ankles, skin pressed into the Georgia dirt.

"I know," I say. "I'm sorry. I'm just defensive because it's Beau."

"Think about what I'm saying, okay? Try to get away while you still can."

I don't want to get away. I suppose, being my friend, she needs to say it. But then again, if she knows I'm all in, why try to call me out?

"Promise me that you'll try," she says.

I can't promise her such a thing.

"Jorie," I plead.

She waits for words that will not come.

"You won't do it, will you?" she asks.

"I can't," I admit. "There are things you don't understand. I know you want to look out for me, and I can't tell you how much I appreciate that, but there's more to Beau than what everyone else sees."

"And you see these things that are more?" she asks.

"I do."

"Tell me about them," she says. "Maybe then I'll better understand."

It's a request I can't grant. "Don't take this the wrong way, but it's sort of his story to tell, you know?"

She absolutely takes it the wrong way. Suddenly, she's stiff, and her look is hurt.

"I'm your friend, Willow. You're saying you can't tell me?"

It's not right for me to discuss his parents, the losses he has sustained, and why he's so guarded.

"I'm saying it's not my place. Surely you understand that."

But she doesn't.

She grows quiet.

"I'm sorry," I whisper.

The once delicious food turns sour in my stomach. I have to choose between my best friend and my boyfriend. Between stories that are not mine to tell and requests to tell them. So I keep quiet and let the silence stretch between us.

36

BEAU

"IT'S BEEN A WEEK already," Grandpa says. "I think I'm out of time."

But it's not his voice anymore. Now, he whispers, and even that is an effort. He's not eating, and he swears it won't be much longer.

In the next room, I hear the television. On my insistence, Charlotte has taken a break from her constant vigil at Grandpa's side. She needed a shower, a meal, a rest from her own mind.

"Ready for that goodbye yet?" Grandpa asks.

He bursts into a coughing fit that cuts off any remaining words. I wait patiently. When he finally stills, I help him wipe a dribble of blood from his chin.

"He's okay!" I say as I hear Charlotte's feet on the ground. "You come back in here and I'll lock you out, so help me."

I suppose another reason I don't want Charlotte in the room when it happens—when Grandpa finally goes— is because I know her, and she won't take well to seeing him pass. Afterward, yes. But the final moments are not meant for her, and she knows it.

There's a pause, and then Charlotte's footsteps retreat.

Grandpa smiles. I'm sure going to miss his grins at the banter between my sister and me.

"I guess I could do that goodbye," I say, mustering every ounce of bravery I own.

I've brought Grandpa his Sunday paper and a cup of coffee, though it remains on his bedside table, untouched. I dread the tradition coming to an end, but I know it inevitably will with his passing.

"I don't want to, though, you know," I say.

"I know."

Grandpa's breaths are worse than I've ever heard them, and this time I believe him when he says he won't see another morning.

"I wish you would have told me about the cancer. I wish I would have had more time with you," I say.

That's about as close to a goodbye as I'll ever give. I'm no good at goodbyes. I never wanted to have to say another one.

"It's the same amount of time, either way. Telling you hasn't increased my days, so don't beat yourself up. Move on afterward. Live life and be free, full of fun and mischief. Don't let my sickness drag you down. Your days are numbered, too, you know. All of ours are. Spend them happily. And please make sure your sister moves on. She deserves every moment of happiness that comes her way. Don't let my death rob that from either of you, you hear me?"

I do, but it'll take time. He must know it won't be easy.

"Remember what I said about"—he stops to cough—"letting the swamp have me."

I nod, hating the thought.

"One more thing, though." His breaths are shallow. "Tell Virginia that I love her. Always have. Always will." He smiles. "And tell her to stop feeding those gators, already."

"Now, you know I can't do that," I reply. "I'd be at risk of her wrath, and I'm not inclined to have her tell me off for this love of yours."

That's when Grandpa laughs for the very last time.

Grandpa was right.

Come evening, he's gone. There as can be in flesh and bone, but gone. I watch for the rise and fall of his chest. It never comes. I check for a pulse. But there isn't one.

"Charlotte!" I say.

My sister bursts into the room.

"Did he…?"

She looks down and sees for herself.

I lean toward Grandpa's ear and whisper one final word before I call the ambulance to take him away.

"Goodbye."

37

WILLOW

"YOU ALWAYS DID SAY that the brightest light casts the darkest shadow."

Gran eyes me suspiciously. The porch swing groans under both our weights, moving so slowly that the source of the rocking could be confused with the wind and not the occasional tap of my foot against the wooden floor to push us.

"Since when do you agree with any of my sayings?" she asks.

Gran reaches a curled old hand into the lime-green bowl that sits in her lap.

"Since I realized what you meant by it," I say. "Love is the light…and the shadow, too, isn't it? Bright and happy but also sad and painfully dark at times. You were talking about loving Mr. Cadwell that day in the kitchen, weren't you? You wanted to protect me from that kind of joyous pain with Beau."

"Willow, you're too observant for your own good."

Gran removes small, chopped chunks of unseasoned pork and chicken—bone and all—from the bowl and throws them into the front yard. The crazy woman.

"Here gator, gator, gator," she calls sweetly.

Wouldn't you know that only seconds later, a gator emerges. Then another. And another. As though she up and called them by their first names. They don't bother getting close to the porch steps. They prefer to stay on the muddy, mossy ground where they can collect their treasured treats and escape quickly. Funny that they are more scared of Gran than she is of them.

"How are my babies today?" she asks, like she's talking to beloved furry friends.

"Lord, Gran. You and your pets."

She grins. "Well, now you know my darkest secrets. I can't stop feeling like these gators need a friend, and I never did stop loving the crooked boy next door."

There's a shine of tears in her eyes.

"May he rest in peace," she whispers.

A car pulls into the driveway, careful to not hit the gators. Jorie steps out of the passenger side and says goodbye to her mother. As though the gators don't bother her one bit, she walks past them and heads toward Gran and me.

"Will you be okay, Gran?" I ask. "I'll cancel my plans, you know I will."

"Don't you dare do such a thing," she says, throwing the last of the treats into the yard, some even into the open mouths of the gators. "Go have fun. Be careful. And if you do decide to give that damn boy your heart, don't make the mistake of giving him the best part of it like I did, okay?"

"But Gran, that's the only way to really love, isn't it?"

I'd rather have my heart infected with love than live a day without it.

...

"Y'all better spring for a new boat soon," Jorie says. "Only a thin layer left to this one. Reminds me of the crust on the pan after your grandma bakes that delicious cornbread of hers. Which, by the way, I'm looking forward to eating when we get back."

I smile at my best friend as I row leisurely through the murky water. Today it's colored like honey, sun shining brightly through it to illuminate an underwater forest of lily roots and green vegetation. A timid breeze softly brushes hair away from my face, and I have to squint through the blaring brightness of the day.

I pat my bag out of habit, just to make sure I have my phone. Never can be too careful, since they still haven't caught the Mangroves Murderer. Pretty sure Jorie and I would make the perfect victims if we don't keep our wits about us. I have my phone. I have the shotgun under my feet. And I have a will of steel. Nobody's taking me from this swamp. And they're sure as hell not taking this swamp from me. I plan on enjoying it, no matter what the killer has done. I refuse to be a jack-in-the-box, stuffed inside the house, waiting to explode out. Life is meant to be lived, damn it. The dead girls, and hearing about Beau's grandpa passing, have taught me that.

Jorie smacks loudly on her gum, blowing bubbles so big they almost cover her face, reminding me of bright-pink balloons. She pops them and starts all over again.

We haven't spoken of our last fight, sweeping it under the rug where we can pretend we don't know it's there. We row under a thicket of leaves. Here, the water points us to a channel, trees like walls on either side.

Jorie sits at the front of the boat, picturesque with the swamp all around her.

There's a spot I'm taking her to where the ground is raised into what could almost be called a hill. The gators don't often trek up it, making it perfect for sunbathing. Gran showed it to me a couple of years back. Said it's one of the only places that stays constantly dry. Unless a hurricane blows through and the waters rise enough, which hardly ever happens. I even brought a bag full of stuff—sunglasses, bottled water, magazines, and a few books. A girls' day all the way. A quiet spot for Jorie and me and no one else.

When we pull up, I slip out my phone and quickly shoot a message to Beau, asking him how he's doing, knowing he's grieving his grandpa's passing and that he and Charlotte are planning the cremation. I tell him that I'm at the hill in the swamp with Jorie and that I'll stop by his place later tonight. I place my cell back into the zippered part of my bag. Who knows if the text will actually go through, horrible as the service sometimes is.

We climb the hill to the top where a perfect circular sunspot awaits us. Jorie smiles at the sight.

"Well, haven't you just found a slice of heaven?" she says. "Come on. Might as well take advantage."

I lay two towels on the ground, which is mostly dirt and rocks and the occasional grass shoots. The rocks are uncomfortable at first, but after a minute, we get used to them. Jorie holds up the books I brought.

"Is this a romance?" she jokes, waggling her eyebrows.

"Yeah, I suppose it is."

She reads the back of all three, picks one, opens it, and rolls over onto her stomach so that she can place the book on the ground while she reads. Then she sits up, as if in afterthought, and pulls off her clothes to reveal a red one-piece underneath.

I take off my shorts and tank top, but unlike her, I have a bikini on underneath—blue with white stripes.

I pick one of the books she discarded and open it. Out of habit, I place a bookmark at the beginning of the next chapter. The sun beats on our skin over and over again until it burns.

Hours pass just like that. Jorie and me soaking up the day, my bookmark making its way farther and farther into cracks between pages, and not a single mention of the murders that tried to taint such a gorgeous place.

38

BEAU

MAKING ARRANGEMENTS for Grandpa isn't easy, and since Charlotte and I need a break from it, and Willow is off with Jorie, according to her text, I invite Pax and Grant over. Charlotte decides to lock herself in her room. Probably best, since Grant won't stop staring at her.

"I'm sorry about your grandpa," Pax says, glancing around the cabin as though he might catch sight of him one more time.

"Me, too," Grant adds.

"Thanks." I sigh. "It's hard, you know? But at least Charlotte and I get the house."

"That's great." Pax smiles. "You can keep your things and memories here."

"But you're not eighteen," Grant says. "Think you can get away with it for a few weeks until your birthday?"

"I think so, yes."

That's the hope. I'll pack Grandpa's things away eventually. Maybe put them in the attic. I don't think I can stand to part with them just yet, or maybe ever.

"I'm not sure what we'll do with the spare room when his things are gone," I say, thinking aloud. "But hey, I guess we'll have space if you ever want to stay the night."

It helps to think of the positive and not of Grandpa's passing. I smile, act like I'm okay with it all. It's better than accepting my friends' looks of pity. Grant humors my attempt at lightheartedness.

"I'd give anything to stay here." He glances at Charlotte's bedroom door. "And speaking of, when are you going to hook me up with your sister?"

He attempts to smile, but I see that it's only halfhearted. Maybe he knows just how bad it hurts to lose my grandpa and just how much I need normalcy at the moment. His jokes and cheerfulness are a routine I welcome.

"Close to never," I reply.

"Come on," Grant says. "You know we'd make a good pair."

"It's better for you if I don't."

"How's that?"

We take a seat in the living room. Flip on the TV. It feels strange to not have Grandpa here anymore.

"Because she'd eat you alive."

Pax laughs, shoulders shaking. "He's right, she would."

Then he turns to me, a slight smile still on his face.

"Would you hook *me* up with your sister, though?"

I grin. "If you're so brave, ask her out yourself."

I'm not the overprotective brotherly type, as they know. They need to have the guts to ask her themselves. She wouldn't settle for anything less.

"You know I can't do that," Pax says, making sure to keep his voice low so Charlotte can't hear us in the next room. "She scares me."

I get that a lot. Not many have the guts to talk to Charlotte—girls or guys. I understand why. She can be downright intimidating most of the time.

"Not me," Grant says. "I'd walk in there and talk to her right now."

"I'd bet my life you wouldn't," Pax replies.

Grant grins and does what we knew he would, which is *not* knock on Charlotte's door or talk to her but instead wish from afar.

Through the open window, I feel a draft of damp air, the kind that signals the approach of a storm, though the sky is still patched with sunshine and clouds. For some reason, it reminds me of the first storm I ever saw in the swamp. And of course, it makes me think of my parents.

The sky grows dark, getting bigger and bigger—an avalanche of clouds.

"You don't have to be scared of it, you know," Mom says, wrapping me in an afghan blanket on the front porch.

Grandpa's cabin is different when it rains. I've only ever seen the Atlanta kind of rain. Drops that plop loudly on asphalt.

"We'll be visiting for the next five days, and if we're lucky, you'll see more," Dad says, joining Mom.

I watch their faces, serene. Dad likes the storms here, I can tell.

"Reminds me of my childhood," he says.

"I'm not scared," I say, even though I'm only seven and I might be a little scared.

It doesn't take but a couple of minutes in the downpour for the waters to rise. Mud gurgles and plops, an alive thing.

Charlotte bounds outside just then, a smirk on her face.

"Look at that lightning," she says.

It rips open the sky. Illuminates the monstrous clouds.

"Perfect weather for family," Mom says.

I learn that night what she means as we play board games by candlelight, the power having gone out with a blown transformer. Mom tells stories of how the power used to go out all the time when storms passed over her island as a child. Grandpa claims he can get the generator, but we don't mind the candles.

The rain calms me.

I don't mean to think of my family, but the rain brings them close to me.

"What happened to you, man?" Grant asks. "You zoning out?"

"Smells like rain," I reply.

"Shit, I gotta go, then." Grant looks warily at his Jeep.

It's open all around. I keep telling him to bring the cover. Swamp storms are beasts no one wants to get caught in without shelter. But as usual, Grant doesn't listen.

"I told him," Pax says, shaking his head.

Since Pax rode with Grant, he doesn't have a choice but to leave, unless I drive him home later.

"You need a ride?" I ask, secretly hoping that he'll decline so I can spend time with Willow when she gets back and her friend goes home.

My look out the window betrays me. Pax sees.

"Nah, I'm good. Go see your girl. I'll catch up with you tomorrow."

It's strange to hear my friends talk about Willow as mine when they wouldn't normally refer to any girl that way.

Grant reaches into his pocket for his keys. He doesn't even make it off the couch before there's a knock at the door.

"Looks like the perfect time for me to go," he says, eyeing the visitors, who are visible through the open window.

"I'll catch you later," I say.

They leave in a rush. Pax offers a final wave, and Grant guns it out of the swamp, trying to outrun the storm.

I face the arriving visitors.

The police are here. What do they want with me now?

Charlotte strides out of her room just in time to see Grant and Pax leave and the police step onto our welcome mat.

"Can we help you?" Her voice is sweet, but her eyes are bitter. Every instance that's brought police has also brought more suspicion on me.

One officer nods in greeting. The other stands stoically, his expression unreadable.

"Do you have a moment to chat?" the officer asks.

"Not if it involves you carting my brother off to that station of yours again. We've been several times. We've answered your questions. He didn't do it, so leave him be. And in case you haven't heard, we recently lost our grandfather. We'd like to have a little peace."

If the situation weren't serious, I'd smile at the fierceness in Charlotte's tone. Her gaze is perfectly icy. Her protectiveness freezes the warm air around us.

"You have my condolences. And I'm not here for your brother." The officer motions toward our living room. "May we sit?"

Charlotte answers immediately. "No."

"Okay, then." The officer shifts, and my eyes are drawn

to the gun at his waist. "We wanted to inform you that there's been a break in the case. The toxicology came back on the second victim. She was drugged, which explains how the culprit overpowered her without a fight." His stare swivels from Charlotte to me, while the other officer remains quiet, allowing his partner to do the talking. "I'm sorry you got mixed up in this, Beau. We finally know for certain, thanks to a DNA swab from the last crime scene, that you are not involved, though we were quite sure you weren't when we discovered your fingerprints didn't match. This is the final evidence."

I perk up at the mention of a DNA test. My feet carry me closer to the officers. I stop just inches shy of the one speaking. I wait for him to say more, my heart in my throat.

The officer places a hand on my shoulder. Pats it gently. "Thank you for cooperating. I know it didn't always look good for you."

"What did you find?" Charlotte's voice is edged with tension. "What did the DNA tell you?"

The officer doesn't show Charlotte the same warmth he shows me. I wonder why that is.

"It told us enough to absolve Beau of any wrongdoing," he replies.

The officer next to him watches Charlotte with an inquiring gaze, tracking her every move—the way she leans against the wall and flips her hair to one side.

"How is that possible? Do you know the identity of the killer? Who is it?" I ask.

They've just admitted they have solid evidence, and I want to know who's responsible.

"We don't know. At least, not yet."

"Then how do you know it's not Beau?" Charlotte asks. "I mean, obviously it *isn't* my brother's fault, and I'm glad he's been cleared, but what led you to this decision?"

For the first time, I notice another van beside the police car.

"If you don't mind, I'd like you to please come with us." The officer is no longer talking to me. His words are directed at my sister.

"What for?" I ask, stepping in her path. I know the look the officer wears. It's the very one he not so long ago reserved for me.

Suspicion.

"Nothing that concerns you," he says to me. And then to my sister, "If you'll please go over to the van there. We have someone waiting with release forms for you to sign. They need to swab your cheek."

"Why?" Charlotte glances quickly at me, worry etched into the line between her brows. "What do you want with my DNA?"

"That's the breakthrough. The sample left at the crime scene told us something we hadn't suspected before. The killer is female."

The only females around the swamp are Willow and Charlotte.

Charlotte walks to them on trembling legs, straight out the door, and all the way to the van. She says nothing, leaving silence in her wake. I am too stunned to follow her. Too shocked to completely understand the officer's words. I replay them, a skipping record in my mind.

The killer is female.

Charlotte is gone for no more than a couple of minutes while they swab her cheek. She returns visibly shaken.

"Charlotte." I watch her approach. "Are you okay?"

She nods but says nothing.

"Here's my card." The officer still waiting at the door

hands me his contact information. "Just in case. We'll be in touch."

He walks back to his cruiser. The van and police car pull away from our house, dirt kicking up behind their tires.

Charlotte shuts the door and walks straight to the kitchen. She pulls pork, onion, and tomato from the fridge and gets to work heating up beans. On the stove, she cooks the meat in oil, garlic, tomatoes, spinach, watercress, and salt. She's making another family recipe, Munggo Guisado.

"What happened back there?" I ask, taking a seat on a stool at the island.

I watch her work, knowing this is what she does when she's upset—cooks. Sometimes for hours on end.

"They swabbed my cheek," she replies.

I wait for more, knowing she'll talk when she's ready. In the meantime, I watch her methodical movements.

"Do you want coffee or tea?" she asks.

"Tea," I say.

I don't offer to help, knowing she needs a moment to herself. Charlotte boils water and before I know it, there's a steaming cup of tea in front of me, sweet enough to leave a syrupy taste in my mouth.

She scoops out the meat and ingredients and piles them on top of the beans. I pat the stool next to me, and Charlotte drops into it with an exhausted sigh. I eat a forkful and almost groan at the deliciousness. Charlotte eats, too, taking bites until about halfway through her portion, when she finally lets her fork clatter to the plate. She places her head in her hands and massages her temples.

"They made me promise not to leave town." She finally speaks, but her voice is void of all emotion. "They think

I did it. I saw the way they looked at me. I have to stay close until the results from the swab are in." She rubs her forehead gently. "God, I'm a suspect. Go figure. Wonder if they've questioned Willow, too. Where is she, anyhow?"

Just then, realization hits me.

"Charlotte. What evidence was left behind? Did the police mention it to you?"

I stand up quickly, abandoning my meal.

"I don't know, something with DNA. They didn't say exactly what."

I reach into my pocket and pull out my phone, glancing at the card the officer left behind. I quickly dial. Outside, the sky fills with clouds.

"Officer Brown here."

"It's Beau." I speak quickly, cell to my ear, suspicion surging through me like an avalanche. "I meant to ask what type of evidence you found at the scene of the crime."

I hold my breath as my suspicions are confirmed.

"A wad of gum."

"I think I know who did it." I race out the door and to the boat, the phone to my ear, my heart pounding wildly. I accidentally drop the card on the dirt ground. Charlotte is on my heels, pulling at the ties and pushing us into the water. "It's Jorie, Willow's friend. She's always around. She was always staying the night at Willow's when the killings took place. And she's always chewing gum."

"Shit." The officer's curses begin to break apart, static turning the line fuzzy. "Hang on a minute. I'm placing a call to dispatch."

"I don't have a minute," I say. "I'm in the boat, in the swamp, going after Willow. She's with Jorie now. Follow the water to the bend and take a left. Willow and Jorie are at the hill there. Hurry."

39

WILLOW

"CAN YOU BELIEVE I finished this damn book?"

Jorie is holding up the romance as though she's holding a dead snake. Above us, the sun begins to dim, a wide band of clouds taking over.

"How you got me to read a whole book without my brains falling out from boredom is beyond me," she says.

"You liked it and you know it," I tease. "I have another one if you didn't get your fill."

"Nah. We need to get in soon anyway. You're looking like a roasted tomato. Ever heard of sunscreen?"

I take out my phone and check the time. Has it really been three hours?

"You think your grandma will still give us lunch?"

"Probably, but we're late," I reply. "Though knowing Gran and her hurt feelings when people don't eat her meals on time, she may make us eat it cold as punishment, since we didn't get there when she made it good and hot."

Jorie rolls up her tan towel, dirt and twigs pinned to it like notes on a corkboard.

"Fine by me. I'll eat it cold, as long as she cooked it.

Bound to still be good."

There's truth to her words. Many nights I've opened the fridge, found Gran's leftovers, and eaten them cold so as to not wake the house by cooking with clanging pots and pans.

I roll my towel up, too, and place all our belongings in the bag, aside from our clothes, which we throw back on over our suits. Jorie carries it to the boat and loads everything up. Just then, I remember my phone.

"I'll be right back," I say. "Forgot my cell."

"Oh, I got it," Jorie says. "Saw it lying on the ground. Don't want to leave that behind. Never know what could happen with the murderer still at large."

Her voice drops a few notches, and she looks around as though he might just pop out at us from the trees. But there is nothing. Only leaves and swamp and the memory of a day well spent. Even still, Jorie's look says that she doesn't trust the bog as much as she once did, and that's a shame.

"I think we're safe," I say as we head toward the boat. "We can't let him take the swamp from us, Jorie. We can't."

Her look changes. "You're right. So what if he's dangerous? We have a gun."

She steels herself, standing taller, though I can see traces of fear still in her eyes.

"So what if he tried to terrorize our town? We can't let him win."

"That's the spirit," I reply.

She nods. "He left bits of his evil here, right? But we can choose to not see them. We don't have to think about the girls or the fear or the amber earring or the bruises."

It's like she's giving herself a pep talk.

"Right, we really don't have to…"

I trail off.

"What's wrong?" Jorie asks.

My eyes settle on a spot over her shoulder. Fear leaks into my veins.

"What is it?" Jorie looks over her shoulder, but there's nothing there. "Talk to me."

The clouds thicken, and shadows crowd the trees.

I never told her that the earring was amber.

I don't know which direction to move. I need to get to the boat, to wherever Jorie put my phone, to my shotgun, but Jorie's blocking me.

I rack my brain, trying to remember what I'd said. I mentioned the earring to her, but I never told her what *type* of earring.

Jorie steps closer to the boat. My mind spins around little details. Jorie lives in the swamp. Jorie is always around. Jorie spoke with the police officers—eating breakfast just fine while the rest of us could hardly stomach it—claiming to know nothing. She spent the night with me several times. I found her at the window one evening. A bad dream, she'd claimed, but she looked wide awake. The next morning, a dead girl was found. Dead girls kept being found, and Jorie was always there in the aftermath.

"It was you," I say.

I take a backward step, unsure where to go.

"What?" she says. "Me? I— No. It can't have been me."

Her laugh is shaky and unconvincing.

"Don't you lie to me," I say.

"I'm not lying."

She is, too. And this time I see it—a flash of coldness in her eyes. How could she have hidden it from me for so long?

She hates Beau. She knows the swamp. She knew all the victims, too. Suddenly, the answer is frighteningly clear.

"You killed the girls." I have never been surer of anything in my life.

Jorie's face transforms. Gone is the shy fear, replaced by a look I've never seen her wear. One of menace and cunning threat.

"You really should not have said that," she replies. "Damn you, Willow. Now look what you've done."

I don't give myself time to falter, I simply run toward the boat. I don't have much of a chance. I'm too far—several yards—and Jorie's between it and me. But I try anyway. I need my phone. I need the shotgun.

Jorie slams into me like a brick wall. We both go down, a tangle of limbs. Something sharp bites its razor teeth into my side, and I wince. Jorie is strong. I push and pull and kick to no avail. I claw at the dirt, searching for anything I can use. And then I feel a rock the size of my palm. I grab it and bring it down on her head.

She grunts and loses momentum, allowing just enough slack for me to break free and run. It's too late for the boat, I realize. Somewhere between me recognizing Jorie as the killer and my abundance of shock, she untied it. The boat now floats down the swamp unattended.

"Damn it," I say.

Jorie is standing now. But I am fueled by adrenaline and instinct. I run toward the swampy waters. Gators or not, I throw myself in. But Jorie is impossibly fast, and she pulls me from the water by my hair.

"Let me go!" I yell. "Help! Somebody help!"

I scratch her arms. It's a futile attempt. There is no one else here.

"How could you?" I say.

Jorie laughs, something dark and deadly, knocking me to the ground, faceup. She binds my hands to the tree with ties that she pulls from a pocket of her shorts. I never would have suspected her of being prepared for a thing like this.

"Funny thing." She tightens the zip ties to the point of pain. "I never leave the house without these. Or this." She pulls out a pocketknife. "I haven't had to use the knife until now, but maybe that's because none of the other girls saw my attack coming. I didn't want to have to use any of this on you, of course."

She laughs darkly, raising the hairs on my arms. There is something inherently evil about the way her eyes focus on me but seem to be looking at nothing at all. Her features shift, as though she's just now letting her hair down after months of wearing it up. She's relaxed.

And it's terrifying.

"I tried to be your friend, Willow," she says. "I really did. Well, not at first, of course. At first, I was using you. You see, I needed more details about Beau. Things I might be able to use against him."

She bends closer to me, her breath smelling of the bubble gum she constantly chews. I back up against the tree, which is difficult to do with my hands bound, but I need to get away from the small blade in her hand. My only chance is to talk her down.

"You never caught on, Willow. You never suspected me. And what's more is that Beau's sister didn't, either. She almost caught me. I snuck in their house, trying to frame Beau, to plant some of the drugs, solid evidence, in Beau's bedroom. I was in the bathroom, where I planned to take hairs from his brush to leave at the next crime scene, when I got distracted by Charlotte's jewelry. I was holding one of her earrings when she and Beau suddenly came home. Heard her outside telling him she had a funny feeling. She's got a sixth sense, that one. I barely got out and didn't realize until later that I was still clutching the earring. Stupid mistake. It's cost me now."

"It was you in the forest that night, then!" I say. "You dropped the earring."

Jorie grips the knife firmly as I look around for anything I can use to protect myself.

"I meant to get rid of it. I'd slid it into my pocket and forgot it was there. I was too busy trying to get close to you. Staying the night at your house let me see when Beau would be home, the right hours to kill so that it looked as though he had done it. Too bad I hadn't anticipated the group of people he had over from the pool staying as late as they did that night, otherwise that murder would have been all the more convincing, all the blame would have been on Beau. Framing someone is a tricky thing."

Tree bark bites into my arms, and I can't help but wonder aloud, "Why?"

"If you'd paid better attention, you'd know exactly why."

But I don't. For all the effort I put into thinking about why Jorie would do such a thing, I still don't understand.

"Do you love him? Is that it?"

She laughs. "Don't be stupid. Of course I don't."

"Then why? What could you possibly get by framing Beau for the murders of innocent girls?"

"Do you remember asking me about the girl who disappeared?"

"Ericka?"

There's a flash of pain in Jorie's eyes. "Yes, Ericka. My best friend."

Understanding dawns and churns my stomach with fear.

Jorie has a vendetta.

"We did everything together outside of school. She left because of him."

At this, Jorie's voice drops dangerously low.

"He broke her heart, her spirit, her life. She left town, and then she left this world. Swallowed enough pills to go to sleep and never wake up. The pain he caused her eclipsed all the years and memories we made together. She used to have fun, laugh at life, spin circles in the rain. She almost always wore a smile until Beau. He broke her spirit. Do you know what it's like to lose your best friend?"

"I have an idea," I bite out.

"No, you don't. I told you the things you wanted to hear, and you played right into my hand. What I had with Ericka was something different. I couldn't stand the thought of her leaving town. Then the call came that she had died. I thought about killing Beau myself, a swift and sweet revenge. But then he'd just get off easy. I couldn't let that happen. He needed to suffer."

"So you tried to frame him," I say. "Well, you did a lousy job."

She reaches out whiplike and hits me in the face.

I wince but hold her stare.

"You're a coward, that's what you are. You're deranged. You didn't have to hurt those girls. They never did anything to you!"

"I cannot let Ericka's death be in vain."

"You could have honored her death. You could

have kept her memory alive in a positive light. Why kill innocent girls?"

"Why not? Why should they be allowed to live when Ericka died? Why should you?"

Her eyes are wide to the point of exaggeration, and an off-kilter gleam shines through them.

"You know, Willow, I think for once in his life, Beau might actually care about someone. Now, he'll have to swallow the understanding of what his world will be without you. He'll have to lose what he loves best. Maybe *that* is the ultimate revenge."

She smiles wickedly and takes two steps forward, dead leaves crunching. She drops the knife just out of reach.

"Better make this look just like the others," she says. "This time Beau will take the blame. I'll make sure of it."

She laughs darkly. I try hard to ignore the stab of hurt in my chest from Jorie's betrayal. I search for any glimpse of the girl I called my friend.

But she's gone. Replaced by a killer.

I breathe as deeply as I can and scream, and scream, and scream, hoping anyone remotely close can hear me. A boater, a fisherman, someone to help.

Icy terror floods my veins as Jorie's cold hands close around my throat, cutting short my cry for help. I try to breathe, try to fight.

"Goodbye, Willow," she whispers.

40

BEAU

"**W**ILLOW!"

I find her laid out on the swampy soil. Body fixed to the earth. Jorie crouched above her, hands around her throat.

"Don't come any closer," Jorie warns.

She lets go of Willow and grabs a knife from the ground. There's something decidedly ominous about her tone. A wind whips around us.

I ignore Jorie's warning and move toward them.

"Don't!" she yells.

My eyes dart to Willow, willing her to stand. I don't know if she's conscious or if she's even breathing at all.

"Let her go," I say.

"I can't do that."

I eye the knife in Jorie's hand. I didn't bring a weapon. There was no time. A decision I now regret, considering that the station and its officers are a half hour out. Willow needs help now.

"Why?" I ask.

I don't actually care why she did it. What I need is

for her to keep talking. What I need is for her to be distracted. I hope she can't see the way I shake with nerves. If only I could touch Willow, feel the warmth of her skin and her soft breaths, to know if she's okay.

A pinecone hits the side of a tree to Jorie's left with a *thwack*.

She turns, and I waste no time. I run at her head-on. But she's quick, slashing out at my stomach. I crumple to the ground, nearly retching from the pain. I don't have time to look at the wound. I need only to get back up.

"Don't fight me, Beau," she says. "Don't make me kill you, too."

A bitter laugh escapes me. It's too late for that. She'll kill me anyway now that I know too much. I stand, clutching my middle, feeling warm, wet blood on my skin.

There's movement behind Jorie, and I try not to alert her. Blending into the tree beside Willow is Charlotte. She grabs Willow's hands and pulls, but the binding doesn't budge. Willow's eyes are closed, and I fear she's unconscious. Or worse. Charlotte searches the ground, finds a rock, and begins sawing at the ties.

Jorie spins around. It's too late for Charlotte to hide.

Jorie cackles. "Did you honestly think you could bring your sister and hope for an ambush?"

I try again to get to Willow, but Jorie rises on the balls of her feet, her movements swift and calculated, swiping the knife at me once more, sending me sprawling backward. This time, she just barely misses.

"Quit fighting me, Beau." A simple command, full of menace.

"The police are on their way," I say. "They know you killed the girls. I told them so when the pieces clicked. You made a mistake, Jorie. There was a wad of gum left at the last murder scene and analysis came back that the saliva belonged to a female."

"You're lying," she says, but I see the fear in her eyes.

"I'm not. How else do you think we figured it out?"

For all the times I've lied, I'm actually telling the truth.

"Is Willow alive?" I call to Charlotte.

I can't tell from where I'm standing, and not knowing is slowly killing me.

Charlotte nods once, and I breathe a sigh of relief. I inhale another shaky breath and contemplate my next move. Jorie is alone. Willow is unconscious. It's two against one, but I'm injured. I won't be as fast or calculating.

With each drop of blood that leaves my body, I feel more of my strength escape. I shudder and struggle to hold myself upright. The pain to my stomach is quick, sharp, and unrelenting, but I attempt to block it out. I have to get to Willow. The thought of losing her is more agonizing than any wound. I don't want my arms to be empty of her. I don't want to never feel her warmth.

I focus on Charlotte's assurance. Willow is alive. We still have a chance. I will never let Jorie win.

"You're done. Give it up."

"No." She sneers. "If you're telling the truth and the cops are coming, then I'm going to make damn sure you suffer the way I have." For the very briefest second, her lip wobbles, and I swear I see a flash of hurt dart across her features. "The way Ericka did."

Finally, I understand. Ericka, the girl who disappeared. Jorie must have known her. Cared for her.

"So you've come to return the favor?" I say as Charlotte creeps steadily closer to Jorie's back. "You want to break my heart the way I broke hers, is that it?"

It hurts to admit some of the blame.

"I want you to know the pain of losing the person you care about most in this world! It's time to kill Willow the way you killed my best friend!"

"I didn't kill her. She left."

"Right, but after she left, she killed herself, so you might as well have forced the pills down her throat. You are the reason she's dead. You, Beau! And you'll be the reason Willow dies, too."

She's crazy, but she's right. I am partially to blame. My actions led Ericka to feel desperate. Maybe if I had been kinder or cared more about how much the breakup affected her, she could have felt differently. I'll never know now, and the guilt of that weighs heavily.

Charlotte moves from behind a tree. I focus on Jorie and not on my sister.

Just another second…

Charlotte tackles Jorie from behind, a tangle of limbs. I try to run to them, but black eats away at my vision, darkness swallowing the trees. I glance down to find the front of my clothes coated in blood.

I fall to my knees. I've lost too much blood. I'll crawl if I have to.

I look up just in time to see Jorie's face contorting with rage. She slashes the knife at Charlotte, and it meets its mark. The skin at Charlotte's forehead separates into a gash inches long. She wobbles and catches herself on a tree before slowly sliding down its bark to the ground.

Get up. Get up!

I silently will my twin to hear me, to summon all her strength and fight.

I can't leave Willow lying there.

I can't abandon my sister, either.

I don't have energy left to save them both.

"Enough of this," Jorie says.

She averts her attention to Willow. "Your turn."

She approaches Willow, and dread makes the hollow in my stomach heavy. She slaps Willow's face.

"Wake up! I want you to look at him as I kill you."

Willow stirs, moaning. I'm not prepared to watch what will happen if I don't get up.

Jorie smiles and turns to me. "I would have made this quick, you know. But now? I don't think so."

Willow is suffering because of me.

Slowly, I rise. Agony shoots through my stomach in waves of torment, but still I get to my feet. I surge forward, walls of blackness eating more of my vision, unconsciousness threatening me with each breath I take. I hear a noise in the distance, a rushing river or maybe a sea of pounding footsteps, but I don't stop to confirm what it could be. Jorie hears the noise, too. She looks wildly around.

I promised to help Willow, to not let her become the next victim, and I meant it.

I use Jorie's distraction to close the dozen yards between us. She doesn't see the discarded, fallen branch in my hand until I bring it down hard on her back, tearing a scream of agony from my lips and causing the cut to pump more of my blood onto the swamp floor.

Jorie screams, too, a wail so high I wonder if the entire bog can hear it. Her legs are lightning fast, kicking out at me. And then she's on me, tackling me to the ground. I wrestle her for the blade clutched in her hand. My movements are slow, wary, and unstable. Before she can drive the knife down on me, I grab for a small, sharp stick within reach of my other hand and stab upward.

Jorie gasps. Her eyes bulge and follow the line of pain down to the point where the stick is embedded just above her left hip. It's not high or disabling enough. My aim is as wobbly as the rest of me.

She reaches for the stick, giving me time to catch my breath, to blink away unconsciousness. I clutch my stomach. If I could just get to Willow and Charlotte, if I could just pull them both away from danger. I spare them a look. Willow groans on the ground. Charlotte blinks in a daze.

With a grunt and a quick pull, Jorie frees the stick from her side. I don't understand how she's still so fast. She favors her good side. Her blade nicks my shoulder. It would have met its mark had I not rolled out of the way just in time. I attempt to rise on shaky limbs, first to my knees, my palms flat against the dirt, and then to my feet. I sway like a leaf caught in the wind.

With every ounce left, I charge her. It's my final effort. It is the very deepest store of energy I own. I have nothing left but this. I meet her with an elbow to the face and a crunch of bone. Jorie screams as telltale silver flashes to my left so close to my ear that I hear the *woosh* the blade leaves behind, so close it nearly slashes my face in two. Jorie catches another elbow to her sternum. She groans, struggling to pull air into her lungs. I lunge forward and grab for the knife in her hand, and she uses my momentum against me, spinning out of the way and shoving me right where my flesh is already severed.

I fall with the weight of realization. I can't get back up. Bile rises to my throat, leaving a sick taste in my mouth. I have nothing, not even a drop of energy left to fight her. Jorie has won, and her cruel smile says she knows it. She stands over me, her eyes trailing my crumpled form. I only hope I've bought Charlotte and Willow enough time to get away.

My eyes find Charlotte, who has come out of her daze. She's near Willow, attempting to help her to her feet. Blood pours into her eyes, and she desperately wipes at it. Willow wobbles and allows Charlotte to lead her to the water's edge, where a boat waits.

If only they get away, it is worth it. I try to convey my love for my sister through the last look I give her. A sob shakes her shoulders.

"You're done, Beau Cadwell." Jorie mocks my weakness with words dipped in victory.

That's when I see it—something weaving in and out of the trees. If I concentrate hard enough, I can keep my eyes open. Until I can't. Until the blood loss weighs too heavily and my lids begin to close.

"Beau."

I hear my name on Willow's lips. I force my eyes to open long enough to see a thundering sea of officers and to hear their command to *drop your weapon*. I don't have a weapon, but Jorie does, and she has no intention of letting it go. Another warning from the police. Jorie raises the knife above me, ready to bring it down on me once more, just moments before an explosion rips the air in two. It's quick, much faster than Jorie. The blade pauses midair. The *pop* of a bullet rings in my ears.

And down, down, down Jorie falls.

Blood drips from her back, blossoming on the dirt. Her mouth opens in a grotesque silent scream. She wildly grabs at the dirt, only feet beside me.

But there's nothing to save her.

Police officers close in from all sides. One relieves Charlotte of Willow's weight and guides her to the base of a tree, directing her to sit while he temporarily bandages her head. Another frees Willow's arms from the restraints and checks the bruises forming around her throat. Two officers move toward me, as well.

Jorie blinks one, two, three more times before her eyes stare, glazed and fixed, open wide, at nothing.

For a moment, I gaze at a dead murderer and fight the urge to vomit. I begin to shake.

"Stay with us," an emergency worker says.

A storm of blackness eats more of my vision until all I see is a tiny light.

Then nothing at all.

41
WILLOW

I KNOCK SOFTLY on Beau's front door to see if he's
up for company. I've come every day for the last week—
since he was released from the hospital—to check on him.

Charlotte answers. "He's in his room."

She opens the door farther for me. In the background,
the television plays softly.

"Thanks." I step inside.

Charlotte wears the look of a girl who isn't quite
as sure as she used to be. It's in the worry creasing her
forehead, the pinch of her brows. I wonder how she's
dealing with the loss of her grandpa and nearly losing
Beau, too. My eyes go to the staples at her hairline, a
wound put there by Jorie.

I flinch at the memory of her—the deceiving best
friend I thought I knew.

"I just finished cooking," Charlotte says. "Beau hasn't
had lunch yet."

She walks to the kitchen, retrieves a bowl, and scoops
something from a pot on the stove into it. She pushes it
toward me. It looks like shrimp and mixed vegetables

and smells like heaven.

"It's *pinakbet*." She sticks a fork in it. "One of his favorites. Why don't you bring it to him?"

I'm tempted to take a bite myself, but I nod and carry it to his room.

Just as I'm about to knock on the door, Charlotte says, "I'll save a bowl for you, too."

It might be one of the nicest things she's ever said to me.

"Thank you," I reply.

"Willow?" Beau's voice comes from within the room.

I push the door open to find him pulling a shirt over his bandaged wound.

"I brought you food."

Beau grins, forgets the bowl, and kisses me full on the lips.

"Hello to you, too," I say through a smile.

"You brought me Filipino food?"

"Well, Charlotte made it," I amend.

He takes a bite. Then another. His face relaxes. Transforms into something purely happy.

"God, I love her cooking. Just like my mom used to make."

"Can I have a bite?" I ask.

He offers me a forkful. I know instantly that I've been missing out. Gran's Southern cooking is good beyond measure, of course, but Beau's family food is exciting where Gran's food is comfort. I take a second bite, relishing the different textures and tastes. Shrimp paste. Seasoned vegetables.

"Why have I never tried this?" I ask around a mouthful.

"We should make a meal together," Beau says. "I haven't cooked with anyone but Charlotte since my mom passed."

I realize that what he's offering me is something special. I nod, accepting. I would love to know that side of Beau better.

"I came to check on you," I say.

By the way he limps over to the side of his bed, it's clear that he's still in pain. I can't see his stomach under the bandage and shirt he wears, but I know from what Charlotte has said that he's on antibiotics to ward off infection and that his wound is still fresh.

"I'm fine." He grimaces when taking a seat on the mattress.

"You know, you used to be such a good liar," I tease.

He laughs. Pats the spot next to him.

"Okay, fine. Truth? It hurts like hell, and I don't regret it for a second."

He props a pillow against the headboard and leans into it. Then eats the rest of his food until there's only a tiny bit of paste at the bottom.

"Thanks for coming," he says, setting the bowl on the nightstand.

"It was this or spend my Sunday in the swamp drawing birds with my parents. Which, as it turns out, isn't as boring as I had originally thought."

I pause, knowing it can't be easy for Beau to hear about family when he's lost so much of his. I take his hand gently. He tucks a strand of hair behind my ear and grins wickedly. Though he looks every bit the boy my gran warned me about, I now know better. He has a softer side. He can be honest and sweet.

"Speaking of family. How are you doing?"

"Not great." He doesn't sugarcoat a thing. "Charlotte and I are taking Grandpa's ashes into the swamp tomorrow. She's not sure if I'm ready for a boat ride yet with my injury, but I'd like to see her keep me away."

I love his determination to honor his grandpa's last wishes. There's something beautiful about his grandpa staying in the place he never meant to leave.

"Do you want company?" I ask.

He shifts closer to me, a rustle of sheets and bedding.

"I think it's something Charlotte and I need to do alone, if you don't mind."

It seems only right that they take him to his final resting place.

"I completely understand. I'll come check on you later tomorrow if you want. I can bring a movie. Text me if you want company. If you need time, I'll understand that, too."

He kisses me again. "Have I ever told you that you're perfect?"

"With your riddles, a person might not know if you mean it or not."

He laughs loudly. Then winces and gingerly touches his stomach.

"So, what movie do you want me to bring tomorrow?" I ask.

"Maybe I don't want a movie. Maybe I want you to bring only yourself. Your company is enough."

I bite back a smile.

"Or I could make food for the two of us," I offer.

"Or you could kiss me and never stop."

His words are playful, but his eyes drop to my lips.

"I could bring Gran's famous sweet tea."

"Well, I can't say no to that," he replies. "Matter of fact, you should get a glass now. Or maybe I can come by with you? Do you ever think your gran will invite me inside?"

This time, it's my turn to laugh loudly. "Let's not get crazy now."

Beau looks as though he honestly believes in the possibility.

"One day, mark my words, I'll walk in that house of my own free will and your gran will welcome me."

"You seem mighty sure of yourself."

He dips his forehead to mine. Speaks so close that our lips nearly touch.

"I'm not going anywhere, Willow. Eventually your gran will see that I mean what I say, and she'll have no choice but to accept that I'm planning to stay. I'll keep coming around until she gives in."

I'm glad he's changed his mind about keeping his distance.

"That might be never," I warn. "She's pretty strong-willed, you know."

He grins. "I like a good challenge."

42

BEAU

THE BOAT GLIDES THROUGH a mess of tangled marsh grass, floating atop a swamp as clear as watered-down tea. The smell of algae and vegetation fills the air, heavier than normal thanks to last night's rain. Charlotte rows gently, taking her time. I am in no rush to leave the final pieces of my grandpa behind.

Charlotte stares into the trees, eyeing a nest of blue jays. If I didn't know better, I'd say she looked close to crying, but it's hard to tell based on how many times she blinks.

I push just a little farther, to an opening where the sun breaks through and shines abundantly, bleaching the sky. It's the perfect spot, fish swimming below, a gator warming itself on the bank, and the two of us in the middle of it all.

We couldn't have asked for better weather, as much as I hate what the day means for Charlotte and me. I stop rowing, letting the gentle current take us the rest of the way.

"It's what he wanted," I say to my sister, breaking the

silence that has stretched since we left.

"Doesn't make it any easier," she replies.

"Never said it did." I take the wooden urn decorated with simple swirls carved into it out from under the seat. I hold it for a moment, needing these last few seconds with Grandpa before he's free to swim with the gators forever.

"We should say something about him." Charlotte eyes the urn.

She clears her throat, stretches out her hand, and waits for the ashes. I'm surprised by her display, but I don't hesitate to hand them over.

"Grandpa." She traces the swirls with shaky fingers. "I love that you took us in when Dad and Mom passed. You gave me a great life. I owe you everything. You made the most delicious mac 'n' cheese."

She pauses, swipes under her eyes, and continues.

"You were crazy in the best way. Remember the time when we were little and you convinced us that Bigfoot was real? We looked for his footprints everywhere."

She laughs. It sounds to me the way dark chocolate tastes: bittersweet.

"You always won when we played cards. I'll never look at another crossword puzzle the same way again. Who's going to read the paper on Sundays now? I don't know my life without you in it. But I guess…maybe you don't have to be gone completely?"

A tear falls. It's the first time I've seen Charlotte cry in years. I have the urge to reach out to her, but I sense that she's not done with her respects.

"I loved cooking breakfast for you. I'll miss that." She sniffles. "But I'll miss you even more. I'm sorry you had to go. But I'm so thankful you'll still, in a way, stay.

I promise to look for you in everything here. The trees. The creatures. The swamp water itself."

She pours ashes into her hand and lets loose a sob.

"Bye for now, Grandpa."

She gives the urn to me — half of the ashes left — and opens her hand. His remains catch a ride on the wind and then sink into the water. I pour the remaining bit into my hand, thinking it feels a lot like the dirt we used to bring into the house on our clothes as kids. Grandpa would sweep it up, grumbling about messes while smiling all the same.

"Grandpa," I say. "I hate that you're leaving us, but before you go, you should know a few things. For instance, I left the whiskey cap open last night, just so I could wake up and smell it first thing. I could almost pretend you were still there, drinking at an ungodly hour, as you sometimes did. And I ate the plate of breakfast food Charlotte made for you, because it only seemed right."

Grandpa will somehow always be in the things I do, in the person I am.

"I loved how we'd collapse on the couch most nights. We'd start out watching television but somehow end up in a conversation about anything and everything. Your voice is the one I hear in my head when I make decisions. You raised me with a strong spirit."

It takes a few breaths before I can continue past the grief that weighs me down.

"I hope you know how much you meant, and still mean to me. I wish we had time for one more boat ride, another laugh, a seat by the fire in winter, our noses in steaming mugs of tea. But mostly I'll miss your presence. It's like Charlotte said, though. You're still close."

He'll always be there in the choices I make. Only this

time, I'll be better than I was before. I'll be considerate of others and fight the fear of opening myself up. His death—and the girls passing, too— is a new life for me.

I take a deep breath. Let it out slowly. "You made me promise. So here it goes."

I hesitate, but only the slightest bit.

"You're free."

I don't open my hand. Instead, I stick it underwater and let the current drag every last ash particle from my skin until there are no more and Grandpa *is* the swamp.

"And by the way," I say. "I'll be telling Old Lady Bell what you asked me to, one way or another. Can't guarantee she'll be okay with me crossing the line, but I'll do it. For you."

I pull my hand from the water and swallow the emotion that clogs my throat.

"I'll miss you."

It's the last thing I say to Grandpa, but it feels right. This. Him. The swamp.

He's gone. And yet, he's home.

43

WILLOW

The sun rises, splashing the sky with pinks and yellows and dusky grays. Charlotte hums a tune next to me, her stare fixed on the swamp. The property dividing line zigzags drunkenly to the left of us, the cabin on our other side.

"Beau will be out in a minute," she says. "He's showering."

I imagine bathing is especially hard to do with a wound that's still healing. At least his stitches have finally been removed.

"I want to say thank you before he comes out," Charlotte says.

"For what?" I ask. "You're the one who tried to save me."

It's been two days since they spread their grandpa's ashes. Jorie is gone, too. The scar from Charlotte's staples lingers. This perfectly beautiful girl now has a mark, and she doesn't seem to give one damn about it. She's alive. That's what matters.

"Yes. But Willow, you're the one who actually *did*

save Beau. You taught him that it's okay to believe in another person. I guess I'm saying that I'm glad he didn't listen to me."

I watch Charlotte's face, but it's impassive, as though she's talking about the damn blue sky.

"And what about you?" I ask. "Are you better for it?"

"I don't know about that. But what I do know is that my brother is happy, and that makes me think it might, just might be worth it to believe in people again."

Slowly and steadily she's making a change. Though I see the wall erected around her, it's becoming more transparent. Her talking openly and honestly with me here and now is proof.

"You gave Beau a reason again," she says.

"A reason for what?"

She smiles, and this time it's not cunning or wicked or harsh. It's open and beautiful and real.

"Everything."

She stands and begins walking back to the house. No explanation. No goodbye.

I want her to say more. I want her to open up. I wish she'd look at me again the way she just did. I wish she knew that she doesn't have to be alone in this world.

"I keep picturing Jorie's wild hair!" I blurt.

Charlotte pauses, back still to me, but I know she's listening.

"I've been thinking of her laugh, her companionship. It's not so much *her* I miss, though there is a little of that, but more the idea of friendship. She was rotten, that one, but that doesn't mean all friends are."

Charlotte still doesn't move.

"Know what, though?" I say. "Your hair is wild, too, and so is your grin. Maybe all this time I was looking for a best friend in the wrong place."

This time Charlotte does turn around. She has an open look, as though someone has scraped away years and layers and buckets full of masked expressions.

She says only one word, but its meaning is worth a million sentences.

"Maybe."

She walks away, through the cabin door. I wonder if she knows that she'll end up coming out the other side and into my life.

The door doesn't even have time to close before Beau emerges. His feet carry him straight to me, though admittedly quite slowly, cautious of his healing stomach.

I weave around fallen pinecones and discarded swaths of moss to meet him halfway.

He says hello by kissing me and kissing me until I can hardly breathe, and I think I like this type of silence more than words.

"Come with me," he says against my lips.

We take a pebbled dirt path, not too far, until it meets the forest. The trees above us sway melodically. Acorns *tap, tap, tap* on the ground as they fall. Wings flutter and soar. And all the while, the swamp babbles as though telling us a story or welcoming us home.

We settle into a good spot.

"Will you stay here now?" I ask.

It's a question that's been bothering me. Technically he and Charlotte still have ten days until their eighteenth birthdays. Could they possibly be put in foster homes? I wonder if Georgia law would allow an almost-eighteen-year-old to be considered a legal adult.

"Yes. No one is interested in messing with us. With Jorie gone, we're cleared of any wrongdoing, and the swamp is safe. We'll turn eighteen and then nineteen and forty and sixty and no matter what age, I'll never want to leave," Beau says, leaning into me and smelling deliciously like soap and marsh.

I never want him to leave, either.

"How about this," I say "we'll both stay here as long as possible."

Beau laughs. "I might be able to agree to that."

A pinecone falls from the tree above, and I watch it roll off into the water.

"How are you doing with losing Jorie?" he asks.

It's hard to bridge the gap between the friend I had and the murderer she became.

"I wonder if I could have done more, somehow saved all those girls," I say. "I miss the Jorie I thought she was, but maybe with time, it'll get easier. I'm convinced something good has to come from this."

Beau watches me, understanding clearly visible in his stare.

"I think you're right that change will come," he says.

Neither one of us wants any of the deaths—the girls, his grandpa, Jorie—to be in vain.

"I feel it, too, you know…the guilt." He sighs and it takes him a moment to find his voice. "It all started with me hurting one girl's heart, but I've decided to be better. More open. Considerate. Thoughtful."

I take his warm hand in mine. I lost a friend. He lost a family member. I gained perspective. I think he did, too.

"What happened with Pax and Grant?"

Both of us suspected them, a little in part because of Grant's jealousy and Pax's quietness. I owe them an apology, even if they don't realize that I'd questioned their innocence. And next time I see them, I plan to straighten it out, clear the slate. Maybe even help Grant learn how to talk to girls so that he can get one to stay longer than ten seconds. I smile at the thought.

"We talked," Beau says. "I apologized for not putting more trust in my friendships with them. Now Grant can see that my life isn't something to be jealous of. I told them that I lost my parents, but I'm not ready to tell them how just yet. It's something, right? I suppose I should tell you that I'm sorry, too."

"For what?"

"For not opening up easily. I'm trying, though."

"I know that."

Maybe he doesn't have an open door to his heart, and maybe that's okay.

"What about the cabin?" I ask.

"Though my grandpa is gone, the house is willed to us—Charlotte and me. You know what this means?" he asks.

I do. It means that he gets to stay my neighbor. It means that he doesn't have to lose everything.

"That you can be in the place you love without worry," I say.

I lean against his chest, gently placing one of his arms around my waist. Beau's lips are featherlight on my temple. Above us, cotton-ball clouds blot an expanse of steely blue sky.

I think about how his cabin will feel with the absence of his grandpa. It's a drastic change for him, one that can't come easily, one that's bound to have a few hiccups. I take a deep breath and gauge my next words.

"Are you doing okay with missing your grandpa?"

He hasn't had a lot of time to grieve his passing.

"It's hard," he whispers.

His fists clench, and he stares off at the trees and leaves and nothingness. And then he does a funny thing. He exhales and grins.

"Before I forget, I'm supposed to deliver a message," he says.

"Oh yeah? What's that?"

"Think you could tell Old Lady Bell that my grandpa never stopped loving her?"

I smile. "I could do that. Believe it or not, she might not mind hearing those words." Then, on a more serious note. "You know you still have me, right? No matter what."

A crow perched above us caws.

"I know."

"You're free, Beau. You suffered another loss, and you survived it. You don't have to live in fear of caring—that's the best part. Without caring, you never truly live."

I'm far from a place of understanding his pain, but his bravery is right here, in plain sight.

He stares off into the distance, only his profile visible. I admire his features, my gaze tracing the strength in his jaw, his shoulders, his body.

"Look at me."

Slowly, he does.

"I'm not going anywhere. You can trust in me, in us. I choose you, Beau. Though you're a little bit wicked, you are also thoughtful and kind and, damn it, I love you."

He stills. And then he smiles the biggest smile I've ever seen in all my life.

"You love me?" he asks.

"So what?" I say. "You love me, too."

He pulls me tighter against him.

"You love me," I continue, "even though you don't

have to and even though you haven't said it, and especially even though you never actually wanted to. You still love me."

I don't care that I'm transparent. I don't care that I've left my heart out on the swampy soil.

"You are completely in love with me, Beau Cadwell, and the feeling is mutual."

He doesn't deny it. Instead, he kisses me.

He kisses me like the sun kisses the sky every morning. Like the forest kisses the shadows. Like murky waters kiss the dirt.

"Willow," he whispers, "I do love you."

I relish the taste of his lips. I press against them again and again until the sun breaks right through the leaves.

"Is that the first time you've told a girl that you love her?"

"It might be the first time," he says.

"By 'might be,' do you mean 'is'?"

"Perhaps. But probably not."

"Or you could be lying right now."

"Or maybe not."

"You are."

"No way to know for sure."

I grin. "Are you feeding me your damn riddles again?"

"Did you honestly think I'd ever stop?"

"I sure hope not."

The sun drips rays over us, and I lean my head toward the sky, letting it warm my face.

"Look at us, Beau," I say as his fingers curl around mine. "The swamp fits us. *We* fit us."

Strange thing about love: it shatters all walls and encompasses all senses and steals the very breath from your lungs. It kisses you good night and greets you in the morning and spins your thoughts with one face. It cries when you cry and laughs when you do and stitches two souls together.

I love him. This boy. I forget what it's like to not love him, and I suppose that's the point.

"The bog can finally go back to being the bog: gator tails and frog songs and, if we're lucky enough, endless nights under depthless stars." My voice softens, and a small laugh escapes me. "Only this go-round, you are *mine*, Beau Cadwell. And I am yours."

His grin speaks of his wicked charm. His hopeful eyes tell me he agrees with every word spoken, and I manage to whisper.

"Forever and ever."

Acknowledgments

Georgia, you beautiful state, thank you for the wonderful, inspiring memories. I wouldn't have wanted to grow up anywhere else. An outpouring of gratitude to the people who made *Wicked Charm* possible. Entangled Teen and my editor, Karen Grove, you are a charm to work with. Stacey Donaghy, agent and friend, thanks for your guidance. Invaluable help came from Amy Horn, who read the first, messy draft and told me I had something worthwhile. Endless gratefulness to my friends Tracy Clark, Kelsey Sutton, and Jenn Marie Thorne for chats, encouragement, chocolate, and Starbucks. You girls have kept me sane. Jay Asher, you are one of the very first people I told about this novel. Thanks for convincing me to drive across the state on a whim, ALA, many laughs, and for showing me the ropes. It was the experience of a lifetime. My precious family: you are adored. Dad, remember the time you encouraged me to call a gator over, and then had me sit beside its head while you snapped a picture? That was fun. Thanks for the walks through the woods, too. Rodolfo, I hope all my chapters end with you. The biggest of all appreciation to my son. I'd pluck down the moon for you if I could, and it'd still never shine as bright as your smile. I love you more.

Grab the Entangled Teen releases readers are talking about!

Pretty Dead Girls
by Monica Murphy

In Cape Bonita, wicked lies are hidden just beneath the surface. But all it takes is one tragedy for them to be exposed. The most popular girls in school are turning up dead, and Penelope Malone is terrified she's next. All the victims have been linked to Penelope—and to a boy from her physics class. The one with the rumored dark past and a brooding stare that cuts right through her. There's something he isn't telling her. But there's something she's not telling him, either. Everyone has secrets, and theirs might get them killed.

By a Charm and a Curse
By Jaime Questell

Le Grand's Carnival Fantastic isn't like other traveling circuses. It's bound by a charm, held together by a centuries-old curse, that protects its members from ever growing older or getting hurt. Emmaline King is drawn to the circus like a moth to a flame… and unwittingly recruited into its folds by a mysterious teen boy whose kiss is as cold as ice.

Forced to travel through Texas as the new Girl in the Box, Emmaline is completely trapped. Breaking the curse seems like her only chance at freedom, but with no curse, there's no charm, either—dooming everyone who calls the Carnival Fantastic home. Including the boy she's afraid she's falling for.

Everything—including his life—could end with just one kiss.

LIES THAT BIND
BY DIANA WALLACH RODRIGUEZ

Reeling from the truths uncovered while searching for her sister, Anastasia Phoenix is ready to call it quits with spies. But before she can leave her parents' crimes behind her, tragedy strikes. No one is safe, not while Department D exists. Now, with help from her friends, Anastasia embarks on a dangerous plan to bring down the criminal empire. But soon she realizes the true danger might be coming from someone closer than she expects…

BREAKING THE ICE
BY JULIE CROSS

Haley Stevenson seems like she's got it all together: cheer captain, "Princess" of Juniper Falls, and voted Most Likely to Get Things Done. But below the surface, she's struggling with a less-than-stellar GPA and still reeling from the loss of her first love. Repeating her Civics class during summer school is her chance to Get Things Done, not angst over boys. In fact, she's sworn them off completely until college.

Fletcher Scott is happy to keep a low profile around Juniper Falls. He's always been the invisible guy, warming the bench on the hockey team and moonlighting at a job that would make his grandma blush. Suddenly, though, he's finding he wants more: more time on the ice, and more time with his infuriatingly perfect summer-school study partner.

But leave it to a girl who requires perfection to shake up a boy who's ready to break all the rules.

NEVER APART
BY ROMILY BERNARD

What if you had to relive the same five days over and over?
And what if at the end of it, your boyfriend is killed...
And you have to watch. Every time.
You don't know why you're stuck in this nightmare.
But you do know that these are the rules you now live by:
Wake Up.
Run.
Die.
Repeat.

Now, the only way to escape this loop is to attempt something
crazy. Something dangerous. Something completely unexpected.
This time...you're not going to run.

Combining heart-pounding romance and a thrilling mystery
Never Apart is a stunning story you won't soon forget.

ASSASSIN OF TRUTHS
BY BRENDA DRAKE

The gateways linking the great libraries of the world don't require
a library card, but they do harbor incredible dangers.

And it's not your normal bump-in-the- night kind. The
threats Gia Kearns faces are the kind with sharp teeth and
knifelike claws. The kind that include an evil wizard hell-bent
on taking her down.

Gia can end his devious plan, but only if she recovers seven
keys hidden throughout the world's most beautiful libraries. And
then figures out exactly what to do with them.

The last thing she needs is a distraction in the form of falling
in love. But when an impossible evil is unleashed, love might be
the only thing left to help Gia save the world.

entangled teen

an imprint of Entangled Publishing LLC